A
SHADOW
ON THE
LENS

Sam Hurcom was born in Dinas Powys, South Wales in 1991. He studied Philosophy at Cardiff University, attaining undergraduate and master's degrees. He has since had several short stories published and has written and illustrated a number of children's books. Sam currently lives in the village he was raised in, close to the woodlands that have always inspired his writing.

A Shadow on the Lens is Sam's debut novel.

A SHADOW ON THE LENS

SAM HURCOM

ORION

An Orion paperback

First published in Great Britain in 2019
by Orion Fiction,
This paperback edition published in 2020
by Orion Fiction,
an imprint of The Orion Publishing Group Ltd.,
Carmelite House, 50 Victoria Embankment
London EC4Y ODZ

An Hachette UK Company

1 3 5 7 9 10 8 6 4 2

A CIP catalogue record for this book is
available from the British Library.

ISBN (Paperback) 978 1 409 18987 9

Typeset at The Spartan Press Ltd,
Lymington, Hants

Printed and bound by Clays Ltd,
Elcograf S.p.A.

www.orionbooks.co.uk

For my grandparents:
Beryl, Gordon, Leonard and Susan

Contents

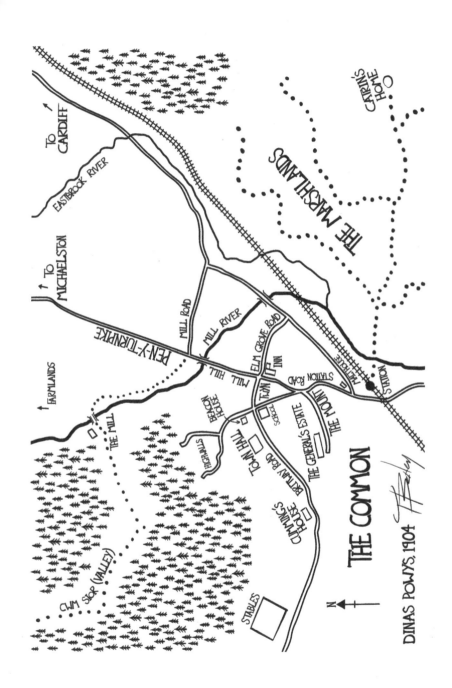

THE COMMON

DINAS POWYS, 1904

TO CARDIFF

EASTBROOK RIVER

TO MICHAELSTON

FARMLANDS

PEN-Y-TURNPIKE

MILL ROAD

MILL RIVER

THE MILL

ELM GROVE ROAD

MILL HILL

STATION ROAD

TURNPIKE

THE MARSHLANDS

CATRIN'S HOME

STATION

THE MOUNT

THE GENERAL'S ESTATE

SCHOOL

BEACON HOUSE

HERMIT'S

TOWN HILL

BETHANY ROAD

CUMMING'S HOUSE

CWM SIOR (VALLEY)

STABLES

N

A Note to the Reader
November 13th, 1913

For years I could not speak of what is written in these pages. It marked *the* change in my life, the death of the man I once was. Only now, as an ever-deepening fear of what is to come plagues me, do I feel compelled to write of all that I have seen.

The account you are about to read is the only *true* one. If you wish to corroborate my story, perhaps with any journal of repute from the time, you will find little – if nothing – of what transpired some ten years ago.

So strange was all that happened, many cannot even begin to comprehend it. Yet still I write this.

Believe me or do not – most think me a madman. On cold nights such as this, I often wish I were.

I

My Arrival – June 17th, 1904

I embarked by train on a fine summer morning. The small windows in the first-class carriage were propped open, and as the steamer gained pace, charging through the green pastures and twisting through the rolling landscape with thunderous rapture, a warm breeze, lined with mill dust and soot, ebbed and swirled about me.

It was a Friday; that Tuesday past I had apprehended a killer. The case in Oxford had taken longer than anticipated and had not been without its challenges. But my work had been done, and seeing a guilty man taken into custody rejuvenated me in a manner that no great elixir ever could. After only two short days at my residence in London (during which time I had received a letter asking for my assistance with a murder enquiry in South Wales), I was eager to return to my duties.

Hence my fine mood upon departing from Paddington, greeting the kindly conductor who inspected my ticket as though he were an old friend. Following my connection at Chepstow I must have dozed, however, for no sooner had I set my gaze out southerly, watching with a strange sense of envy as labourers toiled lazily in the fields, I was stirred by the clatter and rattle of the locomotive dropping speed and pulling into the station at Cardiff. It had been little more than an hour and a half, and whilst the day remained fine, the crisp blue sky had dulled substantially.

I alighted at the short platform as a near endless stream of coal transports ran along the mainline back toward London. Many were headed from the valley routes in the north, the deep pits of the Rhondda and Ebbw Vale. Even over the din of freighters, the hustle of clerks and businessmen rushing to and fro across the narrow platform, I heard the tremendous booming and racket of the great docks just out of sight, little more than a mile south from where I stood. Above the grimy rows of terraced houses compacted and sprawling outward towards the dockyards, I made out the black pillars and white clouds of steam, the dragon's breath of industry, the goliaths that sailed across the Commonwealth from this mighty place. And a mighty place it was, for stood there amidst the chaos of it all, one could not help but feel a little overcome. *This* was the furnace, the heartbeat, of the greatest Empire in the world.

After descending into the station fully, I enquired about my connection, and made haste towards the furthest track from the mainline. A fine locomotive, with two stumpy carriages in tow, began pulling from the station as I clambered the final few steps to the platform. In calamitous fashion and with the aid of a young station assistant, I bundled onto the second carriage.

It seemed deserted and I saw no real need to park my travel case and camera equipment in the racks. They sat in the aisle, rocking gently, as I caught my breath and the train followed the line, bending out of the station.

I watched the world roll past us through the grubby carriage window as we made our way from the centre of the city. We clattered by ever more lengthy rows of terraced houses, the streets a hive of activity, with women busy at their work and children scampering in droves like packs of rabid dogs. The brickwork, walkways and roads were all darkened and dirtied by smoke and fumes, comparable perhaps only to the streets of Brixton town or the ghettos of Spitalfields (my former home). Beyond the workers' houses, I saw the dockyards in greater view and fleets of trawlers and cargo vessels hauled at anchor. The world, it seemed, was darkened ever more in that direction.

It would seem apt to explain the details of my journey, and the full nature of my employment. My trade as a photographer had been passed down to me from my father. I enjoyed the work, though even in the capital the money was poor. After my apprenticeship, and several years of unsteady work, an opportunity had been offered to me by the Metropolitan Police. I'm not ashamed to admit that this securing of work was more a case of whom one knows rather than *what* one knows, for the man who hired me was something of an acquaintance. I take no shame in saying his loose friendship played a vital role in starting my career – too often men let pride get in the way of common sense when it comes to these matters. To turn him down would have been to waste the greatest opportunity ever afforded me.

Forensic photography, as it remains to be called, was something of a fledgling enterprise, a new and specialist field, now incorporated into the wider forensic sciences. Many avoided it, due to the unseemly nature of the work. Though indeed the scenes I saw were ugly (occasionally barbaric), I was vested with one sentiment – there would always be crime, and the need to record it.

Some years passed – I worked at crime scenes throughout the city and I studied in The Yard's dark rooms, morgues and laboratories. In time I earned quite the reputation, both for my forensic expertise and surprising investigatory skill. Many in the force began to see me as an Inspector (a title I feel I do not deserve) in my own right, capable of not only assisting with enquiries but taking on my own cases. My keen eye for detail when examining crime scenes, and a surprising talent for piecing together evidence, brought many a guilty man and woman before judge and jury.

In recent years, and owing to my rather unique skillset, The Yard had relieved me of many of my in-house forensic duties, holding me on retainer as a specialised investigator, consulting on serious crime cases nationwide, often those for which I was requested. Receiving correspondence at my private residence from police forces and constabularies up and down the country was not uncommon at this time in my life. Travelling to assist with a murder enquiry in a small Welsh village was nothing out of the ordinary.

When we arrived in the village of Dinas Powys, the pearlescent blue heavens had re-emerged fully. I breathed in heavily, letting the scorching sun beat down upon my brow as I alighted and stood upon the platform. It was deserted. I checked my pocket watch as the steamer departed with a short screech of its whistle – I was some forty-five minutes early for my meeting. It didn't seem to matter and with an air of calm and relaxation (the last time I should ever feel such ease) I made my way out of the station.

Crossing a wide dirt road, I ascended a gentle set of steps, passing a cottage of some antiquity. Its thatched roof was all but destroyed, revealing the twisted, rotten skeleton of oak timbers and exposed chimneys. A faded sign on the wall read 'Malthouse', though it seemed the place had been abandoned for some time.

A thin trail wound around the derelict, leading to a few more cottages in far better standing. Stretching above the thatched and slated rooftops, I made out the three spires of a dull grey church, each tipped with simple, unembellished crosses. I guessed then that this trail would lead me to the heart of the hamlet, though I chose not to follow it, instead ascending further up the hillock away from the station, where a wide grass verge spread away and out of sight. I would learn that this was the edge of the village common, and as I carried my heavy cases up and over the verge, I realised just how wide an expanse it was.

All was quite pleasant, if not a little inert. Some twenty yards from where I stood, two women, dressed in none of the high fashions of central London, but smart gowns and neat blouses nonetheless, walked side by side along a visible trodden path in the grass. The shorter of the women was barked and yipped at by a small terrier, tethered to her wrist by a thin length of twisted rope. Further off, some four hundred yards perhaps, a young man with flaxen curls rode a fine pony on a dirt road skirting the common's northern edge. With each quick step, the pony shot white and cream dust out behind its hooves.

Perhaps my enthusiasm and good mood got the better of me, for I approached the women too keenly, catching the shorter lady's eye and smiling a little. Innocent as my intentions were, under the circumstances my approach was indelicate. She fell silent and still at the sight of me. With a brief nod of acknowledgement, she pulled with little subtlety on her companion's arm. The pair sharply turned and walked quickly away from me without even a glance over their shoulders, the miserable terrier yanked and heaved by the neck with ruthless thrusts of its leash.

I watched after them for a moment, only turning my gaze away at the sound of hooves thumping quickly across compacted earth. The young man on his pony was out of sight in a flicker.

Somewhat dumbfounded, I walked further onto the common towards a wooden bench, whereupon I set my cases down gently. There was no one else in sight. I considered the encounter, reminding myself that a young woman in the village had recently been murdered and that people were likely nervous (nay, terrified) of anyone they may not recognise. It seemed foolish of me to have expected open arms and warm greetings.

In spite of my eagerness to head into the village, for time is a pressing matter in serious cases such as these, I decided to wait on the common for the hour of my scheduled meeting. It seemed best not to alarm anyone or draw any greater attention to myself than I was already likely to incur. I removed my heavy coat and realised my copy of the *Standard* was still folded neatly in the large inside pocket. *My* copy was something of an inaccuracy. I had found the previous day's paper unattended on the platform at Paddington. I browsed through an account of a meeting held in Manchester between local business leaders and the adopted Liberal MP Winston Churchill. On the page over, nestled in the far bottom corner, I noticed a short extract reporting the recent case in Oxford:

The perpetrator of several salacious murders in and around the Oxford city area has been thwarted by members of the Oxford City Police, working out of the Blue Boar Street station. The accused has not been named publicly but shall be brought before magistrates in the coming week. The Oxford City Force was assisted in their enquiries by Metropolitan Police Special Investigator Thomas Bexley.

I admit now (with some sense of shame for my arrogance, I might add), that seeing my name in print brought a smile to my face. It was not the first time I had been mentioned in a national newspaper, and I daresay I thought it would not be the last. Idling on such things seems so absurd looking back now.

*

Forty minutes later, as I began to gather some of my belongings to make my way toward the village proper, I caught sight of a man waving in my direction some two hundred yards from where I sat. With no one around me, I gingerly raised a hand and waved back to him. That spurred him on and he hurried towards me, half jogging over the fine-trimmed grass.

He was barely five feet five, no more than forty but carrying the weight and purple skin tone of a man who drinks too much and eats poorly. His gasping breaths preceded him and a thin veil of sweat shone dully in the blazing sun from his receding hairline to his heavy jowls. He wore a fine suit, better than the ragged three piece I had on that day. His was dark tan, checked and double breasted with a smart red dicky bow resting against his Adam's apple. He beamed at me and my first impression was that he seemed a friendly type; his greeting was far removed from the earlier reception I had received. I smiled back at him and took a few steps in his direction.

'I guessed you would wander up here from the station. Most do.' He gasped out his words as a dog pants in such weather. He needed to take a breath and compose himself but seemed keen to talk more. 'If you haven't been here before, it's easy to head onto the common rather than straight to the village.' He stretched out a red and sweaty hand. I shook it with vigour, meaning to introduce myself.

'How was your journey?' he rasped at me.

'Fine,' I stammered, trying to wrench my hand from his sweaty grasp. 'Lovely, in fact.'

'Yah,' he murmured. 'Such a shame it is under these circumstances.'

I nodded and watched as he pulled a lime green handkerchief from inside his jacket. He rubbed his face and took several gulps of air.

'Cummings. Robert Cummings, head of the local council.' He smiled as thick, dark veins throbbed from his temples.

'Thomas Bexley,' I replied. He barely seemed to notice. He brazenly stepped past and reached for my luggage case. I moved fast to ensure he didn't carry my camera equipment; the handle on the bespoke case I'd had made was a little loose and likely to break with too strong a pull.

'I've taken the liberty of arranging your lodgings. I imagined the process would be done by tomorrow.' He began walking off as he spoke, back in the direction he had appeared from. I moved after him, my camera case in one hand and coat in the other.

'I'm afraid this will likely take three days, at least.'

He didn't stop walking but remained silent momentarily. 'Really, that long eh? Any reason in particular?'

'No, it is simply not a process we should rush, Mr Cummings.' He nodded without a word.

Crossing the common, we came to a short, steep incline that descended from the expanse of grass. Here, at the brow of the hill, Cummings pointed to a large detached house of fine design and proudly announced it was his. He explained that I could find him there should ever I need him, though from the manner in which he spoke I suspected he merely wanted to show off the property. As we made our way down the hill Cummings further explained how the village square was only a short distance away down Britway Road. Before I had time to get a word in, he began babbling about the history of the village. The man barely took time to breathe before rattling on to another subject.

'How has everyone taken it?' I asked quickly as Cummings paused between his short, haggard gasps for an instant. I thought of the two women who had near fled at the sight of me upon my arrival. Here again, I reminded myself that this was not the heart of a major city like London or Oxford. This was a tiny hamlet where a murder would have a devastating effect on many. 'Awful thing under any circumstance.'

Cummings seemed to growl. 'Dreadful, dreadful thing. It's come as a surprise to some.'

I was taken aback a little by the man's rather brazen tone. 'But not to everyone?'

Cummings shrugged. 'You may learn a few things about the people of Dinas Powys in your short stay here, Inspector.'

'I'm not an Inspector.' It seemed proper to correct Cummings from the outset. In spite of my skillset, I have always felt the title Inspector should be reserved for those who have diligently (often painfully) worked their way through the police force ranks. He stopped in the road and eyed me with an air of confusion.

'The telegram from the Glamorgan Constabulary seemed to say you were. Chief Inspector Brent advised us that your services would be a necessity here.'

I shook my head a little. Either Cummings or Chief Inspector Brent, whose letter to my residence had been nothing but brief, was misinformed.

'A misunderstanding, I am sure, one perhaps I should have clarified when I wired back to the Chief Inspector yesterday morning. Understand I'll be heading up the enquiry now *on behalf* of the Glamorgan Constabulary – I'll work to assist the Chief Inspector and his men but answer only to my superiors at Scotland Yard. Brent wrote to me with the instruction to meet with yourself and your local officer, Constable—'

'Vaughn.' Cummings beamed. 'He's young but has his theory on what happened.'

'He has a suspect then?' We were walking again at quite a pace; Cummings heaved and sighed with each speedy stride.

'Some travellers were camped in the woodlands between here and Michaelston-le-Pit, not far from where the body was found.

They would be the obvious suspects in all of this. If you expect to be here three days, there'll be plenty of time for you to view the evidence we have.'

'In cases such as these, Councilman, I am afraid time is never on our side. When was the body found?'

He glanced at me from the corner of his eye. 'A week ago.'

'Last Friday – the tenth?' He concurred with a nod. I continued, 'The body will need to be examined and documented immediately, along with any other evidence you may have.'

He barely acknowledged what I had said before he cleared his throat and started to prattle on about the village once more, pointing to cottages that we passed.

I interrupted him. 'The girl was local – did she live in the village?'

'Until last week she did.' He chuckled a little, muttering under his breath. He stepped away from me as a cart, dragged by two haggard mules and loaded with a few large bales of dried straw, passed between us. As we continued to pace on he asked quite jovially if I had been to this beautiful part of the country before. He spoke as if no crime had been committed at all.

I deemed then that my first impressions of the man had been quite wrong. Cummings now seemed brash and irritable. I stood and watched after him for a moment or two before calling out to him. He seemed startled that I was not alongside him and waited for me to catch up. Abreast of the man, I lowered my camera case and spoke sternly.

'Is Constable Vaughn available? I would like to speak with him as soon as possible.'

Cummings seemed taken aback by my tone.

'He's on a rest day today,' he spluttered. 'Besides, I'm sure I can deal with most of your queries.'

I shook my head and reached for my case.

'He can rest when I am gone. I'll require all the information he has so far.' I gestured for Cummings to lead on and he did so, though his face seemed to darken to an unhealthy shade of crimson.

The short walk from the common had taken a little over five minutes (if that), yet in that time my opinion of Cummings had altered drastically. His ego was great; his outlook on the murder seemed lacklustre at best. I still did not know the victim's name, and by Cummings' tone and manner, I could already tell he thought little of the deceased woman.

We came into the village square and there I took a moment to pause and gather my bearings. Cummings informed me the village green – a triangular space of grass raised a little from the dirt roads and buildings surrounding it – was known to the locals as the Twyn. He pointed out a few key landmarks, including the school building, its rather large windows all closed in spite of the fine weather. I grew tired of the man's company when he began to delve into his investment and influence in the village's upkeep, hoping then that the young Constable Vaughn would be a more pleasurable (and professional) companion.

I felt the eyes of a few townspeople going about their business, follow my footfalls across the chalky dirt road as we passed the sparsely placed iron rod gas lamps and quaint rows of properties, each with well kept, neat gardens. My lodgings were to be in one of two inns built adjacent to each other. 'The Three Feathers' was emblazoned in black paint across the smooth cream façade. I was grateful to have arrived, not merely to part company with Cummings but also for the sake of my camera case. The handle seemed to be growing dangerously loose under the weight of the equipment I had brought with me.

Cummings continued to ramble on. As we stepped down into the inn's sunken patio, I lowered my case to the floor. Inside my jacket was a smooth moleskin notebook and stubby granite pencil. I removed them, and interrupted Cummings quite abruptly once more.

'An examination of the body will need to be carried out presently. Have Vaughn meet me here; where did you say the deceased was being kept? Time permitting, we shall inspect the scene of the crime this afternoon and begin carrying out questioning first thing tomorrow.'

Cummings shifted awkwardly, trying to smile but doing little more than grimacing at me as I fumbled for a clean page in my notebook.

'What can you expect to find? The body was recovered from there seven days ago.'

I nodded absently. 'There is always evidence left at the scene of a crime, though the eye may not notice it at first.'

Cummings cleared his throat. 'I had imagined this would be a little less ... *intrusive*. More a formality; checking our evidence, that sort of thing.'

I ignored him entirely. 'Where is the body being held?'

'A church – All Saints – in Michaelston-le-Pit. It's a hamlet, but it's always been closely connected to the village. About three miles away.'

I was completely baffled. 'Why on earth would you choose to keep the body there?'

Cummings cleared his throat, seeming to hesitate before answering.

'A few senior figures in the village were ... *uncomfortable* with the body of a murdered girl being held amidst their homes and businesses. It may seem foolish, but people have their superstitions. The manner she was found in ...'

'*What manner?*' My patience was beginning to wear thin.

'Well, she was burnt.'

'Burnt!' I exclaimed, before jotting a single note down. 'You have a whole body though?'

Cummings nodded. 'She was also bound.'

I scowled at him. 'How could her body be burnt yet remain bound?'

'She had a chain wrapped around her.' Cummings' skin was draining of all its beetroot colour to a ghastly shade of pink. I sighed a little – the squeamish fellow would be no use.

'You said the scene of the crime was between here and Michaelston, correct?' Cummings nodded. 'We'll examine the scene *first* en route to the church and the body. What was the victim's name?'

'Betsan. Betsan Tilny.' He spat out the surname as if it tasted rotten.

'Middle name?' I asked sharply.

'Ceridwen, I think.'

'And her age?'

'Sixteen.'

I noted it down before pocketing my notebook and pencil. I reached to take my luggage from Cummings, who still held it in his balled, sweaty fist.

'Fetch your man Vaughn and tell him to meet us at the crime scene. We'll head down there in an hour.'

'I may need longer than that to retrieve Vaughn,' Cummings blurted at me as I turned away.

'As I have already made plain, Councilman, time is not on our side,' I snapped back at him. 'Return here in an hour.' With that he disappeared out of the small patio.

I watched after him for a moment or two, catching the eyes of a few who had been staring at us the whole while from different points across the Twyn. Each turned or bowed their heads as I looked at them. I was accustomed to these sorts of gazes and intrigue when serious crimes had been committed in smaller, closer knit communities. The quiet of the place unsettled me. I carefully took my cases and ducked through the low doorway of the inn's cool foyer. I stepped inside a cramped bar room, with an open cast fire lying dormant but made ready for the eve.

I couldn't help but slouch a little, feeling as though my head was too close to the low-hanging ceiling beams. In a lounge across the other side of the small mahogany bar I spotted a wasted figure slumped in a high-backed chair. His head lolled to one side as if his thin and scrawny neck were at breaking point. After a few moments, I stepped over and lay a hand on the bar, knocking thrice. There was no movement, not even from the old beggar asleep in his chair. I knocked again, this time louder and when no response came still, I leant over the bar, seeing a hatch opened to the cellar below.

I called out in earnest until a misshapen figure appeared from the gloom. He eyed me as he clambered upwards, a husk of a man, with a slack jaw and heavy-set frame. He wore a grubby vest and was balding badly, though he had gone to the trouble of combing what was left of his wiry hair across his ruby scalp. I introduced myself and we spoke briefly; his name was Solomon and he mumbled all his words.

'Copper eh?' He stepped out of sight for a moment and appeared again through a door next to the bar. He knelt so low to get through the door I was amazed he could fit at all – he was nothing if not six feet five.

'Of a sort,' I muttered coolly. He did not seem the type who would appreciate a seminar on the basic principles of forensic photography or investigatory practices.

He lifted my luggage case without another word and stepped back through the tiny door he had come through. I followed into what was a very short and narrow corridor. We passed a small archway that led behind the bar and ascended a narrow flight of uneven stone steps to a tight landing with three doors in close proximity. With a shove, Solomon opened one door and led me into my room.

It was smaller than the bar area I had waited in below. A single bed, a foot shorter than my stature, was poorly made with woven linen blankets and a lone shallow pillow. It rested in the farthest corner. A wooden chair and small table stood against the opposite wall, emblazoned in the early afternoon light cast through a single, misty pane of glass. There was a tin bowl filled with water on the table and a chamber pot barely tucked below the bed.

Solomon dropped my case with little propriety and began leaving the room. I threw my coat upon the bed and lay my camera case down gently.

'I'll need a light,' I called after the innkeeper, stepping over the squeaking floorboards and gazing out the window. Solomon re-entered the room and grunted something inaudible.

'A light – candle or oil lamp. There are no sconces on the wall.'

Solomon muttered once more and slammed the door behind him as he left the room. I deplored the cut of the man, his sloping brow and quiet indignation. I returned my attention to the scene through my tiny window. Laid out before me was the south-east corner of the Twyn, the well-maintained triangle of grass and flower beds of primrose and blood-red poppies. A few trees broke up the green space, with golden light shining through the blossom and leaves like warm embers. I noticed a fountain and trough at the corner of the Twyn and in the middle of the dirt road alongside my lodgings, a gas lamp stood proud betwixt the intersection of four roads.

I made out the large white manor that Cummings had claimed to be the national school. Beside that, seemed to be a postal exchange with a Postmaster's bicycle propped lazily against the wall. Down the Twyn further still, I saw a third inn (The Dragon), seemingly larger than the one in which I resided. It, along with all the domiciles and businesses within view, seemed in pristine condition. No speck of moss lined the tiles, no blade of grass seemed left untrimmed. I thought it was all for my benefit, a charade to maintain appearances. Whether it was for innocent intentions or not, it didn't matter to me then. It only deepened my sense of disquiet and unease.

2

The Scene — June 17th, 1904

Whilst waiting for Cummings to return I examined my camera equipment. My camera — a Lancaster & Son (a superior model to any I had owned previously, bought in the autumn of eighteen ninety-eight) — was in some ways outdated by the time I arrived in Dinas Powys. Much furore was made of the Kodak *Brownie*, and its quite remarkable reels of photographic film, wholly distinct from the glass quarter plates I was trained in developing. The nature of my work would never prescribe me to send reels of film away to be developed and in many respects, I was already stuck in my ways. Still, my camera was a suitable model for the field exposure I generally required. I had enough quarter dry plates with me to make certain I could document the murder scene and the victim's body in fine enough detail. I had also brought with me vials of the necessary chemicals required to develop such dry plates should I need to.

I emptied the contents of my camera case on the floor at the foot of my bed and began to rummage absently through my luggage. Wrapped in a tatty nightshirt was my Enfield revolver; I was quite overzealous in bringing it on all such cases. As I pawed through my clothes and few personal effects, I realised I had no spare ammunition. It seemed to matter little — I had six rounds and struggled to think how I could possibly need them.

With the weighty pistol in hand, I caught the sound of voices from one of the rooms adjoining mine. The words were too faint to decipher, though the tone was unmistakable. An argument was ensuing, a man and a woman. It was short-lived, though I held my breath in vain for a moment to listen. As their voices died away I dare say I noticed an unseemly scratching from the low ceiling above me. Rats, in the loft space no doubt. I followed the scratching as it passed me and my meagre bed overhead. I took no pleasure at the thought of vermin above me whilst I slept.

Barely half an hour had passed since Cummings had left me, though I decided I would rather sit and wait for his return in the warm sun of daylight than the dark, shaded corners of my room. I gathered my camera and around half the exposure plates I had brought with me. Absent of the remainder, and the vials of developing chemicals, my case was far lighter than upon my arrival. I chose to leave my coat, which left me with no pockets large enough to conceal my Enfield. I decided to leave it, doubting I would have need for it at this stage of the enquiry.

I crept out of my room, trying not to alert the rowing pair of my presence. All was quiet as I descended the stairs and returned to the little bar area. I found Solomon tending to the floor with a wet rag and mop. The old man in the lounge was still sleeping awkwardly.

I was famished and decided to ask for a little drink and food. Solomon left the bar area without a word, returning a few moments later with a glass of ale, a chunk of wholemeal bread and some over-ripened cheese. I try to make a point of never drinking whilst carrying out enquiries but assessing the demeanour of the man, I doubted I would be granted a glass of water if I asked. I gave my thanks and ate the bread and bland cheese quickly, sipping at the warm, bitter ale to wash it all down. I left half, finding the silent contempt of the bar an uncomfortable presence.

The early afternoon was as brilliant as the morn, and I wandered onto the Twyn, taking in my surroundings proper. I found an empty bench and sat; the few who had watched my arrival to the village green had all but disappeared. The Postmaster emerged from his office after five minutes or so; he looked at me queerly, in the way a mouse may investigate a breadcrumb as he approaches it. He seemed to stare beyond me for a moment before looking down towards The Dragon Inn. I thought nothing of it then but thinking back, it was as if he were checking that no one was around.

'Good day to you,' I called to him. His wide eyes fixed on mine quite suddenly. He waved a hand timidly before moving to turn away. I called after him once more and beckoned he come over to me.

He stepped onto the Twyn. 'Fine day.'

I nodded in silence. He approached the bench and stood before me.

'You the Inspector, then?'

'Of a sort.'

He nodded as if he understood.

'Heard you were coming – we don't get many visitors here.'

'Nor murders I dare say.' I pulled out my notebook; it seemed as good a time as any to question a local man. 'Did you know the victim?' I asked plainly.

'Everyone knows everyone, more or less.'

I nodded. 'May I take your name?'

He told me it was Jacob Clyde and that he had lived in the village all his life.

'I'll be frank, Mr Clyde, I'll be carrying out thorough interviews with anyone I deem relevant to the enquiry in the coming days. As the Postmaster of this village you may, unknowingly, have some information that will be beneficial to my investigation. If I could ask you a few questions now it would be most appreciated.'

He sighed. 'I have work to be doing.'

'This shan't be long. The victim – Betsan Tilny – what was she like around the village: quiet, hard-working?'

He shrugged. 'I don't know you'd call what she got up to work. She had her way with the lads.'

'In what regard?'

Clyde smiled thinly. 'She was a little *unbridled*. Down to no father I reckon personally. She's got no one except her mother, Catrin.'

'And where does she live?' His smirk only widened at that question. 'Well, does she not receive correspondence?'

He explained that the mother lived on the other side of the railway, in a thatched hovel amidst the marshy bogs south of the village. He gave me some loose directions.

'Well, why does she live there?' I asked, for it seemed by his description to be a terrible place and manner in which to live.

'She has some claim to the land,' he remarked. 'Her family going back and all. She isn't the sort to get letters.' He tapped at his temple and raised his eyebrows.

I frowned at that. 'Are you saying she's deranged somehow?'

He shrugged. 'If that's what you want to call it.'

'How did you come to know of the girl's death?'

'We had a town meeting – up there in the hall.' He pointed to a building just beyond the national school, on the opposite side of the road that Cummings and I had walked down from the common.

'So Cummings informed you?'

The Postmaster nodded. 'Something the General would have done previously but he's getting on now.'

'The General?'

'General Arthur James. He's the Lord of the Manor of Dinas Powys.' He pointed absently towards The Dragon and informed me the General's estate was nestled just a little way from it on the edge of the common. I jotted down the details.

'Cummings made no mention of the General.' This I perceived to be nothing but Cummings' arrogance; perhaps he thought himself leader of the village. 'I shall need to speak with him. When was this meeting Cummings held with you all?'

The Postmaster fell silent, any remnant of the smirk on his face disappeared. He began scratching at his cheek and I beckoned him to speak.

'The body was found seven days ago, so when was the town meeting?'

The Postmaster looked over my shoulder. As I turned to look, I saw a flicker of movement from across the street and the hem of a coat disappear from view into a small dwelling. I felt unseen eyes peer at me.

'Tuesday,' the Postmaster said quietly. When I looked at him next he was already backing away from where I sat. 'Need to be getting on. Good luck with your investigation.'

He walked away without another word. I watched as he climbed onto his bicycle and sped away down the street. I turned back and looked over my shoulder. Someone had been watching us.

When Cummings returned he was twenty minutes late. I marched across the Twyn towards him and cut through his dribbling apologies.

'How far have we to travel?' I barked.

'Not far to the scene along the woodland trail to the north-east. About two and a half miles from there to Michaelston and the church but I can fetch a cart or—'

'We'll walk. And Vaughn had better meet us there.'

Cummings didn't speak much for quite some time after that.

We left the Twyn via Mill Hill. Our thin trail was soon hemmed in by trees and shrubs, held back by low-lying stone walls. Dotted at intervals of a hundred yards or so stood tall and slender telegraph masts with a few thin wires attaching each to the next. The heat of day seemed only to be intensifying with each passing minute and I was quickly enveloped in clammy sweat below my collar. Buzzards and midges bombarded us as the smell of the farmyards to the north and east became heavy in the air.

The trail at the bottom of the hill remained flat only a short while. We crossed a wide and well-maintained bridge that spanned the river running from the north, before our trail split in three directions. Straight before us, the road ascended sharply up an extremely steep hillock. Cummings explained to me feebly that this was the Pen-Y-Turnpike, the road that led to Llandough and further on back towards Cardiff.

'Far easier to take a cart that way to reach Michaelston as well – as I tried to tell you, it could be quite a walk with your equipment.'

I didn't answer. The road to the right (Mill Road) was a stark contrast to what had preceded it. A row of grand stately homes of red brick and white fascias was set back from the wide roadway. The buildings seemed relatively well kept, though each garden appeared barren and unattended. I enquired of this to Cummings, who explained the homes had been finished only the previous autumn.

'Are they vacant?' I asked dubiously. Cummings simply shrugged.

'A few are occupied,' he said casually. 'Clerks and managers from the city.'

I didn't labour the point, and Cummings guided us left off the trail.

We began to traipse along a bone-dry dirt path that led us into the woodlands. The river we had crossed now ran heavily to our immediate left, in a steep gully concealed in places by thick ferns and fallen saplings. Beyond the gully, the earth rose gently, studded with trees that hung towards the path as they grew awkwardly under their own weight. To our right, a field spread away, unkempt and filled with meadow weeds and dandelions. Birdsong and the pleasant trickle of cool water filled the space. Even now I can smell wild garlic as I write these pages, for it grew with great abandon throughout much of that woodland, pungent and strong in the summer heat.

Cummings held his tongue for much of the walk and I admit I was grateful for his silence.

Perhaps a quarter of a mile or so along the path, the ground beyond the river began to ease and flatten. I caught sight of huge glasshouses between the trees and made out the first signs of life: a few farm hands attending to the vegetables and tomatoes growing inside. Cummings explained that the greenhouses were a recent addition to the property of Johnathon Miller, the owner of much of the land. It was Miller, Cummings whispered in hushed tones, who had stumbled upon the girl's body.

Soon after the large expanse of glass conservatories, our path bent left, and we crossed a small stone bridge spanning the river. Here Cummings stopped a moment; standing before us was the mill from which the road we had come along had acquired its name. It was something from another age, its limestone-clad façade daubed in white paint, its misshapen walls all aslant and crooked. Thick ivy exposed only small patches of the exterior; wiry ash trees and thick bramble bushes seemed to contort around the structure. It looked as if the building had grown out of the very ground.

The river passed one side of the mill and a rickety wooden wheel, contained within a lean-to shelter, spun slowly as the water dropped down a sheer, man-made waterfall. A dark coloured sluice, almost green for the moss growing on it, was fixed atop the waterfall.

Worthy of a John Constable painting, I mused, and I meant it with sincerity. The quiet churn of the mill, the smell of damp soil and the light haze of corn dust in the air only enhanced the beauty of the scene. Beams of white light penetrated the upper canopy of a few tall evergreens that shaded the mill and bridge.

My gaze became fixed on a small round window bored into the side of the mill. Obscured in the shadows, I grew certain a figure moved.

A silhouette took shape. The contours of a body, of a face.

The beauty of the place was lost on me as my heart began to beat a little faster.

'This way,' Cummings grunted before I had time to ask who could be inside. Even as we walked out of sight of the mill, I still felt the unseen figure watch our movements. I began to scan the trees around us with ever greater suspicion and unease.

Vaughn was indeed a young man. He had the pasty and blotched complexion of one who has suffered badly from acne in adolescence. His handshake was limp, his palms sweaty and cold. I looked down upon him, and I am not a tall man by any measure. The near black uniform and collars he wore seemed to hang from his scrawny frame in a manner that was far from alarming but almost laughable. He looked like a lad who had stolen his father's clothes.

I introduced myself curtly, laying down my case and opening it carefully to produce my equipment. I made haste to ask Vaughn to show me the exact place where the body was found. We weren't far from the mill, now standing in a meandering avenue filled with colour. Bursts of light shone through leaves of green, amber and dusky orange. To our right, tall ash trees stood stoically, spreading back and high up a slope littered with ferns and the aforementioned wild garlic. There was a similarly steep embankment on the opposing side of the trail. This, Cummings told me, was the entrance to the Cwm Sior, a wooded valley, which I noted down after my introduction to Vaughn.

With a little hesitation, the young officer pointed to our right; concealed by the grey tree trunks was a small clearing, where a wall of sheer granite pierced the rise of the land.

'Cummings mentioned that Johnathon Miller found the victim – what time was this?'

Vaughn seemed to think it over. 'A-around six, perhaps a little earlier. Shortly after dawn. She would've b-been left there from the night before.'

The young lad spoke with something of a stammer. He seemed embarrassed by it and shifted a little awkwardly as I looked at him. I view such things as nothing to a man's character.

'What was Miller doing when he found her?' I asked, jotting down the time of discovery.

'W-w-walking with his hounds to inspect the land at the other end of the Cwm. Was his dog, really, who found her.'

I nodded again and pocketed my notebook. A few minutes later, I had erected my camera stand and aimed the lens straight down the meandering trail of the Cwm to take my first image.

'Do you have a suspect then, Constable?' I asked absently, already knowing his answer.

'Travellers were c-camped out up past Michaelston a little way. Been there for over a week.' He paused as he tried to get his words out. 'Day the body was found they moved on – no sign of them anywhere.'

I replaced the dry plate in my camera and moved a little further up the path to capture another image.

'What would be their motivation?'

'They had their way with her and didn't want to deal with it – savages!' Cummings scoffed and spat as he spoke. I eyed him momentarily.

'I would care for the Constable's opinion.' I turned my gaze to Vaughn. 'What would be their motivation?'

Vaughn glanced at Cummings before clearing his throat. 'The um … Tilny girl was known to be meeting with the tr-travellers whilst they were here. Some of the young farm hands will testify to her coming up and down this track in the days before she, um, she died.'

I nodded and carefully took the plate from my camera.

'Why see to kill her, though? If things had got out of hand why not simply leave?'

Vaughn remained silent for a few moments.

'If they had raped her, they likely feared she would tell the police.'

'Would you have believed her?' I asked plainly.

The young man's eyes widened and he glanced over at Cummings.

'Promiscuous girls are asking for trouble,' Cummings said boldly.

The man's ignorance became clear to me then. 'You would blame the shopkeeper who has his produce taken by the thief?'

Cummings folded his arms and scoffed. 'Come on, man. That's hardly the same thing.'

'In my mind, and that of the law, it is.'

Cummings sighed in mock exasperation. 'I thought a man from London would have a less naïve view on the world.'

I chose not to reply. I took in the scene some more, walking a little way up the trail. It bent shallowly toward the left, and I could see the bushes and wild shrubs encroaching ever more upon the path as it did so.

'How many ways could a man come to this path?' I called back to the other two, now huddled close by my camera.

'Too many to count,' Cummings replied. In that I feared he spoke true.

I stood in silence for a time, pondering and taking the place in. As I stepped back toward Vaughn and Cummings, I spied two figures approaching from the mill. One was far taller than the other, though it was clear that both were labourers, clad in loose shirts and slacked trousers that were all spotted and flecked with dirt and dust. Their skin was deep brown, glossed by the heat of the day. They approached Cummings and Vaughn, greeting the pair as they passed. As the two approached me, the taller man doffed his cap. His nose was flattened, and he had cauliflower ears and visible scars across his lower jaw.

'Great shame about the young woman, Inspector,' he said to me with a thick Welsh drawl. There seemed a genuine regret and sadness about him and I nodded and watched after the pair as they walked on and disappeared from view.

'Who were they?' I asked when I was back alongside Vaughn and Cummings.

'The Davey brothers, Geraint and Lewis – two of Miller's lads.'

'Rugby player? The taller, I mean.'

Cummings nodded. 'Geraint – he doesn't mind a scrap or two either.'

I didn't write this in my notebook then, though I must stress how the brief encounter played on my mind in the coming days.

I set about fetching the camera and stand and asked Vaughn to show me the exact spot where the body was found. He went ahead of me, and as we scrambled through the undergrowth, over loose twigs and fallen leaves, we came to the granite face. There was smooth dirt underfoot. Immediately I was perplexed.

'This is the spot the body was found?'

'Y-yes. Her legs were this way.' He pointed which way the body had lain.

I placed my camera down and moved around the scene a few times, my back pressed against the granite rock face. At one point, I even scampered a short way up the slope to look down upon it.

'You are certain she was found here?'

Vaughn concurred once more.

I shook my head in bemusement. A black scar of scorched earth and charcoaled twigs was scored into the ground. Yet it seemed far too small, barely the remains of a scouting camp fire.

'How badly was she burnt?' I exclaimed a little, beginning to set up my camera to capture the scene.

'Across most of her b-body,' Vaughn said. 'Almost entirely.'

'Can you not see?' I asked, to which both Vaughn and Cummings shook their heads. 'These scorch marks are too small. This would never have burnt her entire body; it would take a significant bonfire to cause such damage. You'd see the remnants, not just scorch marks on the ground.'

Vaughn and Cummings began to stammer over one another.

'It has to be the place—'

'If they kept adding wood—'

'It would make no difference,' I interjected. 'The victim's body would need to be engulfed in flames to allow sufficient heat to cause total immolation. I've seen it before; bodies destroyed entirely in makeshift furnaces. These marks suggest only minimal tissue damage could have been inflicted to part of her body.'

As I took my image and replaced the plate another thought struck me.

'It begs the question why there is a body at all? If the culprit intended to dispose of her why not burn her fully to be rid of her remains? Why not bury her, or throw her in the river? Why dump her so close to the mill, where any remains would very likely be found?'

Neither Vaughn nor Cummings spoke. As I took more photographs, their silence began to irritate me.

'Would either of you entertain the notion that this has been staged?' I growled after a few moments, catching myself before I could say more.

Cummings began to nod his head vigorously. 'As it would if the travellers committed the crime in their camp. They could leave the body here to make it seem another had committed the act.'

'But the question still remains,' I replied, 'why is there a body at all?'

To that Cummings said nothing. I spent the next forty minutes taking photographs of the scene and making notes on the size and shape of the scorched area. With my attentions taken, Cummings and Vaughn stepped away, and it was only as I took my last image that I realised they were muttering quietly to one another. It was more of an irritant to me then than a cause for any suspicion.

Jotting my last few notes, I fetched a short stick and knelt alongside the blackened ground. The charcoal was shallow, though I moved and pawed through it a little for anything that may be hidden. There was nothing and I threw the little stick away with an audible sigh. Questions bombarded me.

The heat of the day had not abated, and the muggy air seemed to take effect on me as I hunched in the dirt. My head began to throb lightly (a result of the half pint of ale, I assumed) and my body seemed weakened, lacking the spritely energy I had felt upon my arrival. I tried in vain to loosen my collar and rubbed the heavy sweat from my brow.

Weary and uncertain of what remained to be learnt from the scene – for it had only succeeded in throwing up more questions than answers – I reached inside my jacket pocket and fetched a thin empty vial. I intended to take a small sample of the dirt, for though it was beyond my competence, I knew of colleagues and chemists who had in recent years begun experimenting with dirt, water and other such earthy things in the hope of shining greater light on crimes committed. It was merely a passing thought, for I was certain that this spot could not be the place in which Betsan had been murdered.

I reached down to fill the vial but instead made a startling discovery. The charcoal and blackened earth were still warm to the touch.

3

The General's House – June 17th, 1904

Cummings and Vaughn were silent when I came back alongside them. I chose not to say anything of the warm soot and charcoal; it was such a strange occurrence that made no sense. Though I had no reason then to suspect the two men, I decided it best to keep my own counsel until I could be certain they played no ill part in the whole affair. I began disassembling my camera stand and placing my equipment back in its case. I tucked the dry plates neatly in a custom pocket that would hold them safe and secure.

I asked Vaughn whether his report was finished.

'Not— not entirely. It's not something I've done be-before, sir.'

The light throbbing in my forehead was rapidly spreading to my temples and I was in no real mood to badger the young man.

'You can finish it as we examine the body this afternoon,' I said sternly, rubbing my eyes as thin maroon spirals and dots began to swirl in my vision.

'A-are you all right, Inspector?' asked Vaughn.

'I'm not an Insp— never mind. Yes, I am fine.' I wasn't. 'Which way would you deem best to get to Michaelston and the church?

Perhaps on the way you could both elaborate as to why the body is held there?'

The pair remained quiet for a prolonged moment.

'To be fr-frank, sir, it m-may not be possible to examine the body this afternoon.' Vaughn was talking quickly as I knelt down to close the latches on my camera case. 'I'm not sure Mr Cummings was aware—'

'Richmond,' Cummings cut in, 'the church cleric, is not here. He's on business today in the city – he helps run a small missionary by the docks. He's the only man who has the keys to the church.'

'You didn't think to tell him of my arrival last night or this morning?' I asked coarsely. 'You surely assumed an examination of the body would be a priority?'

'I can't recall if I discussed the matter with him,' Cummings replied flatly.

A vague answer if any. I looked up at him and thought to question him further. But as I stretched from the floor, I struggled to maintain my balance, my legs feeling weak as the world seemed to blur and lean acutely. Whatever had come over me was worsening quite suddenly.

'Fine. Constable, I'll expect your report completed by the morning. Ensure Richmond is available, so we can examine the body first thing. Mr Cummings and I will meet you at the church there – we'll take a cart along the road rather than walk. We'll make way at nine o'clock.'

Vaughn nodded enthusiastically.

Protocol should have dictated that next we inspect the site the travellers had occupied at the time of the murder. My vision was now spinning uncontrollably, however, and my body felt dreadfully lethargic. I began walking back to the mill and both Cummings and Vaughn followed obediently.

'You doubt the travellers did this then?' Cummings asked me when we were a little distance past the mill and heading back towards the village.

'It seems too easy – many cases are left unchallenged because of easy answers.'

'But surely,' Cummings said confidently, 'they remain the prime suspects?'

I nodded. 'If what you and the young Constable say is true, that the girl was frequenting their campsite in the days and nights leading to her death, then certainly they remain suspect.'

I did little to engage with the pair after that. They bumbled through some questions which I merely ignored or dismissed abjectly. When we were in sight of Mill Hill I stopped for a brief moment to regain my composure. My headache had worsened to a painful migraine; I rubbed my temples and forehead. It's difficult to think straight when one feels such a sharp pain behind the eyes.

'Perhaps you could allow the Councilman and I a moment to talk, Constable. I'll speak with you later regarding your report.'

Vaughn nodded hesitantly, sharing a quick glance with Cummings (which I noted in spite of my discomfort) before walking briskly up Mill Hill towards the village.

'You forgot to mention the General to me, Cummings,' I groaned somewhat when Vaughn was out of earshot. 'I would speak with him before the day is out.'

'I deal with the day-to-day running of the village, Bexley.' Cummings' tone was sharp and cutting – it seemed I had touched a nerve.

'Regardless, he is the authority in this village and I'll speak with him presently,' I repeated. 'I shall drop my things at the inn and you can take me to his estate on the common.'

As I continued to walk, Cummings marched after me. 'How do you know of his estate, or of the General for that matter? I can assure you he shares the opinion that I hold!'

'The Postmaster told me.' I was in no mood to argue and continued the ascent towards the Twyn.

Within a few yards, Cummings barged past me, muttering something about the blackguard deliveryman.

When I was back in the relative cool of the inn, I made straight for my room. I dropped my case clumsily on the bed and sank my face into the bowl of water laid out for me on the table. I held my face under as long as I could before sitting on the bed as the cold water ran down my neck and shirt.

The migraine persisted though I felt momentarily revived. I doused my face for a few more minutes before making my way downstairs. The old man had vacated his seat in the lounge though Solomon remained behind the bar. As I came to the small foyer I turned and reminded him that there was no candle in my room. He didn't answer me.

Cummings was waiting outside, and we walked across the Twyn in the direction of The Dragon Inn. Neither of us spoke.

We headed up a neat road that cut up and across the common a short distance. This was the mount, the trail leading to the General's estate alone. His grounds encroached on the common's border with a large wall running parallel to the road, above which the tops and peaks of tall sycamores were visible. Soon, we came to a large set of tall iron gates, black, with a gold seal and insignia emblazoned in the centre. Cummings pushed against the gates tentatively; they squealed as they opened slowly.

The space was far larger than I had estimated. A wide gravel road, skirting through the exterior gardens and lawns, led to a stately Georgian mansion adorned with large window bays and heavy growths of ivy. Flowers bloomed everywhere, many native though some clearly exotic and rare. Perfume and pollen was pungent in the air, enough to make the eyes water ever so slightly. In the centre of the front lawn a three-tiered circular fountain, topped with an audacious cherub, spouted water softly; it accompanied the chorus of birdsong that echoed and chimed high in the tops of the sycamore trees.

The building was somewhat disjointed, where extensions and conservatories had been adapted or added anew. The main entrance way was off centre, marked only by its small porch, finished with two Grecian-style columns that were undoubtedly made of marble. As we approached the porch, I shifted my gaze to each of the manor's large windows. In a room to the far right on the second floor, I caught a glimpse of a gaunt and pallid figure watching us. He was not hidden, though he seemed a wretched and wasted shape. It was obvious that this man was General James.

As I stepped between the two marble pillars, Cummings pushed alongside me and gently pulled on a golden bell chain. We waited in silence for at least half a minute, until finally, with a loud shift of a metallic bolt, the door opened slowly.

A short, stout figure greeted Cummings with an air of disdain. 'Your weekly meeting was yesterday, Councilman.'

Cummings offered his apologies. 'This is the Inspector about whom I spoke to the General. He arrived earlier today and has asked to speak with the General.'

The woman in the doorway – the housekeeper by all accounts – turned her narrowed gaze upon me, before addressing Cummings in her calm, bristly tone.

'The General left this matter in your hands, Councilman.'

Cummings agreed vehemently. 'I have informed the Inspector, but he still demanded that we come.'

'The Inspector may demand all he likes!' The housekeeper replied as if I were not standing right there, my head pounding mercilessly. 'Today is not a good day for such things.'

I opened my mouth to protest, but from somewhere deep in the gloom of the manor a voice bellowed out. The housekeeper sighed. She disappeared for a moment and we waited in silence once more. Upon her return, she opened the door wide and gestured for us to come in.

'Apologies for my tone, Inspector,' she said quietly. 'The General will see you in a few moments if you would care to wait.'

The housekeeper made her way down the greeting hall we stood in and climbed a flight of stairs to the second-floor landing. Heavy doors opened and slammed, the noise echoed and bounced.

The interior was as well-kept as the gardens. Chequered-tiled floors shimmered in the haze of daylight that shone through the narrow windows of the entrance way. The walls, a light mint green, were all but bare as far as I could see, with the exception of a large portrait of a military officer in his prime. The red coatee, emblazoned with a white sash and ceremonial medals, the feathered bicorne and sleek rapier was the uniform appointed to the British soldiers of the American Revolution.

The piercing eyes of the soldier stared down at me. My mind flashed back to the mill and the shadowed figure I was certain had been inside. The women on the common. The flutter of a coat; horse hooves disappearing out of sight. No matter where I went in the village, it seemed I was always being watched. Now the soldier looked down upon me, his eyes filled with all the blood lust of a man who has seen far too much death. I turned away from the painting after only a moment.

'I take it the General is in a poor state of health,' I whispered to Cummings. He nodded silently.

'His memory.' He shook his head a little and I understood his meaning. A door opened on the landing and the housekeeper looked down upon us.

'The General will speak with you, Inspector.'

Cummings and I moved towards the stairwell until the house-keeper spoke once more.

'You may wait in the lounge, Councilman.'

Cummings' face erupted. 'As Head of the Council I shall be present with the General.' He coughed and spluttered, his skin darkening like a thundercloud. 'You may work for the General, woman, but you forget your place at times.'

'My place, Mr Cummings, is right here, telling you to wait in the lounge.' Her demeanour was wholly unperturbed, her polite, if wholly insincere, smile unwavering. It was clear who would win out in the argument.

'I'll wait outside,' Cummings growled petulantly a moment later. He stormed off as I climbed the stairway and followed after the housekeeper. We passed through a heavy oak door, and down a short corridor. It was well lit and airy, with two large windows looking out to the gardens – I spotted Cummings pacing along the gravel path like a caged beast.

Rooms led off from the corridor, but we continued down to the very end.

'The General is hard of hearing and prone to confusion,' the housekeeper informed me. 'He wanted to speak with you in person, though that is likely on account of seeing you walk up the driveway, rather than any knowledge of who you are or why you are here. Some days his memory is better than others; I'd ask you try not to exhaust him.'

At the end of the corridor, we came to a door with the

three-feathered crest of the Prince of Wales above. The house-keeper knocked twice.

'Five minutes,' she intoned sternly, before leaving me at the door alone. I opened it slowly.

The General's study was dark and gloomy; I was grateful to escape the brightness of the day that only seemed to be intensifying my migraine. The walls were deep maroon, finished with a border of golden flowers that had dulled to a tarnished bronze. The General sat with his back to me, his body concealed by a high leather chair, apart from one grey hand that hung over the arm.

As I walked towards him, I looked upon an impressive collection of military apparel that lined the walls and cluttered the cabinets. There were rifles of antiquity, muskets and pistols with small golden plaques noting their age and origin, an array of rapiers, broadswords, sabres, and a single Arabian scimitar, right up to the decorative castings that covered the dark ceiling. There were flags, medallions, small statues, helms and sashes, buckles and in the farthest corner (far from the natural light seeping in through the windows) a faded, yet pristine red coat. A fine painting of a bloody battle consumed much of the far wall, above a dark fireplace and mantel. To this day, I do not know what battle it depicted.

It all beggared belief, for although I admit I was then (and remain) no great militarist, it was obvious that many of the items in the room were over two hundred years old.

'Quite the collection,' I muttered to myself. In spite of his supposed poor hearing it seemed to stir the General, who murmured something under his breath. I walked into the room slowly and stepped around the leather chair.

The General was a wretched figure in person. His skin was stretched around his thin skull, tucked into the deep pockets beneath his eyes. They themselves were drained of all colour, desperately dark and lifeless. Thick veins sprung out at me, concealed only by a few wisps of grey hair. He had a white moustache that was bushy and unkempt; a thin cigar gave off a spindly trail of blue-grey smoke.

The General's faded smoking jacket seemed to hang off his cadaverous frame. I thought to shake his hand but feared that may exhaust him.

'General, my name is Thomas Bexley—'

He interrupted at volume. 'Harriet says you are an Inspector.'

'Of a type.' I seemed to be repeating myself to anyone who would listen.

'The type that solves crime, old chap? I always liked a good penny dreadful.' He laughed and pointed to another leather chair. I sat down facing him.

'As Lord of the Manor, General, I thought it appropriate to speak with you briefly to outline how I shall carry out my investigation and ask one or two questions. I shan't take much of your time, sir.'

That made him laugh even more, though it was not a pleasant sound.

'I have plenty of that!'

I nodded, trying to decide then if it were an outburst of wit or senility.

'I'm sure you are aware of the sensitive details of what happened. Did you know of Betsan Tilny?' He didn't answer but took a deep drag on his cigar. I produced my notebook. 'Cummings and the young Constable Vaughn have given me their opinion of what occurred. Perhaps you have another view?'

He fidgeted in his seat and stared at the painting above the mantel. I waited a few moments for an answer and got none.

'Is there anything at all you can tell me, General?'

He raised a bony finger towards me and then lifted it toward the painting.

'The King's army rushed 'em, you see. The Grenadiers shafted them from the left and the cavalry flew in like whippets to a hare. They couldn't stop the cavalry! Seems almost a shame really.'

He took another puff from his cigar and I looked from him to the painting. I realised then the extent to which the General's decline was afflicting his mind as well as body. I made one last attempt to gather some information.

'Vaughn believes the girl was killed by vagabonds.'

The General's gaze remained fixed upon the painting, his lips peeling back to a ghastly grin.

'Those Russian dogs never stood a chance.'

I pitied the General as I closed my notebook; it seemed futile outlining how I would proceed with the investigation. I took one further look around the study; at a large writing desk cluttered with papers close to the bay windows; at a stuffed Alsatian standing proudly, its jet black coat matted and thinning in patches.

I stood from my chair. 'Thank you for your time, General. I'll do my utmost to ensure the young woman's killer is brought to justice.'

I took my leave of the old man, heading towards the door. As I passed his chair, the General took hold of my arm with uncanny speed. I was startled, my initial instinct to lurch away from him. He gripped hold of my forearm harder and twisted his neck to look up towards me.

'My heart bleeds for her mother. My duty to her, to the child. That burden – what darkness have I let come to this place?'

His words chilled me; they were filled with cool clarity. His eyes had brightened, alive and focused. They were not the eyes of an infirm, aged man. He fixed onto me for what seemed an eternity and I dare say I struggled to maintain his gaze.

The door to the General's study opened and it was a blessed mercy. The housekeeper, Harriet, spoke though I cannot recall what she said. I felt the General's grip weaken a little, and pulled away from him before turning and leaving the room.

As the housekeeper walked me back down the corridor, I turned upon her.

'Is he lucid often?'

'The General has good days and bad days,' was all she said in return.

So distracted was I by the General in his gloomy study, that for a brief few minutes, my migraine had lost some of its potency. In the bright corridor and stairwell, it returned with vicious venom. I remember pausing and taking grip of the banister, rubbing my eyes with my free hand. The edges of my vision seemed to darken and the world twisted and warped in dramatic fashion.

I recall the housekeeper's insincere tone if not the words she spoke to me. I shook a hand and brushed past her upon the stairs in a discourteous manner. I did not bid farewell as I hauled open the heavy front door and emerged in the agonising light of the afternoon. I made my way down the gravel drive and Cummings appeared alongside me.

'I'm afraid the heat of day has had some effect on my state, Mr Cummings. I had intended to begin questioning but shall retire for a time to my room.'

Cummings ignored me completely. 'Did the General say anything to you? I wouldn't take any notice of the old man, he's quite mad, you know.'

I shook my head, which only intensified the throbbing and sense of nausea. I walked on and Cummings followed. We said very little as we headed back to the Twyn, though he continued to remark on the man's mental state. I am now all too aware that, were it up to him, I would never have seen or spoken to the General again.

4

Diary Entry – June 17th, 1904

I am troubled. This place troubles me.

It's strange to think how fine I felt this morning. Have I become so callous, so insipid, as to take no disheartening from my duties? The death of a young woman seems not to affect me – what else have I lost in documenting the crimes of man?

I am too hard upon myself. It is just this day – WHAT a day! – that has made me feel so.

How different I feel this eve. I sit at the table and write by candle-light, a single candle mind, that I had to ask again for from Solomon. What a trauma to get so basic a thing! I returned from the General's house and feeling poor, retired and rested in my room. That was no later than three, and when I woke some thirty minutes ago (revived in a manner), I swore into the darkness, for that was all there was until my eyes adjusted. The gas lamp in the road outside my window cast a white hue upon my small room, enough for me to read my watch and see it was a quarter past ten.

My head aches – my vision seems to fall in and out of focus. Nevertheless, I feel somewhat better than I did. I have managed to get some more food and water from Solomon, along with the single blasted candle. (But no matches! Lucky I carry my own.)

There is a ruckus in the bar below me, even at this late hour. Good business indeed for Solomon but a rowdier crowd than I would have imagined. I did not stay below for too long. Whatever illness has come to me may hopefully have passed by tomorrow, for it is the last thing I need hampering my work here. Already there have been things I should have attended to.

This is indeed a strange village, something from another time really.

Where to begin, what question or suspicion shouts loudest? The fact there is a body at all, the examination of which will be carried out in the morning, leaves me quite perplexed. We could assume that the perpetrator (or perpetrators) was disturbed in some manner, suspected discovery and perhaps, fearing such, fled from the body before they could adequately dispose of it. Yet the body was not discovered by Miller until the dawn (unless the truth of the matter is being concealed, which for argument's sake, I suppose it is not); if the crime were committed during the night (and it is an if, for until I determine when the victim was last seen, estimating an accurate time of the murder will be very difficult) there would be ample time to hide the body.

And so much space!

Why carry out the crime so close to the mill, where discovery was more likely? With the veil of darkness why not move the body to the woodlands proper? There it could be buried or burnt if that was the inclination. It could be days then till the girl was known to be missing.

My thoughts are thus: either the body was left in its location and state for a purpose (though the reason remains unclear) OR the time of discovery (perhaps even the discoverer) is incorrect. If the crime were an act of passion, it would perhaps make more sense – the perpetrator could have panicked and fled the scene, maybe even seen to try and foul the remains in such a manner as to destroy any connection to himself. Yet the scorching of the earth, relative to the burn marks that Constable Vaughn has described to me, do not correlate, meaning the injuries inflicted could not have been done in the same spot the body was found. This theory, that the killer panicked in a moment of frenzy and tried to defile the body where it lay, is therefore null and void, as her final resting place cannot be where she was burnt.

What then of the accusation that this was an act carried out by travellers, somewhere toward their campsite in the woodlands? It is a possibility, for they could have moved the girl's body, staged the scene close by the mill to conceal their crime. Intuition tells me this is false, however; the idea seemed such the moment Vaughn and Cummings expressed it to me. Far too neat, far too easy – these matters rarely are. AGAIN, why would they leave a body to be discovered? It makes no real sense.

It seems to me that the body was left for a purpose, to invoke fear or send some message, perhaps? The charcoal felt warm to the touch this morning, but that I now question. If it were warm, it would have been a fresh burning, an outrageous idea. By my own admission I had been feeling unwell since noon, and with credence to Occam's Razor, I accept now that I was mistaken in my thinking. Yet the scene remains a staging of a sort.

Vaughn's report may shed some more light on the whole affair. The Lord General did little to help with that – had I known his state . . . no, I am lying even as I write. I would have still gone to see him for the sake of my enquiry and to rest any niggling doubts about his character. I distrust Cummings for the simple fact that he seems keen to be done with the matter quickly. He hoped I would merely confirm his and Vaughn's opinion, make a warrant for the arrest of any travellers within one hundred miles and pay my last respects with a shot of brandy before returning to Cardiff on the last train of the day. I have no evidence to suspect him of any foul play and I am giving him the benefit of doubt – it is likely he is as fearful as all those who live here, and is simply willing his theory to be true.

I am keen to learn more of why the body is being kept so far from the village proper. *Cummings mentioned some superstitions on the part of these people. I imagine they fear that some cruel spirit – Beelzebub himself! – shall cast a lasting curse upon the place should the body remain in the vicinity. Perhaps that is an unfair presumption – a discrimination of sort – upon these simple folk. In a sleepy shire such as this, it is all too easy in the bright light of day, with the songbirds whistling and the mediocrity of life being played out around you, to dismiss such fears as old wives' tales for children who have not done all their mother's chores.*

At this late hour though, with the heavy black of night as company, with the whispering of draughts through crooked rafters and the hollow, unnatural hoot of the night owl unseen, the mind wanders to its darkest corners and thinks of all too dreadful things.

The entire time I write I have been glancing – glancing through the window, glancing over my shoulder, glancing towards the bed. Since my arrival I have dealt with the discomfort of being watched, and the feeling lingers now into the night. Each flicker of the candle makes me turn and watch. The shadows seem to startle me, something looming in my peripheral vision, moving against me as I cast my head down towards the paper. It is foolishness, of course, though far harder to dismiss than I, a rational man who fears no God, would dare admit to anyone.

There remains the scratching from the ceiling; I shall not sleep easy with rats moving above me. Such vile things.

The revellers have left and the bar rests quiet now. I should as well, for I am weary, and would be rid of this sudden illness that has taken hold of me. I would not have bothered sitting and scribbling this entry if it were not for the shadows and the eerie hue of the gas lamp.

Let me muster some courage to extinguish this candle.

5

The Road to Michaelston –
June 18th, 1904

Some phantom in a nightmare must have roused me, for I woke suddenly with a terrible flutter in my heart. The dawn had not arrived, though the inky darkness of night was beginning to lighten. My shaking hands were blue as I looked at them, so too were the sheets on my bed and the walls of my room.

I sat bolt upright and took deep breaths to calm my nerves. The ache in my head and body lingered from the night past. I was feverish, my entirety seemed drenched in oily sweat. I cursed the damn illness that had come over me so suddenly on this errand.

In the gloom, I managed to take some drink I had remaining from the night previous. My shoulders and neck felt stiff and I sought to move and pace a little around the room to energise my body. It only did to exhaust me. When I collapsed back into bed, I held my eyes shut in an effort to return to sleep.

It is funny what a bad dream and darkness can do to you – the two combined can banish sense and reason. I lay there for perhaps an hour or more, till the first streaks of light dispelled all the horrid things I had dreamt and returned my sanity and courage.

I was dressed and fully groomed by eight thirty – Cummings was to collect me at nine. I scanned over my notes from the previous day, trying to gain some inspiration or a more rounded idea as to what had happened. Nothing came, and I mostly sat wiping the sweat from my brow, before checking my camera and stand. Testament to how badly the nightmare had unnerved me, I felt compelled to tuck my Enfield pistol in my case with my equipment.

When I left my room, I heard whispers and muttering from the couple in the room across the short landing from mine, no doubt the pair I had heard arguing the day before. I stumbled down the narrow stairwell and found the bar as I had left it, though a few chairs were lying on their sides and the tables were in need of a thorough clean. As I waited, I noticed the old man, asleep once more in the lounge opposite. His head lolled to one side in the same manner as when I had first lain eyes on him, only now his shirt and herder's cap were of a different sort. The sight of him brought on quite the spell of nausea, and as I bowed my head towards the floor, Solomon appeared before me with irritation etched across his brow.

He brought me a mug of weak, lukewarm tea without a word and a few moments later returned with a plate of boiled eggs. I thanked him and inhaled the tea rather than drank it.

'A full house then,' I gasped when the mug was empty.

Solomon said nothing.

'Are there guests in all the rooms above?' I asked once more.

Solomon glared at me. 'No one here but you,' he murmured.

'Come now,' I replied groggily. 'What ruckus was that yesterday if not your other guests? I heard them as I left my room this morning.'

He maintained his cool gaze and I decided to leave the point, guessing then that it was his family occupying the rooms above.

'Is there a physician in the village?' I asked. He shook his head and left me alone.

I sat for a few more minutes, mustering the strength to stand and leave the bar. With my case in hand I made to the door and stood in the small outside patio of the inn, feeling the chill of the morning rush against me. It was welcome but did little to alleviate my fever.

It was a fine morning by all accounts. The pastel dawn had been replaced by hazy blue skies, unbroken by cloud in all directions. Everything was still. A church bell rang out with rhythmic authority; it was nine on the hour. A door slammed across the Twyn, though I saw no one stir. A few minutes later, I caught sight of the Postmaster leaving his office. He seemed to hold still for the briefest moment, looking straight at me. He made no move to approach but sped away on his rickety bicycle down Station Road.

As I watched after him, the disturbing sense of disquiet returned to me. The stillness of the Twyn suddenly became unnatural rather than serene. It is hard to explain such an intuition, one that is completely unfounded. But I was certain, as with the previous day, that behind the gothic windows, obscured in the darkness of their rooms, people watched me.

I turned on the spot and looked all around. Indeed, in that moment I saw the flicker and twitch of curtains rustle here and there. My paranoia it seemed was justified – it would remain fully ignited until the day I left Dinas Powys, with no real pause or reprieve.

Some ten minutes later, I heard the clatter of a wagon approaching the Twyn. It seemed to take an age. As Cummings appeared in view, sat atop a dusty haycart dragged by a thin shire horse, I succumbed to another spell of nausea and dizziness and barely acknowledged his greeting.

'You don't look well, Inspector,' he pronounced. By now I had decided not to bother correcting my misplaced title – I hadn't the energy.

I clambered onto the driver's box and slung my camera equipment behind me with a regrettable clatter. Cummings gave a light shake of the reins and we slowly moved away, looping around the grassy Twyn and heading back down Mill Hill. Cummings informed me the journey would be no more than twenty-five minutes and that Vaughn was already waiting for us.

The cool morning air whistling gently past us felt wonderful. Cummings asked me my opinion on the matter at hand; I chose to say as little as possible.

'Until an examination of the body is carried out and questioning begins there is little to say. Too many things do not correlate to paint a clear picture.'

'If I may be bold, Inspector,' Cummings said warmly (too warmly in fact, for it was obvious then that his manner was feigned), 'perhaps you are overthinking the matter. This all plays into the hands of those damned gypsies – they've left the girl and a scene so confused wholly on purpose. We with good heart spend days trying to uncover the truth whilst they scurry away, never to be caught.'

In truth, the man had a point, though his insistence that the crime was committed by travelling vagrants was becoming more than a little noteworthy.

'Do you have some experience, Councilman, that gives you such prejudice against travellers?'

Cummings grimaced. 'Such dirty, vile—'

'Your duty,' I cut in before he could say too much, 'is to assist in uncovering the truth of this murder, not in placing guilt on anyone you deem somehow lesser than yourself.'

'Now really, Inspector, that has never been my intention.'

'Then unless you have credible evidence to support your

claims and theories, do not question the manner in which I carry out—'

I stopped mid-sentence. We had descended Mill Hill, crossed over the river and were now approaching the base of the Pen-Y-Turnpike. A large wagon, laden with wrapped meats, sacks of flour and other such provisions, stood at a standstill before us, its nag waiting stoically at the base of the hill. An argument was ensuing between the driver and another man. I quickly gathered that this man – the road keeper – was not allowing the driver to make the ascent up the hill, deeming his load far too heavy.

Cummings pulled up the cart, climbed down from his perch and approached the two men. In spite of his being there, the argument quickly descended into vulgarities before each man grabbed at the other's collars. Cummings quickly separated the pair, leaving them swinging their arms maddeningly with no real contact.

I made no attempt to interject, feeling dreadful, light-headed and hot with fever. The three bickered for a few minutes until their voices began to simmer down. It seemed an agreement was met.

Cummings returned to my side.

'Joseph is heading to the farms near Michaelston,' he informed me. 'We'll take some of his load.'

I nodded, groaning a little as Cummings stepped back towards the hill. I followed, in no real mood to help but compelled to hurry things along. In spite of my torpor, I lugged a few flour sacks and two whole butchered mutton from Joseph's cart to our own. Joseph's cart still seemed dreadfully overburdened, but the road keeper was soon satisfied. Together, he and Joseph began leading the horse and cart up the steep incline.

Cummings and I watched after them. He offered me a

cigarette, which I declined; I have a taste for tobacco, but my throat felt wretched and dry.

'Damned fools, the pair of them,' Cummings muttered as the two men began barking at one another some way out of sight up the hill. By now we had been at the base of the turnpike for almost half an hour and the cool of dawn had burnt away entirely. I removed my jacket and tie, unbuttoning my shirt and rolling my sleeves so that, from a little way off, I looked indistinguishable from the few farm hands we saw heading to and from the mill. We returned to our cart and waited for the road keeper to return.

'The body at rest in Michaelston,' I said quite bluntly, pinching at the bridge of my nose as the haycart, the road and everything else in my line of sight shuddered before me, 'explain that to me.'

Cummings took a slow drag on his cigarette. 'I told you yesterday. These people have their superstitions.'

'Of what nature?' I persisted.

Cummings spluttered, 'Look, I don't share the opinions of many who live here – it is not my role to judge as you, this very day, made plain to me.' His cigarette had burnt to a stub and he flicked it to the floor. 'Many years back, some foo— someone got the notion that a, *thing* – a presence, spirit – whatever you may wish to call it, lurked in the woodlands around the village. They call it *Calon Farw*, the deathly heart or some nonsense. Now, people blame *it* for the girl's death, though the state she was in, they think it's not finished with her. They wanted the body held *in a church* and All Saints had a vacant cellar. They're certain it will come back for her.'

'So what of those who reside in Michaelston – surely they were not pleased when they learnt the body would be kept with them?'

Cummings hesitated and mumbled. 'They came to stay in the village, for the time being at least.'

I shook my head. 'You cannot indulge such nonsense—'

'Indulge it!' Cummings blurted. 'Do not come to this village, Inspector, and tell me what I may or may not do. I had *no choice* in the matter when everyone wanted her body away from their homes, their places of work. It's not my fault these people are not like you or I. Out here, far from a city, from real civilisation, you cannot blame them for having all manner of fears and worries, especially when such a thing as this has happened.'

On this point I couldn't help but agree, thinking back to the night previous and the very real feeling of a presence being with me in my room at the inn. A vision from my faded nightmare flitted quickly in my mind.

'So that is it? There is no other purpose for her body being there?'

Cummings placed a hand against his chest. 'There is no other reason, Inspector. In truth, it is probably the best place for her, for your enquiry if nothing else. No one has been able to get to the body since it was moved, not that anyone wants to go near it.' He fell silent then, his face draining of its colour.

A voice called out and the road keeper waved at us from the base of the hill.

When he came upon us, I insisted we make way immediately, my patience worn away almost entirely by the delay and my contemptible fever.

The road from the peak of the turnpike was narrow, with untamed hedgerows and thick bushels of brambles at either side. We cut through the rolling hills and outcrops of tall trees, passed a few cattle sheds and an abandoned farm house, all at a sullen and sedate plod. We made no sight of Joseph ahead of us, nor of anyone travelling in the other direction.

'Many of us saw this coming,' Cummings said quite suddenly after we had sat in silence for some time. 'Well, not this entirely, but you get my meaning. Whether you agree with me or not, Inspector, girls who act out are likely to get themselves into trouble. I imagine half the cases you have in London—'

'She only has her mother, is that right?' I interrupted as I stared out across a golden field of rapeseed. Cummings nodded.

'Yes, Catrin. I daren't say I knew anything of the girl's father being around. As a matter of fact, I can recall a strange fellow staying in the village for perhaps a month – if that – not long before the mother started showing. I'm certain he abandoned her when he realised. That class of man was bound to breed a wayward daughter. Catrin is no better mind – encouraged her, *activities*.'

I asked him what he meant.

'She was selling herself, Inspector, undoubtedly. Why else would she have been frequenting these travellers? No other reason than that in my opinion, and there were some rumours flying around the village before she died.'

'Rumours of what sort?'

Cummings seemed to grow uncomfortable. 'She was something of a flirt with the young farm hands. The millers, too. Led them on, if you take my meaning.' He pulled right on the reins to skirt a large pitfall in the dirt road. 'Miller especially warned them of her. Of her sort really – this thing is not uncommon outside of the city.'

I thought then of the two men, the Davey brothers who I had seen the day before in the woodlands close to the scene.

'Would any of the farm hands testify to that? That she was a harlot, I mean?'

Cummings only shrugged. 'It's no great secret amongst the village. Remember how I told you yesterday that some were not surprised.'

'Whether she sold herself or not, it lends no credence to the belief that she ought to die.'

'Of course not, but you must admit, Inspector, it greatly enhanced the risk that a terrible thing would happen to her. Here's our turning.'

Just then he pulled the reins so that we almost came to a complete stop. He yanked left and the nag took us down an ill-formed track that skirted off the main road. Our line of sight was obscured on either side of the track by thick-bushed trees that rose high from tall, steep banks of dirt. The heavy foliage arched overhead.

The air seemed to grow even warmer as we headed further down the track and a dank smell rose around and followed us. The trail snaked through the land, enclosed and sheltered from view. Our pace was still slow, and each turn seemed to find another and another, so that soon it felt as if the road would never end. Birds and other animals rustled and called in the greenery that surrounded us, though quickly such noises became unnatural and strange to me.

My state of paranoia deepened both suddenly and terribly, spurred on by my fever and raging suspicions.

I seem to recall growing certain that our journey was but a dreadful ruse and that, isolated in this space, incapable of any escape, I was to be met with a miserable end, a gang or more waiting for us with clubs and sticks and shovels ready to bury me somewhere in the outlying fields. Figures stood and moved about us in the heavy undergrowth, before vanishing in an instant. Bright eyes, wide and bulbous, white, bloodshot and filled with malice and hideous intent glared at me before blinking into darkness. Voices chattered, in hushed and bitter tones. I did not speak, nor think much upon the girl or anything other than the beasts and men lurking and watching in the shadows behind the trees.

Something glistened deep in the gloom, far up on the bank. A knife. More than one. Teeth jagged and sharp!

A few spots of water dripped down from overhanging foliage. When I looked at my hands, they were red with glossy maroon blood.

The horse vanished, Cummings too. I moved alone on the wooden cart as something nimble, chattering – laughing! – began to consume each precious gemstone of daylight, piece by piece. I didn't try to cry out or flee, mesmerised as much as terrified by the spectacle. Dread spoke plainly of all the terrible things to come, whilst reminding me of every ill thought I had ever had. The claws of branches reached out towards me with ever closer swipes and lunges, grabbing at my hair, my neck.

The eyes still watched, though now they were the eyes of serpents: yellow, green, sliced by a thin dagger-blade pupil that focused on my beating heart and throbbing jugular.

The voices began to mutter in unison, their words unclear but their intent quite obvious. They were taunting me, chanting. Their words grew steadily louder. Louder. Louder still.

The path faded completely.

I was submerged in the darkness of a deep pit.

Their voices grew louder. Louder.

My body shook. My eyes darted all about me.

The last splinter of light flickered from existence.

Louder. They spoke ever louder.

A compulsion took hold of me – to reach in my case and fetch my Enfield. I had enough bullets to ward off any attack.

Cummings roused me, his words at first like echoes from a far-off place.

'Inspector. Inspector!'

He shoved my side and with a start I came to, catching my breath as if I had been holding it. I hacked and wheezed for a moment or two, reeling and scanning the tree line.

I must have muttered some nonsense before regaining my senses. I took a few deep breaths before apologising to Cummings, who looked at me with real concern.

'You are unwell, man,' I heard him say.

To that I nodded. He was right.

6

All Saints Church – June 18th, 1904

I rubbed my face, felt the heat and sweat on my skin and the throbbing veins in my temples. I looked around; the unbroken blue sky had gone, now shrouded in bright white cloud that weighed upon the air and made it dense and cloggy.

We stood amidst a handful of tiny cottages, all of which had thatched roofs and poorly constructed exteriors. They were rustic, on the verge of collapse, older even than those that surrounded the Twyn at Dinas Powys. Beyond were the farmlands, and Cummings informed me that further north, carrying along the track we had arrived on, was the Old Court Farm and Manor that presided over much of the land.

We pulled up alongside the man Joseph, who was waiting on the road with his cart still fully loaded.

'You took an age,' he cackled as we stepped off and began moving the goods back to his cart. 'Were you lost?'

Neither I nor Cummings answered. When the task was done, Joseph hopped upon his wagon and set off without a word of thanks.

I fetched my case and headed into the grounds of All Saints church. It was a small space, littered with a few crumbling gravestones and memorials. The church itself was of a simple construction, furnished with only a few discreet glass windows and a stout bell tower.

The place was deathly quiet, devoid of bird calls or even light breaths of wind. I stopped in the graveyard and looked behind me, towards the cottages and the wheat fields. It seemed nothing was moving except for Cummings tending to the haycart and his horse.

I heard a voice call my name and turned to see Constable Vaughn emerging from the church, alongside a priest of some standing. Cleric Richmond was tall and well built, with stocky forearms and such deep lines across his face they appeared like cracks in bone-dry masonry. His eyes were heavily deep set, shrouded, in a fixed expression of scolding. His robes seemed dreadfully unbefitting, far too short in the legs and arms.

Both he and Vaughn remained in the arched entrance to the little church. Vaughn greeted me as I approached, and I cleared my throat to introduce myself to Richmond.

'Bexley,' I rasped.

He offered his hand with no word of welcome.

'I hope this has not been too distressing for you and your congregation, Reverend,' I said in a cordial manner. He only shook his head a little. Vaughn handed me a thin dossier – the report he had completed on the case. I tucked it under my arm as the cleric gestured for us to step inside.

The nave of the church was draped in shadow. What little light crept in through the small and grimy windows was augmented only by a range of beeswax candles spread along the aisles and as far back as the altar. Like its exterior, the church interior was simple and unadorned. Thick cobwebs seemed to hang everywhere, and heavy plumes of dust drifted with each of our steady footfalls. Though it should have been cool, the place was stifling, the air too thick to breathe.

Richmond led us down the aisles. The heady smells of moth-eaten prayer cushions along with the stale air only seemed to worsen my state. The camera case in my hand felt heavy as I looked toward the altar and at the twisted, ill-formed wood carving of Christ upon the cross. As we passed the altar, I saw the dust lie thick upon a copy of the King James Bible.

By all appearances, it seemed the church had been abandoned. I knew then that Cummings had not been telling me the whole truth of this place.

Richmond led us through a narrow doorway beside the altar. The light inside his vestibule was even poorer than in the nave. The room was not small, but was so badly cluttered with bookshelves, stacks of plain wooden prayer stools and an oversized writing desk, that it was barely large enough for us. The few lit candles cast a fiery glow upon our faces. Richmond looked devilish in such light.

He pointed toward the corner of the room, and beside a rusty wood stove, a hatch was opened in the floor, revealing a few stone stairs descending into darkness. The hatch was barely wide enough to fit a grown man.

'How on earth did you get the body down there?' I exclaimed, taking a few steps toward the hatch.

'With g-great difficulty, I'm afraid,' Vaughn replied. 'It was the best place for her.'

'I'm not sure any of this has been in the girl's best interest,' I replied.

I dropped my case and knelt beside the hatch. The air around it felt colder, though the reek of the girl's rotting corpse hit me full in the face. I admit I recoiled, caught between such a foul smell and the dry, dusty air of the vestibule. Coughing badly, I managed to stand, though my footing was unsteady. The fever was afflicting me ever more and I asked Richmond for some water. He cast me an irreverent stare and muttered that he would need to fetch some.

'We shall need all the light you have as well,' I groaned, rubbing my brow. 'I require the exposure for the camera. Fetch all the candles you can find.'

'I'll fetch them,' Vaughn chirped before leaving the vestibule. Richmond continued to stare at me whilst I glanced around the room.

'I understand this may make you uncomfortable, Reverend,' I said, meeting his gaze for a moment. 'But as soon as this is done the body can be buried properly.' I paused then, thinking how best to say: 'It seems the church has not been used for some time.'

Richmond nodded his head slowly. 'You're quite correct.'

'Mr Cummings—'

'Would be best to speak to on the matter.' Whether it was merely the flickering of candlelight across his face or his true displeasure, he seemed to grimace for a brief moment, before leaving the vestibule without another word.

I shook my head in contempt – Cummings had surely been lying to me.

I began making ready, setting my case down upon the writing desk. I removed the camera mount before checking over the plates I had brought. Before Vaughn or Richmond returned, I reached for my Enfield and tucked it in my trouser waistband. Its weight, and the butt of the revolver against my back, were nothing but reassuring.

I walked around the room and took hold of a bronze candelabra with three short candles. Vaughn returned a few moments later, bringing with him a grubby jug of lukewarm water – in which I promptly soaked my handkerchief – and a few short candles.

'Reverend has g-g-gone to fetch more candles,' he whispered, glancing over his shoulder.

'He is a quiet man,' I replied, striking a match.

'He is upset by all this.'

I nodded. 'And Mr Cummings?'

'Outside, sir. Shall I fetch him?'

'No, we have more pressing matters at hand. Fetch your handkerchief and soak it here,' I said, pointing to the jug of water. 'You will need it for the smell.'

Vaughn turned rigid.

'You want m-m-m-me down there with you?' His eyes darted from me to the little hatch in the corner.

'I'll need your help,' I muttered sternly. 'You can ensure the candlelight is best for exposure.' I was shaking quite frantically and took a moment to be still, for a wave of nausea and scorching pain spread from the tip of my brow to the muscles around my eyes. I rubbed my face again and dabbed my wet handkerchief around my temples.

'Our duty is to carry out these unpleasant tasks, Constable.' I sighed and took the now lit candelabra and handkerchief in each hand. 'I shall lead us down and you merely need fetch the lights and bring my equipment behind me.'

I said no more, for I could see Vaughn was shaken by the thought alone of heading into the church cellar. As I stepped over to the hatch, I rallied him with a stern word and he moved quickly behind me. With the briefest pause, my grip tightening on the candelabra, I stepped through the hatch into the darkness.

7

Stepping into Nightmares –
June 18th, 1904

As I immersed myself into the cellar proper, the bitter cold consumed me. My candles flickered a little and I held them out feebly to the darkness at my left, where the cellar spread away from me. I saw nothing for the darkness was as solid as the damp stone wall to my right. I set my back to it and slowly began to descend the shallow steps.

I took deep and steady breaths to calm my nerves. The wretched, festering smell of the body burnt through my hand-kerchief. It was an effort not to gag, for the air-tight cellar had compounded the stench beyond anything I had ever experienced. With each breath, I thought myself inhaling the girl's tortured spirit.

I slowly left the dim sphere of light cast from the room above. Soon, I was engulfed in true darkness, that which has a presence to it, a weight. Such darkness imposes itself upon you so that you do not move or walk in quite your usual manner. It consumes rational thought, sense and logic whilst feeding the heart panic and sheer dread. Each step downward I took was a miserable one, for each tested my courage and reserve, already beaten and bruised by the fever and the strange sights it had brought on.

All manner of wicked thoughts began swirling through my

mind as I approached the final few steps. My back slid against something spongy on the wall, cold moisture seeping through my shirt. I lurched forwards and lost my footing, collapsing off the steps and stumbling downward, blessedly only a foot or so below to the solid floor.

'Are you all right, Inspector?'

I turned and saw Vaughn's shrouded frame looking down from the vestibule above.

'Get down here, man!' I tried to be forceful but tremored as I spoke. I heard Vaughn's reservations but kept my gaze upon him as he stepped through the hatch and made his way down.

I wanted to wait for him, to have someone beside me as I moved forwards. But I didn't; I needed to shed light into the place and banish the foolish fears that, like hundreds of thin spiders' webs, were taking hold of me.

I held the candelabra out before me. Its soft glow pierced no further than a foot or two. I thought to throw it into the pitch – a childish notion, of course. The handkerchief to my nose seemed useless, for the smell was only worsening. My steps echoed throughout the cellar and I guessed then that it stretched the length of the church above.

'Where is the body?' I whispered to Vaughn.

'At the end,' he replied, still close to the hatch.

I moved on, unable even to see the edge of the walls to my left or right. My only reference was Vaughn and his single candle flame. He held it close to his face, so that when I turned (for I seemed to turn back every other short step) I saw his petrified eyes glistening faintly.

'For God's sake, get down here,' I growled to him, his little candle bouncing as he took another hesitant step.

I noted a soft trickling of water, likely through a breach in the cellar wall. The floor was damp and uneven in patches, but in the flicker of my light I began to see small pools and puddles dotted across my path.

A moth crawled along the hand holding my handkerchief – I batted it away, catching only the faintest glimpse of its speckled brown wings, before they vanished into the black. To my right, in the direction it flew, I glimpsed the faint outline of furniture propped against the wall. Stepping over, I saw some crates, filled with emptied wine bottles, and a few chairs, their felted seats moulded and dank. Here, water dripped lazily from the ceiling above.

Vaughn began dry heaving, still perched only midway down the stairs. He dropped his candle. It tinkered down the steps and came to rest on the cellar floor. He would have vanished completely, if not for the faintest light coming from the open hatch that struck the curve of his back as he remained doubled over.

I moved a few steps towards him.

'Are you all right, Constable? I'd advise you to continue coming down; the smell only worsens, and if you leave now you may not have the stomach to come ba—'

A knock, a faint dull thud, came from the darkest end of the cellar. It was enough to stop me where I stood. I listened intently but heard nothing more than the drip, drip of water and Vaughn's heavy breathing.

'I'm sorry, Inspector—'

'Come down now, Constable,' I said firmly. My eyes were fixed on the gloom from where the knocking sound had come. I began moving slowly back into the darkness towards the far end of the cellar, with tentative steps over the wet and slimy floor, my arm stretched outright. Hot blood, laced with fever, charged and throbbed through my beating heart and body – what effort it took to bring one leg in front of the other!

Something crawled across my neck.

I brushed at it, but to no avail. I thought for a moment it was only my raging imagination, but the itching crawl was too persistent, too regular to be a phantasm. It sped down beneath my shirt before I had chance to brush it away. What legs it had clawed into my flesh, prickling as it moved. I tried at first to hold my nerve, reaching around my back with the hand clasping my handkerchief. But when I felt its girth, a body of some sort, half the size of a golf ball, I began to panic and swirl.

It was trying to burrow into my flesh just below my left shoulder blade. I shrieked, dropping the candelabra to the floor with a piercing clatter that extinguished two of the little flames. I think Vaughn was shouting to me from behind though I cannot be certain. By then I was tearing my shirt away (I pulled at least three of the buttons clean off), pawing blindly at the wicked thing. It lurked upon my back just beyond my reach, so that I convulsed and spun like a madman, shaking myself to loosen its hold.

It gave off a dreadful natter, like iron files scratching against one another.

Finally, I managed to stretch in the right manner, clawing at the terror with the handkerchief in hand, squeezing it a little as I did. Whatever it was, for even now I still cannot imagine, it had a tough outer skin and very soft insides. I pinched it in my hand and flung it off me. When I searched upon the floor, I saw only the smallest glimpse of movement, scurrying into the gloom out of sight of the candlelight.

For a moment, I still turned and twisted, crying out with each panted breath. Grabbing the candelabra from the floor, I looked up toward the ceiling, seeing nothing of course for it was too high. I had flung my handkerchief away with the dreadful creature. The true, awful smell of the place, like rancid meat and burning sulphur, hit me. I tried to take shallow breaths, though my nausea near overpowered me and I felt on the verge of collapse. Some compulsion made me take hold of my pistol.

I felt more itching across my back and began sweeping and spinning once more. It was then I noticed Vaughn shouting to me.

'Hurry, there are more things unseen. I need light!' I cried at him, hoping he would come to my side. Instead I heard him quickly speed back up the steps to the hatchway. I thought to rush after him, but held still. *Things* scratched and moved around me. I had heard such scratching recently – the rats in the ceiling above my room at the inn.

I wheezed and spluttered, flinging my arm around with the revolver, aiming at nothing. The sole candle did nearly extinguish for the way I shook it around, my hands unable to hold still.

Something passed over my foot and I kicked out madly, yelping once more.

I shuddered in the cold, my shirt loose and unbuttoned, exposing my chest. The scratching only intensified, a cacophony of natters and dreadful claws on cold stone. It was closing in on me and my tiny ember. I yelled out, to try to banish such things, but the echo of my voice seemed only to fill me with more fear.

I began to speak to myself, vainly trying to hold my nerve.

'What game is this? Some foolish revelry?'

I clenched my eyes shut and felt excruciating pain in my temples.

Then something began speaking back to me from the far end of the cellar.

I stepped further forwards as the voice spoke in muted tones.

'Speak up, if you will. I am an officer and I am armed – this foolhardiness will not stand.'

I heard a thud to my right and aimed my gun. Strange laughter began to bounce around me, augmented and unnatural, queerly pitched as if drowned in water.

'Vaughn,' I shouted fearfully. 'There is someone down here!'

I continued to step forwards as the laughter grew louder. The cold worsened suddenly. The last speck of light from my candle began to dwindle and die, which aroused such a state of panic in me that I began to bellow and holler in the direction of the stairs.

'For God's sake, hurry, man! Hurry!'

Things whispered, the whispers of beasts not men.

Whether this next part of my account be true or not I write what I remember seeing and hearing in that moment. I glanced over my shoulder towards the stairs and hatch leading upward, distant now, seemingly too far to reach. A soft creak, the faint hue of lights in the vestibule fading, fading. Then darkness and the snap of a lock being shut.

I was speechless at first, unable to comprehend what was happening. Then the truth of the matter hit me – that it was indeed a ploy and I was being held in the cellar for some obscure and malicious purpose.

'Vaughn. Vaughn, you coward!' I yelled, hurtling back towards the steps. I lost my footing and clattered to the floor.

There I sat, shaking in a heap, alone in darkness. I hurriedly reached in my pocket – my matches, I had forgotten they were there! I struck one quickly as a strange breath of wind grazed my skin. I returned my gaze to the depths of the cellar. The voices spoke once more, though now they said my name with dreadful clarity. In the dying light of my match, I made sight of a shape within the gloom. It had edges and right angles – something misshapen upon the top.

The match extinguished completely, and I dared not move to light another. Everything fell silent.

When exposed to true darkness we revert to something less human, something feral and timid. I sat blind, hearing nothing but the panting of my rasping breaths and the haggard beating of my racing heart.

That moment remains the calm in my nightmares since, the pause before such terrors emerge and wake me from my slumber.

Something brushed against my back, rubbed against the bare skin of my chest. It was warm, dry like bark in parts, greasy and sticky in others.

I could do nothing for not even my pistol remained in my hand. I shook and quivered. My breathing was erratic, my nerves electric, sensing every tiny speck of dust and movement of the air. I had no need to clench my eyes shut for there was nothing but darkness before me.

It was torture, sitting before an unknown horror. I pleaded for it all to end.

Then I felt the hot breath of someone close to my ear.

'He never left, he still remains. The demon of this village.'

I mustered the last of my courage to speak.

'Who ... who whispers with such foul tongue?' I whimpered like a babe.

There came no reply. I seemed unable to catch my breath, for the air had all but gone from around me.

Suddenly the candelabra at my side erupted, engulfed in a ball of white blazing fire that ignited the room and revealed all its dreadful horrors. The fires licked against my flesh. I shrieked as I burned alive. I tried to cover my eyes, but they were held, fixed upon what I saw before me.

Sitting upright atop a wooden table, was the smouldered and mangled corpse of Betsan Tilny.

She was looking at me, her half rotten face split by a twisted smile. She had no eyes however. Only deep black holes stared at me.

8

The Body – June 18th, 1904

My recollection of those dreadful moments, alone in the darkness of that cellar, has taken many years to reform in my mind. It was not wholly clear what had happened for so long; only snippets and flashing images came to me, most often in deepest night. It is clear to me now, only because I have spent so many wasted hours reliving it, screaming aloud, knees bent, praying for some light, some shimmer of salvation to emerge and rescue me.

I cannot tell you what happened after Betsan appeared – Constable Vaughn told me I was lying unconscious on the floor when he and Cummings found me. I remember little of my revival, but it seemed to take a great deal of time. I slipped in and out of consciousness for almost an hour, though they did not divulge whether I spoke or not.

Eventually I came to with a start, seated in the vestibule, cool rags and cloths laid about my neck and shoulders. Regardless, my whole body felt terribly hot, as though I had fallen asleep beside a kiln or baker's oven. I gasped for air and retched dreadfully to my side, the dusky, maroon rug on the floor spinning and looping as I did.

Vaughn knelt beside me then and made me drink, though I reeled away from him at first, tormented by grave visions and memories. After struggling to push him away, he held my shoulders firmly and spoke to me slowly. Only after a few long sips of water, did I understand what he was saying.

'Do you rem-remember what happened, Inspector? D-do you remember?'

At first, I could not understand the manner of his tone. His eyes were wide, staring into mine as if searching for something. I took more water, and after catching my breath a little, shook my head.

'There was darkness. Something on my back. The—'

I saw fire and hollow eyes staring at me. I began to tremble and ran my hands through my greasy hair.

'There was something on my back.'

Cummings stepped into view behind Vaughn. His expression was stony, severe. 'You are delirious, Inspector,' he grumbled. 'You were raving down there. Vaughn came to fetch me as I was gathering candles and we found you in the darkness.'

I shook my head at first, recalling the cold air and an awful gnawing sound. Cummings stopped me before I could start.

'Your fever! You are unwell – even upon the road I said so.'

I protested for a time, describing the sensations I could recall, the things I had seen. I felt like a child, convincing his parents of the grizzly beasts hiding beneath the bed; the pair looked at me regretfully. Vaughn continued to give me water and left my side a few times to fetch more. He dampened another rag and handed it to me; without thought I began mopping it upon my brow.

Gradually, my better judgement began to return, the madness of what I could recall becoming apparent, as one comes to understand the waking world after a vivid dream. (Everything seemed to be dreams that day and then the sudden waking from them.)

I listened to Vaughn's account once more, how he had seen

me screaming in the shadows, how I must have thrown down my candles and stumbled through the pitch.

'You … y-you closed the trap door,' I muttered accusingly at one point, my brow furrowed as I thought upon the sound of a lock being shut.

'Well, of course he did!' Cummings snapped. 'I told him to. The lad said you were waving a gun around for Chri—' He stopped himself with a huff.

I nodded then, though Vaughn looked as me as if I had wronged him badly. I sat in silence for a moment or two, drinking more as I did. After a few minutes I felt truly foolish.

'I'm sorry to you both,' I said, buttoning up my shirt (what buttons remained). 'This damned illness has taken hold quickly. It is quite unfortunate.'

Vaughn stood and looked at Cummings, who stepped away and leant against the vestibule wall.

'There is … um … there is no need to apologise, Inspector,' Cummings said. 'Perhaps though it would be best to suspend your enquiries.' He shifted, glancing to Vaughn as he spoke. 'This fever seems to be impacting your judgement.'

'It has caught me off guard, Mr Cummings, but my judgement remains sound.'

'You may argue that. But no one would be given this task in your current state.'

He was right. I could not deny it. But never had such a thing happened before and as I stood, pulling off the damp rags about my neck and shoulders, I felt a greater sense of determination to carry out my work.

'I shan't let a fever get the better of me again, Mr Cummings. For however much longer I remain here, be it a day or two. This work must be done.'

Cummings clearly wanted to disagree. He shook his head and looked down toward the floor.

'You need bed rest.'

I ignored him, taking a rag in hand and wiping my eyes and forehead. I looked about my person and to the small writing desk with my case upon it. I saw, then, the candelabra, its short candles still extinguished, though I made no sight of my pistol.

I turned to Vaughn and held out my hand.

'My gun, Constable.'

He fidgeted, thrusting his hand into his pockets and glancing at Cummings for some reassurance.

'Per-perhaps it is best we keep it safe for you, sir. You were waving it about quite madly; should it have accidentally fired—'

'My gun.' I held my hand firm and stared at him.

He shared another quick glance with Cummings before turning back to me, his eyes round and soft. He puffed out his chest to speak then seemed to collapse inwards. With an audible sigh and slump of the shoulders, he stepped towards a cabinet by the door and retrieved my pistol. He held onto it for the briefest moment before handing it back to me. I placed it in the open camera case.

'How much light is down there now?' I asked as I took hold of the camera stand.

'More than before,' Vaughn replied quietly. 'Though we will n-need much more.'

I have documented many forms of body decomposition in my career. One of the first cases I was assigned to – prior to any investigative role I had earned and solely when I was a photographer – regarded a young man who had failed to pay adequate interest on debts owed to a local creditor of East Ham. He was dragged from a public house in keen view of many witnesses and wrapped in the chain of a derelict tug boat, before being slung into the river under the cover of nightfall.

That was in the first week of January eighteen ninety-two; the Thames was sub forty degrees for much of that month. When the man's body was recovered some ten days later, it was almost in perfect condition upon first view. As he lay on the slab it was a different matter – his skin peeled away with but the lightest touch of the coroner's tools.

When a body is buried in heavy soil, the gases inside the corpse have no way to escape, resulting in expansion of much of the stomach and intestinal tract. The body eventually bursts around the gut and what is left of the internal organs seeps and mixes with the dirt and soil. Exhumation of a victim buried in such a manner is a pitiful thing, for the body is beyond almost all recognition and even the facial features can be bloated, distorted and twisted, in a dreadful manner. However long the body has been buried greatly influences the ferocity with which the insects and creepers have devoured it. Little more than a skeleton remains after four weeks.

I have seen all manner of tortuous deeds and harrowing acts performed upon human flesh, many too foul and disturbing to be noted in detail in these pages. I have seen a body frozen by the elements, only examined after thawing for forty-eight hours. I have even seen the remains of a man left to fester in a vat of potent chloric acid, so much so that his body had deflagrated to something barely recognisable as human.

Believe me when I say I have seen some dreadful things.

But one can cope with such sights, separate them, if you will, from the rest of the psyche. A coroner's room is nothing but a physician's laboratory. We live in such an age of advanced medicine that the body upon the slab is nothing more than a piece of meat, a scientific study, an anomaly or peculiarity. Do not misunderstand me, for I am not so callous as to be unaffected by such things. Merely it is the case that I have come to process and isolate these disturbing scenes from the rest of my life.

When I speak of this case, you may blame my fever, my delirium, the horrors I claim to have seen in that cellar. Perhaps blame my suspicions, the isolation I felt in that tiny village and the heightened state of paranoia it had wrought upon me. Whatever you may think, understand that the girl's body was, in many respects, the foulest I have ever laid eyes on. And to this day I wish I never had.

Let me divulge only a forensic overview – that detail which is of grave necessity. The girl was burnt, for a relatively brief time. This is clear, for whilst the skin was almost entirely blackened and blistered, it, along with near all other muscles and tissues of the body, remained intact. A distressing sight nonetheless; the girl's facial features in particular were distorted, the ears and nose destroyed entirely. All but the left hand and wrist had been exposed to the flames.

Further damage was inflicted upon the body in the form of deep lacerations around the joints of the limbs, arms and neck. This damage was clearly exacted after death and burning. Bizarrely, whilst these lacerations were of reasonable depth, they were inflicted upon both the front and back of the body, as though someone tried to remove the limbs entirely.

All manner of other injuries and brutalities enacted upon the body will remain undisclosed here. I feel they would only serve as a dishonour to the murdered girl.

'Where is Richmond?' I asked, setting my camera stand down at the foot of the table. The body shimmered in warm candlelight; I stared at it morbidly, though could not keep my gaze on the girl's empty eye sockets. The cellar was now reasonably lit, with at least thirty candles spread throughout its entirety. It was still not enough, and Vaughn was already gathering more.

'He left soon after we arrived.' Cummings stood at my side. 'I was talking with him a while, though he wouldn't listen. You must understand he is unhappy with all of this.'

'Yes, I had a feeling.' I turned to fetch my camera. 'Though it seems this church has been abandoned for more than a mere week, Councilman. Perhaps you forgot to tell me the whole truth of this place earlier today.'

Cummings' face turned scarlet just as Vaughn came scampering down the stairs.

'We'll discuss the matter later,' I said curtly, before instructing Vaughn where to set the pillar candles he carried. Thirty minutes later I had the camera in place and the candles arranged to maximise the exposure.

'There is no guarantee that these will be clear, but it will have to do.'

I paused a moment before taking my first picture, using the camera stand to hold my balance, as everything whirled around me. The fever was unabating.

After replacing the plate, I moved around the table and removed the cotton cloth laid across the girl's midriff and thighs. I heard Cummings tut and murmur his disapproval. I ignored him and returned to my camera to take another image.

I took eight in all, two of the body's entirety, others of the lacerations around the limbs and two of the face and neck. When I was satisfied, I returned to the vestibule and brought Vaughn's completed report down into the cellar (quite the struggle, for standing at the hatchway looking downward, every fibre of my being screeched at me to run away and never look back). I read it as he and Cummings stood in silence; it did not take long for it was very brief.

'You have failed to note a few things, Constable,' I said, already making notes at the foot of the report. 'And there is not enough detail.'

Vaughn muttered an apology. 'I've never written a murder report before, sir.'

I did not browbeat the young man but beckoned him to stand close to my side next to the body.

'The lacerations around the arm and neck were made with something slim and very sharp – likely a butcher's blade, a boning tool of sorts. The cuts were sliced through quite neatly, time taken, if you understand my meaning.' I pointed to each delicate slice as Vaughn nodded.

'Here at the legs, however, notice the lacerations were made with something far clumsier; a cleaver, perhaps?'

'Why would someone do that?' Vaughn asked uncomfortably. I shook my head, continuing to make notes. Black spots danced across the page and already I could feel the deep throb of the fever's scorn, pulsating up the back of my neck towards my temples. I tried not to show any of my wavering state.

'Were there any items of clothing in the area or upon her person, any burnt remains?'

Vaughn shook his head.

'Jewellery, a necklace or a ring perhaps?'

Vaughn shook his head once more.

I moved around and gently lifted the girl's left, unburnt hand. The fingers and wrist were horribly cold and stiff.

'There is blood, here. Can you see it?' Vaughn leant in a little closer to where I pointed. 'Just below three of her fingernails. Whatever attack took place, she lashed out and drew blood from the assailant. She was defending herself, meaning she inflicted defence wounds, scratches no doubt, upon her killer.'

I wrote in silence for some time, as Vaughn inspected the hand and fingers.

'This rules out a few theories,' I said quietly.

Cummings seemed baffled. 'What can you possibly learn from this?'

I closed the report and began scribbling in my notepad.

'Well, we now know this was not a sudden, violent act of passion. Had it been so, the assailant would not have desecrated the body in this way, other than the burning.' I looked at Vaughn as an idea came to me. 'Are you aware of fingerprint analysis? Scotland Yard adopted it as a serious practice a year or two ago?'

'N-no, sir.'

'We each have unique markings on our fingers, a trace of which is left when we touch anything, even another person's skin. Had the perpetrator known of this, they may have wanted to burn the body to remove any trace of themselves.' I shook my head dismissively. 'I doubt they were aware of such things, though it's made me think. We'd be wise to record the victim's fingerprints. They may be relevant moving forwards; did either of you see ink upstairs?'

Vaughn hurried away and returned not two minutes later with a small bottle of rusted brown ink. Under the curious eye of Cummings, the pair of us set about recording each fingerprint on the girl's unburnt hand, marking them on the last page of Vaughn's report.

'Burning,' I continued as we set about this, 'is often the means to which a criminal attempts to dispose of a corpse. This body was not fully cremated however and the scorch marks where the body was found do not correspond to the burn wounds inflicted. My first inclination would be to suggest the killer attempted to destroy the body with fire – though failed as it is not always an easy task – and then set about staging the scene close to the mill. With only a little more thought, though, I strongly doubt someone who killed the girl spontaneously, with no premeditation, would have set about that course of action.'

'I d–don't follow, Inspector,' Vaughn uttered.

'Why risk being caught defiling the body in this manner and staging it where they did? Only a fool would do so. Had the crime been spontaneous the girl would be found dead, but her body intact – so to speak – for the assailant would have panicked and fled the scene. Or there would be no body at all, for the assailant, mustering some sense, would have disposed of it.'

'Meaning what, then?' Cummings asked.

'We have to accept now that this was an act of premeditation, or at least not an act of passion, as it were. The killer wanted the body found and has taken much effort to defile it in this manner *and* to stage the scene. To be blunt, the time taken to torture the girl, and then desecrate her corpse to this extent, would support the notion that the girl was killed somewhere else entirely and brought to rest where Miller found her. Due to its proximity and the vast amount of unattended space, we can assume the girl was killed somewhere in the woodlands.'

'That would support our theory then,' Vaughn chirped excitedly, 'that the travellers could have done this in their camp.'

Cummings was nodding. 'They have strange ways, the gypsies.'

'Strange enough to implicate themselves in all this, make themselves prime suspects even? I have noted your opinion on the matter, Councilman, and it is still in consideration. But we have a few leads to follow up on, particularly regarding those who frequent the woods for work and the like.'

'What leads – how on earth could we link anyone to this?' Both Cummings and Vaughn seemed baffled.

'If this was murder by a single man, he is quite depra—'

He never left, he still remains. The demon of this village.

The words burnt in my mind, spoken by a thousand voices a thousand times in an instant. My body weakened and I daresay I even gasped aloud. Whether Vaughn or Cummings moved or spoke I cannot say, for it took a great effort not to let myself fall to the floor. Blood boiled in my veins.

The voices silenced; my strength returned.

'Depraved. Ill and violent. Undoubtedly he would hold a keepsake to commemorate the deed – I am afraid most men of this sort do.'

I pointed at the pale skin of her cold hand.

'To draw blood, she must have done some visible damage. We need to look for anyone with scratch marks about their person.'

9

The Woodland – June 18th, 1904

By the time I returned to the clean air and stood amongst the gravestones outside All Saints, my fever had diminished somewhat. The fresh air helped invigorate me further. The day was still close and clammy, the cloud above darker than the morning. Yet I was glad to be out of the dust and shadow of the church and its cellar, though the sight of the corpse weighed heavy on my thoughts.

The world around us remained deathly still and quiet.

Cummings locked the church doors (for the cleric Richmond had not returned) and asked Vaughn if he would be travelling back to the Twyn with us.

'Yes, perhaps we can discuss the c-case a little more,' Vaughn said brightly.

'Actually, Constable, I think I shall walk back. Take in the air.' I trailed off a little then; I had a passing sensation of tiny claws burrowing into my back. 'The fever and all.'

Vaughn seemed to hesitate for a moment. 'A-are you sure? With respect, Inspector, you need bed rest. To hallucinate in such a manner—'

I nodded. 'I appreciate your concern, but I would take a walk.'

I set my camera case on the back of the cart, checking then that my notepad and revolver were still about my person.

'The travellers, were they camped far from here?' I asked Vaughn as he hopped up to the driving box.

'Well, they … Um.'

'Quite a way,' Cummings interrupted. 'You have to travel up toward the Old Court Manor and take the trail right around back to the edge of the Cwm Sior. They were somewhere in the north fields, just before the woodland.'

'I heard they were up further, on the trail headed towards Saint Andrew,' Vaughn chipped in. The two men began debating.

'Never mind,' I said after a moment. 'I shall take a walk and see what I see.'

I pointed further up the road, in the direction Joseph had headed with his overladen cart. Cummings gave me some loose directions and I began on my way.

'I should talk with you later, Mr Cummings,' I called over my shoulder.

He gave his reply and began turning the shire horse and cart. Soon after, I heard the rickety rig leave Michaelston and when there was silence again I stopped for a moment. I was certain, from where I stood upon the road, that I was the only living thing in some distance, for not even a vagrant thrush or blackbird could be seen soaring across the skyline.

Nothing, for all I could see, would suggest that a travelling band had made camp. There were no signs of fire, no cart or horse tracks in the earth. The thriving wheat and barley was untouched, the locks and chains barring the gates of the fields undamaged and unbroken.

By now I had been wandering for near two hours. Vaughn and Cummings had been uncertain of the camp and I did not think outright that they intended to mislead me. There was much I had not seen and had I been inclined to, I would have pressed on through the woodlands and surveyed the land further to the north and west. But I was tired then, in mind more than body, wrestling with the facts of the case and battling the creeping fever that simmered throughout me. The skies had continued to darken and soon after half past four, the heavens opened, cascading heavy rain down upon the land.

I found my way back to the rocky trail that led to Dinas Powys and continued along. Soon the rolling fields were left behind, replaced by dense forest, untamed shrubs and bramble bushes. I was entering the Cwm Sior and the bank of trees marking the foot of the woodland to my right began to grow steadily steeper, the canopy hanging over me in ever more precarious fashion. Soon, the bank was replaced by a tall cliff face, that ascended some hundred feet or so. It was wholly impenetrable, lifeless albeit for a few daring saplings that grew in shallow cracks and crevices. My path wound at the foot of this cliff face, with a steep incline of greenwood, scouring upward on the other side of the gorge.

I was sodden, drenched and dripping, my forehead hot whilst the rest of my body shivered. I wound through the tight ravine, losing myself at times, returning to the dark cellar, with the single flame of the candelabra in hand.

I heard the strange voice again, felt breath against my ear, the sickly touch of burnt flesh against my bare skin.

The demon of this village.

The trees rustled the words to me with each wisp of wind. Over and over, I heard them, no matter how hard I tried not to listen or to convince myself it was the fever. But soon I was talking to the trees as they spoke to me.

'What happened to you?' I recall mumbling, as though I were speaking to Betsan herself. 'What happened to you?'

There came no answer. I have no memory of passing the scene

where the body was found, or the mill, though I surely must have, for well past five of the hour I 'awoke' as it were, at the foot of the Pen-Y-Turnpike hill.

The inn was filling up with revellers by the time I barged through the small door, hacking and coughing as I did. The room fell silent for a moment, as eyes turned upon me with grave intrigue. I trudged through the small space without a word, passed Solomon at the bar who offered me drink and food.

'Mr Cummings left your case upstairs. Said he'd be back later.'

I didn't respond and made my way to my room quite desperately. I stripped off my clothes and climbed into bed, weary and unable to think straight. I must have slept suddenly, for my next memory is of a knock at the door and a figure shrouded in darkness entering with great clamour.

'Inspector, are you awake?'

It was Cummings, guided by candlelight. He carried a plate of food with him, which he set upon the writing desk, before lighting the other candle to better illuminate the room.

'What time is it?'

'Nearly half past nine. I thought not to wake you but in your present state I decided it best you take food.'

He sat down at the writing desk as I hauled myself upward in bed. I thanked him quietly, as I rubbed my face and eyes. As with the morning, I was dank with sweat.

'You're obviously a man of great pride, Inspector,' Cummings said softly. 'I respect that. I understand your drive to carry out your work and neither I nor the Constable would question your determination. But you are unwell; your actions are rash.'

'You lied to me about Michaelston, Cummings?' I said coolly, with no real regard for the man's pleasantries. 'Why the girl's body is there. Why it was abandoned.'

Cummings spread his arms in mock exasperation.

'You prove my point! I told you no lies of any kind. People wanted the girl's body in a church – All Saints seemed the best place for her.'

'It's been abandoned for years,' I replied, my voice dry and croaking. 'It was plain to see today. You told me those who live in Michaelston came here temporarily, after the girl had been killed.'

Cummings shrugged. 'Perhaps I was not clear. Some years ago the families felt disconnected from the village proper, there were newer properties available to them.' He paused and scoffed a little. 'There is no great secret to it, Inspector; you can ask anyone around.'

'You're hiding her from everyone,' I replied. 'You've left her out there alone.'

Cummings scoffed once more. 'For God's sake, man, she is *dead*. Not just that but brutally killed! I made plain earlier that these people are simple, they have their beliefs, their fears as we all do. It's bad enough thinking that your friend, colleague, neighbour could have done this but their *Calon Farw*, their foolish bedtime story scares them even more so.' His face was turning scarlet. 'Besides, what bloody difference does it make if the girl is out there or not, or if I didn't make the matter plain before now? You think I have some part in this, something I wish to conceal?'

I didn't answer him, and we sat silently for a few awkward minutes. I felt a sharp pain in my back, just below my left shoulder blade. I stretched a hand to it absently, unable to reach fully.

'I have tried to call for a physician but have been unable to get hold of one,' Cummings said slowly. 'You're unwell and you know it. What you saw, what you *think* you saw today—'

'I know. I know,' I interrupted him. 'And I told you earlier it shall not get the better of me again.'

'It has,' Cummings exclaimed. 'Solomon says he heard you raving in your sleep after you returned here earlier, soaked through to the bone. Did you even find that damned campsite?'

I shook my head. Cummings threw his hands up again.

'There is no shame in saying you are unwell. It makes nothing less of you, but what will, what certainly will, is the manner in which you go about this enquiry. There is no great mystery here, no conspiracy.'

'There is a murder, though, Councilman, one that cannot be explained.'

'To you perhaps,' Cummings proclaimed with a raised voice. 'The body was staged, you say? Why do it, to what motive? To throw the scent, of course, to stave off the constables, to ensure this bloody band of gypsies is not followed or held under suspicion!'

He seemed to fall back in his chair and slammed his palm against the writing desk.

'You lose yourself, sir,' I muttered.

'I do, I do,' he replied, rubbing his brow.

'Your conclusion, whilst plausible, remains unjustified. You have no real proof for your claims. Too many things cry foul and, speaking frankly, it is in your interest that another party committed this crime.'

He started at that. 'So, you do think me covering some truth?'

'No, merely that you have drawn a conclusion, a favourable conclusion, and now seek to fit the evidence to it.'

'Bah!' he snapped, standing from the chair and pacing the small space before me. 'Then what is your opinion, what have you concluded?'

I sighed. 'Nothing. Truly, it fits no brief, if you will.'

He made his way for the door then. 'You should rest more,' he mumbled.

'I'll need to start questioning the villagers tomorrow,' I said plainly. 'Vaughn may need to gather individuals, and we'll need a place to conduct interviews. I'll start though by visiting the mother first thing.'

He stopped at the door.

'Catrin. She is in mourning – I doubt you will gain anything from her.'

'Yet I shall have lost nothing when I do.'

Cummings left then without a word and I sat upon the bed in silence for quite some time. The room was cold, and I soon sought to fetch some dry clothes from my luggage case. In a loose-fitting shirt and a pair of cotton bottoms, I sat at the table and ate the small plate of meat, potatoes and gravy. I was famished and consumed the meal quickly, feeling more alive when I had.

Darkness was setting in by then and the glossy hue of the gas lamp on the road outside filled my room. I fetched Vaughn's report and my notebook, sitting with the two candles close to the pages. I found a telegram tucked neatly behind the report, sent to Vaughn from Chief Inspector T. C. Brent, the very man of the Glamorgan Constabulary who had written for my services. It informed Vaughn of my arrival, and the actions I would carry out. I thought little of the telegram then.

At around half past ten, my eyes grew heavy. The words upon the pages of my notebook began to blur and my skin began to tingle and prickle with irritation and heat. My dreadful migraine was creeping back. The fever was relentless, and I cursed quietly.

The murmur and rumblings of the bar below escalated suddenly. Voices began yelling, profanities and vulgarities, insults were thrown. Glass smashed against a wall, light spilled into the darkness below my window as the front door was thrown open. Two shadows emerged, squaring off in the light of the street. One was tall and well-built, and I recognised him from his stature alone. He was one of the Davey brothers, Miller's lads I had seen the previous day.

By now the rain had passed, and in the gloom I could see both his raised fists, and a smirk spread wide across his face. He said something to the other figure, a stocky man at least a foot shorter than he. They barked like feral dogs, goading one another. It was all very brief – the short man lunged and Davey threw two quick jabs with his left fist and floored the man with a dreadful uppercut to the jaw. The short man crumpled, unconscious before he hit the ground. Davey thrust his hands into the air, stumbling backwards, drunk. A few people cheered, some called out. Solomon appeared then and waved Davey away whilst a few other figures attended to the man on the floor. One of them was Cummings, his face shaped by fury. He yelled at Davey to move on and seemed to try to revive the unconscious fellow. Davey disappeared in the direction of Mill Hill whilst the other man was hauled from the ground and dragged in the opposite direction.

Within five minutes everything was still. I thought about Geraint Davey for a little while, the way he had looked and spoken to me that previous day. My intuition implored me to speak to him, and as all good investigators do, I listen to my intuitions.

I yawned, meaning to write a little in my diary.

The candles on my table flickered. The gas lantern at the cross roads dimmed. The room fell to darkness, all except the two fine orange embers that glowed across the little table.

The air grew cold as dread overcame me.

I moved to turn and look behind me, twisting my neck slowly, fearing what I would find with me in the room.

The gas lantern suddenly grew brighter, the candles on my table re-ignited. The room was flooded in soft light again. It gave me such a start that I sprang from my chair, knocking it backward with quite some force. I swirled in the room to find there was nothing but the bed and my shadow.

The dreadful scratching from the ceiling started once more.

10

Diary Entry – June 18th, 1904

My fever is deepening – it has brought with it such terrors.

I cannot trust anything of myself, of my senses. I have seen such things, so unnatural and perverse. Not of this earth, of this place – nothing could be more unreal than what I remember laying eyes upon today, what I smelt and heard.

Yet there they were before me, as solid as the pen in my hand, as tangible as the paper on this writing desk.

Reason dictates I hold steadfast against such supernatural things, for they are but a fiction, a dream world. I am a twentieth century Descartes, deciphering reality, justifying what can be real and what is but fantasy. And I am sceptical (I admit quite fearful) for what was surely real today could only be true fantasy. And what fantasy I experienced felt very, very real.

The wound upon my back (what wound, for there is none to be seen!) stings as I write these words. I see her face, that most dreadful expression, the black holes of her eyes, whenever I look upon shadow.

What a fool! My hand shakes as I write of such things!

To turn to other matters then – to talk of the grave case at hand.

What of the enquiry? It has thrown all manner of questions and no answers make themselves clear. Suppose Cummings is right, suppose he has been all along. His suspect is the most obvious, a wayward gypsy, a bandit of sick mind and intention. A naïve young girl, selling herself to dangerous fellows – what is so uncommon of that? Nothing is more common on the streets of East London.

Why then does it not sit right; why does it feel too neat for such a wicked thing? Why do I feel it is but a narrative being pressed upon me by the Councilman?

Is he suspect, perhaps the suspect? What motive could spur him – concealment: truths to which he will not admit? Involvement – could a man of his type have a part in such a vulgar thing, a butcher's crime? And what of Vaughn, for he would surely be complicit. And who else, for until I begin questioning, I cannot know of anyone's whereabouts, motives, desires, passions, insecurities, resentments . . .

It is now a priority to begin interviewing those in the village, a task that should already be underway (were it not for this fever I'm sure it would be!). First the mother; she may have noticed a change in the girl's demeanour in the days leading up to her death. Then the miller who discovered the body; he may divulge some new information missed by Vaughn and Cummings. Then the miller's workers (including Geraint Davey) – the farm hands as well – who may corroborate Cummings assertion that the girl was selling herself. Then all others, one by one until some truth is made clear to me. Perhaps it shall come quickly.

Perhaps. Perhaps I shall have greater suspicions by this hour to-morrow.

Perhaps I shall sleep and be rid of this insufferable fever by morning. In spite of the rest I take, it seems only to be worsening.

II

The Mother – June 19th, 1904

I awoke sprawled across the floor, the candles but dwindled pools of wax upon the table. I barely moved for ten minutes, for my body ached so terribly and the wretched fever had only intensified.

A great deal of effort was needed to haul myself upward and I clambered against the chair of the writing desk, cast to one side as if I had fallen from it. My diary was open, some pages bent and dog-eared, my fountain pen nowhere in sight, its ink daubed across the desk and floor. The top page of my diary was scratched and scrawled, words etched in as though carved upon stone. I had no memory of writing them, though they were surely made in my hand.

I could barely think straight, barely move even, for it were as though a savage infection had taken hold of my entirety and I were greatly pained just to exist and breathe. At some point I rose nonetheless, though I knew in what vestige of coherent thought I had, I should take rest or even, in spite of Cummings' previous failed efforts, call upon a physician.

I have no real idea of how long it took me or what hour of day it was, but I left my room with my notepad, pencil and pistol (my fountain pen I discovered at the foot of my bed), stuffed into my heavy coat pocket. My temperature oscillated wildly from fiery heat to freezing chill. I nearly fell down the narrow stairwell, and stumbled into the bar area in an unseemly fashion, clenching my eyes shut as dark purple prisms exploded across my vision.

Outside, I stood in the sunken patio of the inn waiting for Cummings, certain for whatever bizarre reason, that he was to escort me to the mother's dwelling. Church bells roused me; the sights and sounds of men and women moving across the Twyn for Sunday prayers. I didn't care then whether they noticed me or not.

I was in no real state to question the mother, knew damned well it was wrong of me to trouble her on a Sunday. Yet I was compelled to do so, for I needed information. I needed to know what happened, needed to understand more of Betsan and how she died.

I recounted what the Postmaster had told me of where the mother dwelt and headed out of the Twyn alone.

Here, it would seem fitting to note thus. I write of my encounter with Catrin Tilny as best I can, for the details were hazy even in the days immediately following our conversation. I make no attempt to paint Catrin as anything more or less than she appeared to me on that day. With the benefit of hindsight, I wish now that our conversation had not been hampered so badly by my illness, and Catrin's initial reticence. Often, I have wondered how things may have been different had I returned to her after our first meeting.

With some regret I admit now, that it was not merely the distraction of other matters that kept me from speaking to her once again, but something more akin to a lack of nerve.

The railway track marked the frontier of development south of the village; there seemed nothing of the land beyond it. I doubt even now that anything of significance has been built there, though it has been ten years, and much, of course, can change in a decade.

I remember heading to the station to cross the railway line. Standing on the platform, I watched as a few figures mingled close to the edge of the common in their Sunday best. Church bells rang out, dull and monotonous. The sound was something to focus on nonetheless, as I skipped thoughtlessly across the sleek tracks of the line before disappearing into the marshy landscape beyond.

I recall wandering, misguided by the Postmaster's loose directions and my wavering pyrexia. My shoes, bogged down, sunken in waterlogged mud. Midges – I, flagging badly, cursing, muttering, slipping in entangled undergrowth. All is something of a blur, until at last (after mere minutes or half a day) I smelt smoke and came in sight of a dishevelled dwelling.

It was arcane and ancient to say the least, a relic, far more so than the cottages and farmhouses of the village and Michaelston-le-Pit. The Postmaster had called it a hovel and that seemed a great exaggeration, for it was far less substantial than even that. It was built of mud (though its base was lined with large stones, packed together with clay) and rounded, the thatch roof thick and misshapen so that the whole structure seemed to lean to one side. A thin trail of smoke stretched skyward from a small opening in the peak of the roof. Adjacent, a chicken coop and run of sorts was built and fenced in by low stone walls and brambles wrapped and spun to form a fence. There were no animals in sight.

I inched slowly towards the little entrance way, an arched opening with a woven reed door propped clumsily, concealing what dwelt inside. A pungent smell of dank, rotten vegetables hit me, exacerbating my now constant nausea.

'Hello?' I called brazenly, stumbling over an array of pots and metal skillets left lying in the dirt. I continued to creep around the structure and saw a little wooden shelter leaning against the house, a cover from the elements if nothing more. There was a bench and a small open fire with a black stove pot stood atop it. Here sat the Tilny mother.

'Hello,' I called again. She did not turn to me.

I stood and watched her. She was grey and thin, her fine white hair untamed and loosely plaited down the length of her back. Her aspect was severe, all bones and right angles, her nose sharp and pointed, her brow furrowed and wrinkled. She toyed with some needle work, hunched over it, twisting at the material with quick thrusts of her wrists. Her withered arms were exposed to her shoulders, so pale that thin trickles of purple veins were clear to see even from where I stood.

I stepped over towards her though she paid me no attention. She seemed such an aged creature, so old that I doubted for a moment she could be the mother of the young Tilny girl. She was nothing if not sixty. Yet her taut face and petite frame bore some resemblance to the body lying in the cellar of All Saints church. I felt a chill in the air, so similar to that monstrous place.

I staggered a little, overcome by a fit of coughs. She turned on me then, her crisp blue eyes puncturing the landscape.

I greeted her once more.

'You're the Inspector.' Her voice was high and abrasive, like nails on a blackboard. '*We* thought you'd be here sooner.' She turned her gaze back towards her needles.

I stared at her for a moment, perplexed, before scanning the area. There was nothing but trees and the untamed wilderness.

'I'm seeking the mother of Betsan Tilny.'

She only nodded and muttered in shallow breaths. I stepped closer still.

'Are you the girl's mother?' My voice was rasping, my throat hot and dry.

'Only one she ever had.'

I was dumbfounded. I moved within a few yards of her and waited to see if she would speak some more. When she continued to sit in silence, I produced my notebook and crouched on my haunches. At her level, I looked upon her with greater scrutiny. It seemed she had barely eaten in some time, the bones of her frame protruding through her dirty blouse and faded blue apron.

'Mrs Tilny—' it was enough to get her started.

'Mrs!' she shrieked, her eyes still fixed on the material in her hand. 'You think I have had a man, I ever had need of one?'

I frowned before starting again. 'Ms Tilny,' for I thought it best to not excite her further, 'my name is Thomas Bexley and I work for the Metropolitan Police in London. I understand this is a very difficult time.' She remained unmoved. 'Can I offer my sympathies and assure you we are doing all we can—'

'*We* is you! No one else would care do anything for my daughter in death. It's why you were brought here.'

My head pounded and I thought how to go on.

'I'd like to ask you a few questions about your daughter, particularly regarding her behaviour in the days leading to her death.'

'Murder,' the mother said sharply.

I nodded slowly for she was quite right. 'When was the last time you saw your daughter?'

'Four days ago,' she said simply.

I stayed quiet for a moment, hoping she would correct herself. She only continued to work her needles.

'Forgive me, Ms Tilny, but I'm afraid your daughter was found deceased on the tenth of this month – she's been dead for well over a week now.'

She seemed to smile, a thin little smile that was barely noticeable. Then she turned to look at me for the first time. 'Have you seen her yet?'

The pit of my stomach fell away as I saw the dark hollow eyes and charred skin.

'Yes, an examination of the body was carried out yesterday.'

She shook her head a little. Then I truly saw the family resemblance, for I had seen that smile the previous day, as the girl's dead body had sat up and glared at me despite those empty eyes. I began to cough and wheeze uncontrollably. When I was somewhat composed, I reached a hand towards her and whilst she didn't flinch, she eyed me as a snake looks upon a rat. I gently clasped her forearm.

'I know this is hard, but we must talk of your daughter. It is imperative we find those who are responsible for her death.'

She wrenched her hand away from me with a dry, sadistic yap of laughter.

'Place me in irons then, Inspector. She was my daughter, my love, and I let this happen.' She hit her wrists hard together – twice, thrice – what smile there was erupted madly before vanishing with no trace. She stared at me with such vacancy for an instant before falling completely silent and returning her attention to her needlework. Grief takes on many shapes and voices, but it is always recognisable.

'It is all too easy, Ms Tilny, to torment ourselves with what should have, could have been done. It will serve no purpose in this matter now though.'

'Regardless I know my guilt,' she hissed quietly. 'Ask me your questions.'

I nodded, fumbling for my notebook and pencil. 'Betsan lived with you, *here?*'

I could not hide my intrigue in the ramshackle dwelling.

'Since the day she was born,' the mother replied quietly. 'Think what you will of this place but never have I needed a man to buy me a home, gather me food, provide for me, buy me little dresses and hats to wander about in.' She spat into the dirt by my feet. 'This home, this land, *is mine*. Would have been Betsan's . . .' She trailed off then.

I nodded. 'Do you frequent the village often?'

She shook her head.

'But Betsan did?'

She nodded slowly.

'Betsan was found close to dawn on the tenth; had she been home the night previous?'

The mother shook her head, her jaw visibly clenching under her thin skin. 'Hadn't seen her the day and night before that either. Wasn't the first time she'd stayed out, sleeping God knows where.'

'Did she have many friends in the village, anyone she was close with?'

The mother shook her head once more.

'Did she have work?' I continued.

'What difference does it make?'

'I'm trying to piece together what happened to Betsan in the days and hours leading to her death; who she met, who she spoke with. A key part of that is understanding how she occupied her days.' I stopped then, thinking how best to approach the rumours of prostitution.

'She came back with money, not just ha'pennies, mind. Quite a bit of money.' The mother growled, jabbing her material ever harder with her needles. 'More and more it seemed lately. And I know what you might think, what you'll go on to ask me. Betsan was young and naïve and pretty. I don't know how she came by that money and I don't want to know.' Her voice quivered at the last.

I nodded. 'One line of enquiry concerns a group of travellers who were believed to be in the area in the days – perhaps weeks – leading to Betsan's death. Did she say anything about that to you?'

The mother shook her head wildly. 'She didn't say much at all to me in the last few weeks. Whatever she was keeping to herself made her happy, though.'

'In what regard?'

'In the way all young girl's keep secrets from their mothers,' the old woman sneered.

I felt a pulsing pressure building in my right temple. My stomach churned and I was certain I would vomit.

'Could you make a guess what such a secret could be? Did she plan to leave; did she have plans for the both of—'

'I don't know!' she yelled at me and it near sent me reeling in the dirt, for the volume and scorn she reached was shocking. I maintained my balance, but the world seemed to change all around me, the light dimming. I scanned the wild bushels and twisted trees, suddenly certain that figures in hiding watched us both. Footsteps ruffled, close by, far off. I tried desperately to ignore them.

By now I was gravely in need of a drink of water.

'Have you seen her yet?' the mother asked once more.

I nodded my head, rubbing my eyes, sweat running heavy down my cheeks and neck. 'Yes, as I said, the body was examined yesterday.'

'I saw her,' she replied flatly.

I was taken aback. 'You ... you saw Betsan's body?'

'Not her body. I saw *my daughter*, Inspector.' Her smile was returning. I told myself she was delusional, grief-stricken, desperate to see her child once more. But that smile had darker meaning. It filled me with such fear, as the movement and clamour of those in hiding grew in volume.

'You have my sympathies, Ms Tilny, but understand this is no matter of folly. Your daughter's killer remains unchecked, whether they reside in the village or have fled entirely. Forgive my candour but you must be as frank and clea—'

Something sped through a thick growth of nettles in my line of sight.

'Did … did you see that?'

'I know all too well my daughter is dead, Inspector …' she continued talking.

Things blurred; the world left me. All went black if only for a moment for I was still balanced (barely) on my haunches beside the old woman when everything snapped back into view. Whether I asked for water or not I cannot say, but I remember taking a drink from a small clay mug and thinking miserably on my state. I was unwell, and the illness was only worsening.

'Those *fools*,' the mother cackled, 'think this is all some *monster*. Have you heard that yet?'

I nodded, dazed.

'What happened before …' She trailed off, her words replaced by whispers that battered me from all sides.

The demon of this village.

The demon of this village.

'What? What happened before?' Whether I said the words aloud I cannot be certain. I saw the mother speak a while longer, tried as hard as I could to listen to what she told me. But I was lost, my body engulfed in unseen fire, my senses forgotten – for nothing of what I saw or smelt or heard was truly real. The mother's bony features exaggerated, oscillated, grew and shrunk. She seemed to tower over me and I became so fearful of her, of her arcane hovel, of the marshlands all around us.

The leaves of the trees turned cold and grey. The mud and the dirt turned crimson and red.

The whispered words bombarded me mercilessly.

The demon of this village.

'I ... I shan't take up anymore of your time,' I mumbled, terrified.

I stood and circled the hovel quickly. Then I turned and found the mother standing, the little scrap of material in her hand. She hobbled over to me slowly. I noticed then the light shining through the bushes and leaves of the trees, vanishing piece by piece. The sky overhead – the very sun! – was being extinguished for ever. She took an age to walk to me – I wanted so badly to turn and run.

When she was before me, she reached out and clumsily thrust her needlework in my hands. I recoiled at first, the cold of her touch feeling now like reptile skin. I looked at what she had given me. I saw it was a tatty ragdoll, a doll of a girl, a doll of her daughter, no doubt. She patted me with fingers that did not feel human.

There were tears in her eyes, fat and heavy and ready to roll down her cheeks. Her mouth moved but her shrill voice was lost.

Do not look for her with your eyes, for you will not find her.

The words were distorted, low and booming. My chest tightened as my heart thundered. The face of the woman before me contorted and changed. Her blue eyes began to shrink and shrivel. When they were gone, she looked at me with empty black hollows.

I think I gave my thanks. I think I offered my sympathies once more. The mother nodded her head as her skin began to congeal and burn with no sight or flicker of flame. Her mouth moved as she spoke to me. The words were not hers though.

They seemed to come from everywhere all at once.

Do not look for her with your eyes.

12

The Discovery – June 19th, 1904

I wandered for such a time, that when I emerged from the swamps and returned to the station, it must have been the middle of the afternoon. I raved as I moved – lost – my sanity gone, my mind overrun by fever. I clasped the little ragdoll in hand and spoke to it, as though I were questioning the girl herself.

'What will you not speak of?' I muttered at the doll. 'What happened to you, Betsan?'

My attentions were all but fixed upon the ragdoll and I barrelled ever more questions at its blank, expressionless face.

I must have walked up to the common, for my next recollection was standing in the wide spreading field. Something of a crowd had gathered, and those who found me, knowing me as the Inspector and calling me thus, seemed gravely concerned for my manic state.

Whether they tried to bring me to heel or sedate me through talk and pleasantries I am uncertain, but I brushed them aside, no doubt, and wandered to the farthest edge of the common (for what reason I cannot tell). Perhaps Vaughn had been amidst the crowd, or a runner sent for him, but I recall his speaking to me sometime that afternoon, where I lampooned him with all bluster and bombast, rambling of the mother and her strange ways.

I cannot recount Vaughn's words, but know he was gravely concerned for my state, that I had succumbed fully to the fever and may perhaps require admission to an infirmary. He led me off the common no doubt (for I must have been quite amiable by then) and we returned to the Twyn slowly, whereby I was taken to the inn and my room, stripped to my waist and left in the bed. Vaughn brought provisions of water and damp rags, along with a strange herbal concoction that was bitter and unpleasant.

I slept, and I dozed, and I dreamt, and I muttered and groaned, the little doll for ever staring at me from where Vaughn had set it on the small writing desk.

However many hours passed I am uncertain, but light still streamed through my little window as I leapt from the bed, overcome with a powerful compulsion I could not fully comprehend. Something, it seemed, had dawned on me in my hazy consciousness, something I struggled to fix or focus upon.

Do not look for her with your eyes.

I vomited from nausea, moving too fast from my resting place. Everything spun as I collapsed to the floor; a hammer smashed against the interior of my skull. No matter the pain, my compulsion was stronger, and I clawed towards the little table to pull myself upwards. The bowl of water sat next to the doll; Vaughn had filled it to the brim. I plunged my face into it, splashing water against my neck and back and chest with no real care. The floorboards were soaked when I was done.

I moved towards my camera case. Someone had gone to the trouble of tucking my Enfield inside (I presumed this was Vaughn, for Cummings would surely have seen to take the gun from my possession entirely). Some of my sensibility must have remained, for I felt it best to conceal the gun below my bed's thin mattress. Then I scrambled through my case, collecting all of the exposed plates I had used at the scene and in the cellar of All Saints church. I stuffed my pockets with the vials of developing chemicals I had brought with me and hastened from the room, bungling down the stairs.

Eyes looked at me with concern, suspicion, judgement as I came into the bar area. I barely gave anyone seated drinking a thought, though I daresay I must have appeared an escapee of Bedlam, bare-chested and sodden with water. This was surely compounded by the manner in which I passed those who stood around and made to gain Solomon's attention.

I dropped my photographic plates onto the bar top, knocking drinks as I did. Voices grumbled and cursed me. I believe someone gave me a light shove and told me to calm down – I barked at him which seemed to gain Solomon's attention.

He moved out of sight for a moment, appearing alongside me in the bar as I continued to mutter and bellow.

'Upstairs, Inspector.' Solomon manhandled me, bundling me out of the room. I resisted his heavy frame and grabbed at him, trying to speak with him at first before yelling as we crashed through the small door leading to the stairwell.

'Your cellar!' I cried. 'I need to use your cellar.'

'You need rest.' He muttered something more under his breath.

I thrust an elbow in the man's abdomen unwittingly and winded him badly. He recoiled from me and bent over double. I turned upon him with some concern though it was short lived, for my compulsion would not abate.

'The cellar, man. I must use it! I am ill, I know, but this is no act of fever.'

I talked on as he took a few heavy breaths and straightened up slowly. He shook his head, his round face plum red as he scowled.

'I shall tell the Councillor of this,' he said quietly.

I nodded frantically. 'Send for him. Vaughn too. I shall not be long down there and they will need to see – I think they shall need to see what I may find.'

I was quite delusional, of course, for I could have had no real idea of what I was soon to discover. Only that strange compulsion drove me, and for many years I have pondered what brought it on. Solomon looked rightfully confused and stood silent for a moment, glancing from me to the little door on his left that led behind the bar.

'You act up, it'll be a clout,' he growled.

Without another word, he slowly opened the little door and led me behind the bar. The revellers watched on in silence, as Solomon knelt and yanked at the hatchway which opened with a great creak of the hinges. I retrieved my stack of dry plates as Solomon stepped downward into the cellar.

'I'll light all the lamps,' he mumbled as he became submerged in the gloom.

'No, no,' I said excitedly as I stepped down after him. 'Light only one. I need the place to be as dark as possible.'

I shall not bore you as reader with the intricacies and histories of photographic processing, for whilst many a professional and amateur enthusiast may labour upon the subject for hours on end, the layman need not care for talk of exposure times and gelatin solutions. Many shall not read this for some in-depth analyses of my development process, though I admit to you now, what photographic development I did in Solomon's cellar that night, would not conform to the strident standards required of a police enquiry.

Until now, I have spoken to very few regarding my time in Dinas Powys. Of those to whom my greatest confidence was previously given, some defended my rather unconventional development methods. Others argued against them, suggesting

I was perhaps foolhardy in my efforts, allowing uncontrolled light to expose my plates and obscure the images captured, prior and during the development process. It is plausible, though even in retrospect, considering my poor state, I lament such claims.

For those who now read this, you may go so far as to question my skills as a photographer; to explain away what I claim to have seen in those images (for what is surely my greatest regret is that I have no evidence to support my claims) by way of my eagerness or lack of skill at the very time the plates were exposed, in the woods and church cellar. 'It is likely,' you may say, 'that the focus was incorrect, or ample time was not given during each exposure; that what is claimed to be visible, was surely caused by movement of the camera.' To that dispraise I merely laugh and do not dwell.

Cast such doubts if you will, or call me fainéant, but know I hold my reputation as a professional above all else in this matter, and let me assure you, that what was revealed in those photographs was not put there by the dishonesty of my heart or the ineptitude of my hand.

The cellar was small, cramped and dark, laden with barrels and bottles of spirits. Solomon lit a small oil lamp which he hung from a hook on the low rafters. I swirled and searched for a usable space, clearing a narrow shelf littered with a few tools and other trinkets. I swept all these to the floor, despite Solomon's protests.

I removed the vials of chemical spilling from my pockets and asked for water, both hot and cold, and large pint glasses. As Solomon made his way up the little steps I called after him.

'And dishes, shallow plates, tin preferably. And a thermometer if you have one.'

He only grunted back at me.

Each photographic plate had been individually wrapped in thick black paper sleeves after exposure, which I had stacked in order. Solomon returned several times, bringing with him a metal pot of steaming water, large jugs of cool water, three pint tankards and various dishes, bowls and plates of all sizes and shapes. He told me he had no thermometer to which I did not answer – by then I was already combining chemicals.

'What is that?' Solomon asked, watching me with cautious fascination.

'It doesn't matter,' I said rather facetiously. I was impatient, keen to be working. But Solomon remained close by and some small awareness of my discourtesy implored me to answer him properly.

'This,' I said, lifting a small ounce vial, 'is metol.' I lifted another brown bottle and dabbed some powder into the mixture, estimating somewhat, for the fine measurements on its side were barely visible.

'This is sodium sulphite, what we call the preservative.'

I must have seemed quite menacing to Solomon then, my face glossed in sweat, cast in the dim light of a dipped oil lantern, my eyes wide and shifting, jabbering on about strange chemicals as though I were the mad doctor of a Robert Louis Stevenson novella.

'This is hydroquinone – the developer along with the metol. Here then, we add sodium carbonate, a little more … a little … there! With this we finally add a fraction of potassium bromide, a fraction to restrain the development.'

I admired the concoction as Solomon asked me what it was for.

'I need something to mix it with,' I murmured, completely ignoring his question. 'A ladle or spoon, clean, mind you.'

Solomon scrambled back up the stairs. Whilst he was gone,

I filled a large shallow dish with cool water, tipping in a small fraction of acetic acid to form the stop bath for the developed images. I set this to one side of the little shelf. Solomon returned as I prepared a final solution for fixing the images. He brought with him an array of wooden spoons and metal ladles.

I mixed my solutions in silence. When I was satisfied enough, and had laid out three large metal dishes containing the developer, stop bath and fixing solutions, my hands were shaking with anticipation. My skin pulsated, as hot blood, like thickset tar, coursed through my veins.

'Dim the light some more,' I said quietly. When Solomon hesitated, I pushed past him and reached for the oil lamp. The room was shrouded in such darkness then that Solomon and I were but crimson faces, demons rising from an inferno. His pale eyes were fearful – not of the darkness but surely of me, for I was not myself, not the tempered man going about his enquiries, but a being unhinged, fired like a salamander.

'I shall fetch the Constable,' he said quietly and left without another glance at me. By the time he had closed the little hatch above, I was already submerging my first plate in the developing fluid.

The first two negatives revealed nothing, or perhaps I should say nothing untoward. I remember feeling a sense of frustration, one that spurred me on to move with a greater sense of urgency. It seemed I was searching for *something*.

The soft glow of light through the tree leaves, the thick trunks and the dense foliage of wild-growing garlic and ferns, shone with a silver luminescence against the dull black canvas of the clouded sky. Vaughn was visible in the first image (though absent from the second), his dark police uniform now a silvery white.

He stared into the camera lens, the features of his face clear enough to see his curious expression.

I began developing the third plate, rocking the little dish gently to ensure fresh fluid remained in contact with the emulsified plate surface. The scorched black earth where the body was found appeared first, before the surrounding dirt and leaves came clear. It took some seven or eight minutes to develop the images before they were placed in the stop bath and fixing solutions. In truth I could have taken more time. But my frustration was growing rapidly, the compulsion that had driven me down below the bar still raging with my fever.

I skipped the fourth and fifth plates knowing them to convey various angles of the scorched earth and surrounding ground. In the sixth and seventh images I had focused on the wall of granite, casting the camera lens upward to reveal the overarching canopy and gentle slope of the wooded hillside. Neither of these images revealed anything to me, and as I set the eighth plate into the developing fluid, I reviewed each one again, standing close to the oil lamp so I could scan through every fine detail.

'Nothing,' I growled despondently, though I knew not what I hoped to find. I prowled around the little space then, impatient, agitated, raving.

By now it had been an hour or so since Solomon had left. I expected both he and the Constable to emerge in the cellar at any moment. I slouched onto a heavy cask barrel and tried to think straight. I spoke to myself, scratched at the sides of my face and smacked my hands against the cool stone wall behind me.

'What is it? What is it?' I repeated to myself, on and on, before falling silent, staring at the floor of the cellar as beads of sweat fell and dripped from my forehead. Each minute dragged past, so that eventually I pounced across the dark room to glare down at my next submerged negative.

There was the scorched dirt, a whitened scratch in the foreground at the base of the image. There too were the trees rising upward with the land, the undergrowth and ferns spreading away, arching with the curve of the landscape. There, dashed across the image amidst each well-formed leaf, were the blackened clouds of the skyline.

And there, just obscured behind a narrow trunk, perhaps thirty yards from where the camera stood, was a face. Unclear, blurred, but visible. A face was staring at the camera.

I pulled the negative from the tray, and held it close to the oil lamp, incapable of words or real understanding.

I could not believe what I was seeing.

Then I was submerging the next plate, my vigour and sense of urgency renewed. I watched it as the dark sky emerged first, then all manner of deepest shadows, the specks of the trees, the outline of each trunk, the bumps and shallows of the land as it spread into the background.

There was the figure, closer now, silver, glowing, the head and upper torso clear, the shape of a woman, a young woman no doubt.

Then the next image, similar to the eighth, and the last of those taken at the scene. The woman was much closer again, almost fully revealed, a few yards from where I stood with the camera. The thin features of her face were clear, a small but sharp nose, thin arms and body, not unhealthy but merely petite. Her hair was so white in negative, it was surely darkest black in life.

Then the depths of All Saints church, and the girl's body laid upon the table, the cracks of burnt flesh revealed as white bolts of light across her skin, the hollows of her eyes, emblazoned in silver fire.

The ghoulish figure reappeared, lurking at the head of the table, looking straight into the camera lens.

Then the body lying horizontally across the image, her left hand, that which was not damaged by flame, visible and at her side. There I noticed something strange, for a thin band, a ring no doubt, was clearly visible on the fourth finger. It glowed as hot as lead, and I recalled with what sanity I had then and there, that no such ring had been present before. In the background, the numerous flames of candles, each positioned at varying heights, appeared inverted as black pools of deepest darkness, wells that engulfed all light rather than projected it.

The macabre figure, standing alongside the body, looking down upon it.

How close she must have been, so close to me in that dreadful church cellar.

Close enough to whisper in my ear. Close enough to touch my skin.

I developed no more after that, and whilst I cannot recall the manner or time in which I fully cleaned and fixed the images to ensure their permanence, I next remember sitting upon the stone floor, the oil lamp in my hand. The negatives were spread about me in no real order. I picked through them, staring at each one with an indescribable fascination. I don't recall being afraid – the fever had burnt away my fear by then. I was merely fascinated; I looked upon the negatives as a naturalist may observe embalmed insects or fossilised flora, with enquiry and curiosity.

I looked upon a ghost, the ghost of Betsan Tilny, hiding in the trees of the woodland and standing beside her cold, rotting corpse.

I looked upon her ghost as though it were nothing extraordinary.

My silence, my solitude, was broken sometime later – how long, I do not know. A voice spoke out to me quietly.

'I-Inspector?' Vaughn was standing over me. Cummings, just

behind him, was staring wide-eyed at the negatives on the floor. Solomon too was looking at them, or at least down at me. As I looked past him, to the flooding light of the bar above, eyes peered down into the cellar, staring at me gravely.

Whether these words be true or a fiction of fevered memory I cannot be sure, but I recall them being uttered and believe the weary voice who spoke was mine and mine alone.

'She is here. Betsan is here with us.'

13

The Grip of Fever

Most in my position would not see fit to write of the two days that came after I was found, crumpled on the floor of Solomon's cellar, gazing at my negatives. This, after all, is a memoir, one of sorts anyway, an account of fact be it a subjective account. As reader, you may not accept what I say to be factual but must merely accept that *I* believe it to be so. Yet in those days that followed I admit to you that I lost all grasp of what was real and what was total fantasy, so much so, that even I cannot be sure what (if anything) of my account is true.

There is so little to recall, so few flashing images of daylight, of unknown people coming hither and to, attending my needs and washing my face and body, that for some time I thought it unnecessary even to touch upon the subject, albeit to say: I lay in a state of near paralysis; I barely ate; I thought myself close to death.

My diary entries would beg to differ – there are many strange and fantastical entries in it from the darkness of night on the morning of June twentieth to the eve of June twenty-first – I remember writing none. Some I recognise as being in my own hand. Others I cannot say.

I have laid out extracts of these entries (what were the most legible and understandable) as they were written. I have not included any notes or abridgements for they would be redundant – read what was written and make of it what you will.

14

Diary Entries – June 20th, 1904

I have stirred from such a deepest sleep, from such a dreary depth of dream, and have awoken in a nightmare's grasp, where nothing real is as it seems.

I fear I understand, for all is truly come to hand and I feel but a spectator, carried along like a dinghy on the waves. Trapped amongst this ruin, this aged place, this village of inexplicable isolation. These walls of my chamber are not that which hold me, for I know I am TIED UP, BOUND now to this place. Perhaps this will be my end – perhaps I am to die here.

If so let this be my will and testament of type – that what I have is little and what I take with me be even lesser still. See to my fair cousin, for I have always been fond of her and she will surely deal with all my legalities. Strange to think now of what I have when in truth it amounts to so little. To have a child, a daughter, was always my quiet hope.

I feel Betsan with me now. Not as one feels a sense of peace or unease, not as a presence. I feel Betsan with me in the most real of ways.

Her hand is upon my shoulder, her fingers are moving to the back of my neck.

*

This be a record – for the enquiry this be a record. Take heed of my trembling hand.

She stands close to the chamber door. Her back is to the wall and I shall write whilst she stands, hurriedly, for she will surely go as fast as she has come. She stands with her back to the wall and watches me as I sit at the desk. There is no street light, no stars or moon, for this, it would seem, is darkest night, blackest night – THE NIGHT – for no night could ever be much darker. I write only by the light of a single candle; how its flame contorts her!

Her movements are unnatural, grotesque. I dare not scream for fear she will consume my very breath.

She raps her fingers against the wall, tapping with a strange rhythm. Something upon her left hand seems to glow dully. In this light it is like a beacon to a wayward sailor. My eyes are drawn to it, though it is never wholly clear.

With each sudden movement she makes I recoil, no matter how hard I try to hold still. Her face is concealed by her dark hair.

I've moved twice towards my camera case, lying on the floor close to where she stands. On each occasion, she has inched away, closer towards the door, as if signalling her intent, to run and flee should I act against her will. So, I merely sit, scrawling as fast as I can.

I am building the courage to talk to her, though my questions seem foolish.

I have just asked her, 'Who killed you, Betsan?'

She will not answer me.

'Why were you to die then?'

Still, she stands in silence.

I have survived the night. Seems a hollow victory, for I am no better off, my fever has not broken. Cummings was seated at my bedside when I woke, claimed a physician had been (though I cannot recall, my waking hours being so little) and that my prognosis was poor. The

*fever must break tonight or tomorrow if I am to stand any chance –
little else can be done. It seems certain then, for the fever only worsens.
This surely is my lot.*

*Cummings spoke to me a little about the investigation. He seemed
eager to know who (if any) I held suspect. He rattled on nervously
about the travellers and their motives; wondered if I held a report
or dossier he could give to the Constabulary that would surely be
sent for. I would not tell him much, nothing really, for now as ever
I hold my suspicions of him. Even on my death bed I maintain some
Machiavellian cunning, some semblance of myself – an investigator to
the end! I assume he is in possession of my negatives, though I forgot
to ask for them. I doubt he has let them out of his sight, nor will he let
many in the village see them. They may already be destroyed. There is
little I can do about that now.*

*I dreamt of Betsan last night, saw her as well I am sure. I have
failed her. I know I have failed her.*

*Solomon had left three candles alight upon the little writing desk as
darkness drew in. The man carried a plate of food with him, even
offered some to me at my bedside. I could not eat if I wanted to. He
closed the windows and left me then to sleep. Maybe I did to a degree,
for next I recall the candles flickering, dimming so that the flames
were barely visible.*

*I knew then Betsan was coming, for no wind or draught could
extinguish the lights in such a way. In the dim light I waited and
felt the room grow cold.*

*Still now I sit and wait. I wait for my end or for the girl's spirit,
whichever should come first.*

15

Diary Entries – June 21st, 1904

Daylight has brought with it no comfort or joy, for this may be my last morn upon this Earth. It will not be long now; my breathing grows laboured, the pain ever more.

I am no God-fearing man, for I have seen too much sorrow, too much evil and misery, to have faith in such as God. Like I am soon to be, God is surely dead. Yet I am still fearful, like all men when they see their end, knowing there is no hope.

I wish I were more the writer, more the thinker, so that I could finish with some strings of poetry or impart some deep philosophies of the meaning of things and how to live life. All I can think of is the girl, Betsan, and those who may pick up the enquiry after I am gone. To them then I shall write, for I have little else to give than my suspicions, my doubts and intuitions.

It would be such a foolish man, such a superstitious devotee of silly stories of hauntings and spirits who would believe the ghost of Betsan Tilny visited me in my final few days, my short time in Dinas Powys. If you are an Inspector (for upon my final end one will surely be sent) you WILL CALL SUCH THINGS NONSENSE and not waste any time scanning through photographs or allowing dark cellars and wicked whispers get the better of you. And that is good, for a murder has been committed and above all else, a killer remains at large, one who must be brought before a court and judge.

My work so far has revealed the scene of the crime to be staged. The girl's injuries have been inflicted for effect, for a purpose, though that remains unclear. The girl did not return to her mother's home the night before her body was found; the testimony of those in the village (and what was said by the girl's mother) point towards potential prostitution.

My next intention was to begin questioning those in the village, beginning with Miller, the man who discovered the body. Dull, old-fashioned police work; patience and some careful reasoning is needed to ensure adequate alibis are given. A travelling gang may still have played some part in this affair, though my intuitions believe this is not the case. Search out the surrounding areas for any sign of their camp nonetheless.

I believe the girl was killed in cold blood, not in the grip of any act of passion but with premeditated callousness. Should the killer be a local man, he would surely take great delight in the clamour upon the body's discovery – the rumours, the whispers and, of course, the spreading fear. He would also be enacting a fine deception, playing on the superstitions of those who fear some dreadful spirit that lurks within the wood (I defy to acknowledge such superstitions here, for in spite of all I have seen and heard, in these, perhaps, my last rational moments, I cling desperately to logic and reason. This was a crime of man, enacted by man and nothing more).

The girl was surely tortured, her death even possibly the result of her burning. Yet the lacerations around her limbs and neck were most certainly done after she was burnt, implying that the killer had both TIME and PRIVACY – SECURITY as well, the assurance that he would not be found. The proximity and scale of the woodlands suggest she was likely killed somewhere out there.

Someone will know something, someone will have noticed a change in personality, an absence from the dinner table or at the bar after working hours. Your task is a painstaking one, but also one of logic, for in time you shall surely smell a rat, cross reference two statements that do not correlate. Then you will have your suspect or suspects, for this could be the act of a few loathsome fellows (though more likely it is the action of a lone man).

If you have men able, search for where the body was kept during (and possibly after) the killing. This village has numerous farms and properties, each with cattle sheds and barns, abandoned outhouses and forgotten shacks. The abandoned hamlet of Michaelston-le-Pit is a likely place, and I advise you begin your search there. Whilst it was some distance from the scene of the body, it is isolated and remote enough that no one would likely find Betsan or disturb her killer.

Heed these words and you will surely clap the guilty man in irons before a week is out. Drag him before a judge and see that justice is done.

When that is settled, when this village can rest safe in the knowledge that the killer is in chains or on way to the gallows, THEN take the time to look upon my negatives, the images I have developed. Look at them with the greatest scrutiny, with the logical, sceptical mind of an investigator.

Maybe I am mad. Maybe you will see nothing but trees in a forest and a dead corpse lying upon a table.

I'd like to believe I have not succumbed to madness. I'd like to believe you will see all that I saw in those images.

At first, you will likely dismiss them and this whole tale as nonsense. Blame my fever, call me a liar, a forger, an eccentric – all such claims of this type. Run through all of them and settle on one if it helps ease your mind and let you sleep at night. Most sane and reasoned men would do so, for the prospect of the dead lingering amongst the living is as frightful as it is absurd.

Perhaps though, sometime in the future, when the cold wind rattles against your chamber window and the dark shadows on your wall create a menagerie of dreadful beasts, you will dwell on this place, on my words and the images you have seen. In those moments, when fear and doubt and questions race through your mind uncontrolled, perhaps you will be compelled enough to think me not a mad man.

In the darkest hour she spoke to me. I could not see her, for a single weak candle was all that lit the room, and her figure, hid just beyond its reach.

She wept. And I felt her pain.

She watched me in silence. And I wanted it all to end.

16

The Storm Sets In – June 22nd, 1904

Though it may be hard to believe, truly that fever should have killed me. My formative diary entries would suggest I had *some* strength in me, *some* fight and give. But they tell nothing of the darker hours I lay awake, groaning and weeping, writhing from the pain coursing through my body, the attacks of panic and pleas for help and mercy. They give nothing of the true misery of those days and nights, the powerlessness I felt.

How then did I survive; how then am I alive at all?

I awoke to the pale light of a clouded dawn as though it were the first time I had looked upon the world for a great age, as though I were only now returning from some dreadful realm. I had no idea or recollection of how long I had lain in my small chamber. My head hurt, though I knew it was but a shadow of the pain I had endured. My mouth felt dry, and I thought better of calling out.

As I began to move, my body tingled, particularly my lower legs and feet, for I had clearly been lying near motionless for some time. My bedsheets were heavy with sweat and gave off such a musk that I took to clumsily collect them in my hands and throw them to the floor. In time, I gingerly swung my legs from the bed and sat facing the small window, focusing on nothing but the dull light.

My stomach growled, and I gathered my thoughts in such a slow and precarious manner that it was perhaps not for another half hour that I made to stand and stretch my body. Only then did I seem to acknowledge the torn and tatty pages of my diary, strewn close to the bed and further around the room, some scrawled in pencil, others blotched in black ink. I stood and paced across the floorboards, moving around the pile of damp bedsheets, collecting each scrap of paper as I did. I set them upon the table, alongside the large bowl of water that was once again filled to the brim and the menacing ragdoll, lying on its side.

The little doll stared up at me, the black stitching of the eyes seeming to grow larger as I stared back. I reached down slowly, gently wrapping my hand around it. The doll was cold and unpleasant to touch – after only a moment I dropped it, childishly turning it away so that the face was not looking at me.

It was a bleak and miserable day outside. The heavy clouds above were unbroken and unending, rolling from the north where they seemed only to grow darker. A storm looked imminent, ready to break and shatter the heavy, warm summer air.

I washed my face, and feeling so unclean all over, took to spread out the bedsheets across the floor a little, whereupon I stripped off my pyjamas. I took the large bowl of water and with one unseemly and indelicate movement, thrust the contents over me, so that water cascaded from my head to my knees and ankles. It was such a brash thing to do but I felt no regrets as heavy drops fell from me onto the filthy bedsheets where I stood. The water was bitterly cold, though I felt much more a man alive than a walking corpse as I dried myself a little and moved to get dressed.

When all was done, and I had buttoned a fresh shirt to the collar, I turned my attention to the diary entries. Upon my first reading they did not shock me as one might expect, for although I had no great recollection of the previous few days, I had a strange sense of fingers moving across the back of my neck, of a figure, standing with me as I sat and lay close to death.

When I had scanned through the pages (separating those I knew to be by my hand from the strange, nonsensical scrawl), my thoughts turned to the enquiry and the interviews I so desperately needed to begin. I recalled my negatives, briefly assuming, as I had written, that Cummings had taken charge of them. I wondered what he had made of the girl's ghoulish figure appearing in the images.

It was *then* that I was hit quite suddenly by the enormity of it all, the absurdity of what I was accepting and believing to be true.

I remember the sensation quite well, as if a shot of lightning erupted throughout my chest and paralysed me instantly. As I sat at the small writing desk and watched the thickset black clouds draw closer, seeing the first drops of rain spit and glance against the window pane, I became quite overcome with emotion, panic-stricken and overwhelmed.

Ghosts! Here was I investigating not only the murder of a girl but the appearance of her ghost! Madness, surely – logic, rationality, precedent gripped my mind and called me fool. I was being had, this was all some ruse, some lark of the killer, some deceptive way of throwing me off course. And how I felt then such an entanglement of emotions, for I was both foolish and naïve, for if such as ghosts were indeed real, then I knew *nothing* of our real world. What foundation of knowledge or beliefs could I stand upon? Surely now there was an afterlife of sorts, though I had had no such faith in any before. What of a God then, or any manner of other whispered tales of nightmares that one dispels as a child?

I began to read through the diary entries once more, blaming the fever and its madness. I didn't simply want to look at my negatives then but *needed* to desperately. They could surely dispel all such nonsense of phantoms. I assured myself of this, and for perhaps five or ten minutes I became quite resolute on the matter.

The fever had made me see a ghost. *The fever* had made me see Betsan.

It was undoubtedly the most rational conclusion. I clung to the idea gladly, even if it meant I had embarrassed myself or looked a fool. I even laughed aloud at one moment, shaking my head at the thought of how my colleagues would crow and giggle when I recounted the tale. I would surely never live it down, for ever to be known as Bexley, the Ghost Hunter, the Crypt Inspector.

I laughed as I tried to convince myself that nothing I had seen or felt of the girl's waking spectre had been real. I laughed until I could hardly breathe.

When I finally left my room it was with an unnerved sense of purpose. I returned almost instantly, fetching the Enfield from beneath my mattress and shoving it in the deep pockets of my heavy coat. It was just past nine in the morning, though as I took one final glance out of the little window, I saw no signs of life or movement on the Twyn, now being soaked by a deluge of rain.

As I turned to leave I caught sight of the little doll, still propped on the desk facing the wall. I thought of the mother, how I would no doubt need speak with her again in due course.

The demon of this village.

I winced, as though the words hurt me.

I quickly grabbed up the doll, thrusting it in my pocket along with the pistol. There were other matters to attend to first. I left once more and after climbing down the narrow stairwell, came upon Solomon, who leapt quite dramatically at the sight of me.

'You're awake! And out of bed.'

I nodded and moved past him, stepping into the bar and sitting on a rickety stool. Solomon followed me, babbling about bed rest, what Cummings had told him, how I had been close to death.

'I'm hungry,' I stammered, my hands still shaking, the shock to my body and the raw emotion unabated. 'And need a drink.'

Solomon left for some ten minutes, returning with a messy plate of eggs and bread along with a small mug of weak tea. I devoured all as he stood opposite me behind the bar. With a mouthful of food, I gestured to a dark brown bottle of Scotch whisky behind him. He seemed confused for a moment, before setting the bottle down on the bar in front of me. I removed the cap and poured a drab into my tea mug. I downed the lot in one, as Solomon watched me in complete silence.

My nerves seemed a little calmer then and I closed my eyes for a few moments, taking deep breaths and clasping my hands lightly together. My head and neck ached badly; I still felt nauseous. My arms were weak from inactivity; my chest rattled a little with each deep intake of breath.

'I'll get Mr Cummings,' Solomon mumbled. I opened my eyes and shook my head.

'I shall speak to him in time. First, I need to send a telegram. Quite urgently. Is there an exchange?'

Solomon looked baffled for a minute. 'The Beacon House, just across the Twyn, up Highwalls Road a little way.'

'I assume Mr Cummings took my negatives – the photographic plates I developed down there?' I pointed to the hatch at Solomon's feet.

He shrugged. 'They're not down there.'

'Did you see them?' I asked.

'Yes,' was all he replied. I stayed quiet for a moment waiting for him to speak.

'And?' I barked.

He didn't answer, fetching my plate and mug. 'You should rest some more. You're unwell.'

I moved without thought, reaching over the bar and grabbing Solomon by the scruff of his grubby shirt. It was caused by the fever, its effects still lingering. I pulled him towards me with quite some force, so much so that the tin mug he carried crashed to the floor.

'Do you believe in ghosts, Solomon?'

I spoke in hushed tones, as if we two were conspiring in a dreadful secret.

Solomon reacted swiftly; he dropped the dirty plate and cutlery on the bar and shoved me away with one meaty hand. His eyes were wide with shock, his face flushed.

'Are you mad? If it's the *Calon Farw* you're talking about I'm no bloody fool! I know there's nothing out there in them woods.'

He collected the plate and cutlery and left the bar without another word. I thought to shout after him but instead lurched off the bar stool and headed out onto the Twyn.

The rain by then was frightful, both heavy and cold, so that it beat against the ground with great ferocity. It scratched against the exposed skin of my face, penetrated through the thick layer of my coat within but a few short paces. It was most uncommon weather for the season.

I moved quickly and headed across the Twyn. No more than a hundred yards from the inn was a neat white cottage, two storeys with a small well-kept garden of heather and pink roses. A thin wire draped loosely from a small partition close to the upper windows and connected to a dark telegraph mast erected just outside the front gate. I had seen these masts continue at irregular intervals, down Mill Hill and up along the Turnpike towards Cardiff.

As I opened the garden gate, I saw a face watching me from a window looking onto the garden. The front door opened before I could knock, and a woman, in a pristine navy dress with a crisp, white shawl draped around her shoulders, beckoned me in.

There was no greeting space or foyer to speak of, for the front door led straight into a wide kitchen with cluttered Welsh dressers and brown tiles lining the floor. The rain dripped from me, and a puddle quickly formed about my feet as the woman looked me over. She was perhaps fifty, short but of such a proud and straight posture as to make herself seem taller. Her chin was raised a little, so that she looked down her nose at me, her eyes narrowed, her lips pursed.

'You're the Inspector?' Her voice was deep, her heavy accent, lavish and rolling. Her tone was as stern as her features.

I nodded. 'Of a sort. I need to send word to the Glamorgan Constabulary.'

She moved around me slowly, her eyes fixed to mine.

'May I ask why?'

'It's a police matter,' I said impatiently. In truth I intended to ask for more men.

She nodded, her face blank and expressionless. She silently moved out of the kitchen through a low door. I followed after her, into the adjoining front room of the small house, where the brown tiles of the kitchen floor continued. It was sparse, furnished only with a few wooden chairs and a dark fireplace, clean and well swept. Against the far wall, towards the back of the house, stood a wide desk. Upon it sat a large Morse key, fitted with numerous wires that ran across the desk and up the wall out of sight.

'The line has been down, some two days,' the woman said. 'My husband, Mr Wilkins, has been affecting repairs as best he can, though the cabling has never been good from here as far as Llandough. With this storm, things are only likely to be further damaged.'

She fell silent then, clasping her hands together and staring at me with her cool unbroken gaze. It was unsettling, that along with the manner in which she pursed her lips and twitched her nose ever so slightly.

'Show me,' I said bluntly. The woman – Mrs Wilkins – seemed quite taken aback.

She huffed and moved over to the Morse key. After sitting herself down in a laborious fashion and attending to the necessary wiring, she began keying in a message.

'There's no signal – I can't send or receive anything.' She turned on me as I leant forward. 'See for yourself.'

She mumbled under her breath as I pawed at the copper key. I had no real knowledge of telegraphy, but it seemed quite clear that the machine was completely inactive.

'May I say,' Mrs Wilkins said slowly, 'that this is quite improper, Inspector.'

'How soon will the cabling be repaired?' I snapped at her.

Mrs Wilkins exclaimed a little at the manner in which I spoke, standing from the chair in dramatic fashion.

'This storm is only set to worsen and will hamper all repairs – not even the trains are running along the line. *As I have already told you*, there is little to be done.'

She moved then out of the cold room into the kitchen and opened the front door to the howling wind. With little pause I took my leave, only stopping in the doorway for a moment as

Mrs Wilkins bid me a curt farewell. She seemed to straighten her back even more as she spoke to me:

'I'm sorry, Inspector,' she said as the rain flooded her little garden. 'But we are completely cut off.'

17

The Miller's Account – June 22nd, 1904

'How are you even standing?'

I didn't wait for Cummings to invite me in but brushed past him and stood in the short foyer of his house. I fought the urge to shake the arms of my coat and dash raindrops across the fine gold-leaf wallpaper.

'Would you have me still ill, in bed?'

Cummings scoffed and slammed his front door shut. He grumbled and fidgeted, clearly lost as to what to say.

'We thought you close to death.'

'Would that be preferable?'

'Of course not.' In that moment he did not meet my gaze. 'Though your fever was ferocious, man, worse than many of us have seen.'

'It has passed,' I muttered, knowing full well I was still quite unwell. The cold rain had cleared my head somewhat, however, so that I could cast aside all thoughts of the paranormal and focus my attentions on the case at hand.

I wiped my soaked hair from my forehead. 'And it has wasted valuable time; our killer has gained ample opportunity to conceal or distort evidence.'

Cummings' face flushed, though I made sure to speak before he could get a word in.

'We will have to redouble our efforts, begin questioning the residents and cross-examine anything that seems out of place. I'll need you to find Vaughn.'

'Are you mad? You are in no state to carry out an investigation or any sort of work. Last we spoke you were delusional, raving.' He stepped towards me and thrust a fat finger in my chest. 'Seen your ghost again, eh? Seen Betsan wandering in the dark hours of night? That's what you told me of last time we spoke.'

'You saw my negatives,' I replied coolly.

'So what? A few images of trees, the girl's body.' He shuddered then.

'You still have them? I'd have them back.'

Cummings shook his head. 'All you'd do is stare at them and see things, phantoms in the woodlands.' He stepped close to my face, though now my patience was wearing thin and I took a hold of his shirt. It was the second time that day I had grabbed at a man's collar.

'Muttering, yelling in the night, scrawling pages of nonsense and crying into the darkness. And you call yourself fit, fit to lead an enquiry without pointing a finger at the wrong man or tearing people's lives apart.'

He thrust my hand away from his shirt and retreated from me. We both stood glaring at each other for a few moments.

'I intended to ask for assistance, though it seems the storm has cut us off from Cardiff or anywhere else for that matter. The telegraph lines are down, the trains not running. Until I can gain the aid of the Constabulary, I will set about my duties and carry out enquiries.'

A rumble of thunder cut my words short. Outside, the rain began to lash across the common with ever greater ferocity.

'This storm will not last for ever. When it has passed more men, in a better state than I, will be sent for. Should you try to disrupt this enquiry or stand in my way I will have no choice but to ensure charges are brought against you.'

I realised then that I was clasping the handle of my Enfield quite tightly in my pocket, though I had no idea why. My thoughts were still addled, disjointed and hazy. I loosened my hold on the gun with a sigh and a small shake of the head. Cummings didn't seem to notice.

'All right. All right, fine.' The pallor of his complexion had dulled substantially, his words far less shaken and agitated. 'What do you plan to do?'

'I shall start at the beginning. Johnathon Miller, he found the girl's body. I'll begin by questioning him. Would he be at the mill now?'

Cummings nodded a little. 'We spoke last night. He's only just noticed damage to the mill and was afraid the storm may cause more. I imagine he will be down there. What would you have me do whilst you question him?'

'Fetch Vaughn. Gather whoever you can, preferably labourers from the mill and farms first. Have them meet at your town hall this afternoon. It will serve as a makeshift headquarters for our enquiry. I will question each one by one.'

Cummings rolled his eyes at that but nodded in silence. I made to move past him but stopped with my hand upon the front doorknob.

'My negatives, Cummings. I'll have my negatives.'

'I don't have them,' he replied plainly whilst holding my gaze. I felt a sudden rush of panic overcome me. It seemed he was telling the truth.

The woodlands were a different realm from those I had admired on the day of my arrival. The smell hit me first; no longer the sweet scent of dried hay and wild garlic, now the dank rankness of sodden soil and spreading moss. The air down here was still stifling in spite of the rain, trapped beneath the heavy canopy. The forest sprawling upon my path to the mill creaked and groaned at me; branches splintered and fell out of sight. No thrush or other songbird swooped or danced, for the world in every direction seemed dark and miserable, drained of all colour and life.

I hacked and coughed as I approached the mill, my body already weak from what little excursion I had enacted that morning. Now, as I carried my camera equipment, my back began to throb and burn ferociously as muscles, unused for such a length of time, worked and grinded to keep me moving.

I had decided to photograph the mill, in spite of the reservations I had. I say with no shame that as I walked, still haunted by my fever, I feared what may lurk in any more images I took. I had no intentions then of developing any whilst I remained in the village. I knew however that the mill may be of some importance, and photographic evidence may be relevant for a subsequent enquiry or future trial. Despite my anxieties, some rational sensibility was returning to me.

So dark was the day, distorted by the sweeping rain and thick swirling cloud, it was not until I was but ten yards or so from the mill that I caught sight of two figures, working with hammers and split lengths of timber. I called out, though it seemed neither man heard me.

A voice called out my name from behind me. I turned.

Betsan's burning spectre lunged into my thoughts.

I lurched where I stood, the loose handle of my camera case giving way. It fell to the wet path with a clatter. I tried pushing the dreadful sights from my mind, cursing as fiery pain surged behind my forehead and temples. The illness still skulked within me. I reached down and awkwardly hauled the case up.

'Miller?' I called out again. To this the taller of the men turned. By now I was close enough to see his features wrinkle and twist in confusion.

'Who's asking?'

I didn't reply until I stood before him. I set down my case gently and stretched out my hand; Miller looked at me quizzically.

'Bexley. I'm here about the murder of the Tilny girl.'

He eyed me for a drawn-out moment; I thought best to let my hand fall back to my side.

'What y'want?' he croaked over the pitter-patter about us.

'I need to ask you some questions, about the day you found the body, and take some photographs of the mill, though in this storm it will only be the interior.'

There came a rattle and thud, as the other man, seemingly trying to board up one of the mill's small glass windows, let slip a length of timber. Miller turned and growled at him.

'Bloody fool! Get on with it.'

As the other man looked back, with slacked jaw and eyes blinking quickly in the rain, I recognised him vaguely as Lewis Davey. He and his brother Geraint had passed by the scene where the body was found on the day of my arrival. I had not paid Lewis much attention before, though now I saw how dissimilar he was to his brother. He was neither tall nor broad, lacking the fine features and commanding presence of Geraint. Lewis was short, hunched, his hairline receding though he was surely younger than twenty-five. His eyes were small and his skin quite poor; he looked at Miller in such a queer way, his speech slow as he apologised.

Miller grunted at him and Lewis near recoiled, dropping his gaze and collecting the wood from the floor.

'Fool,' Miller snapped.

I cleared my throat. 'As I said, I have questions regarding—'

'I answered plenty the day I found 'er.' He moved away from me and opened the door of the mill. Warm light spilt out briefly as he stepped through – the door shut with a crack behind him. I glanced at Lewis working, before collecting my case and following Miller inside. I almost walked straight into the man, who seemed surprised that I was still there.

'I told ya, I already answered questions. That lad Vaughn spoke to me before moving the body.'

Gently placing my equipment down once more, I pulled my small notepad and pencil from the inside of my jacket. The air inside the mill was thick and musty; my eyes felt dry and irritable in an instant. 'That doesn't matter, I'm afraid. *I* have questions to ask you now.'

I could see he made to protest though I wouldn't let him start.

'This is a serious crime, Mr Miller, and to be frank, I need to ensure I gather all the facts accordingly.' I jotted down Miller's name at the top of a fresh page. 'I understand you've a busy workload at the moment. Business is going well, I gather.'

He grew guarded at my passing comment. 'You been investigating me then?'

I shook my head with a frown. 'No, no. Mr Cummings explained you had recently expanded. The large greenhouses just along the trail.'

'Oh,' he muttered quietly. 'Yes, things are going well. Mr Cummings has been very good in assisting with getting the work completed. He's a good man, the Councillor.'

I feigned a smile.

'You found the girl whilst walking with your hounds, correct?'

Miller grunted at me then.

'What time?'

He sighed and nodded his head. 'Not long after sun up, around six.'

'Between six and six thirty?' I asked. He nodded. 'I'm aware of the injuries the girl had sustained before her death but tell me in your own words how you found her.'

He folded his arms and shrugged. Outside, a dreadful squeal was silenced by a sharp snap. We both turned at the sound: no doubt a large tree limb breaking and falling to the ground close by. It sounded awfully human, nonetheless.

'They'll be coming through the bloody rafters at this rate. Look, I told Vaughn before. She was bound up in a chain; her face and arms were all burnt up. Eyes gone, hair bloody. It wasn't pretty – dogs would have started gnawing on her if I hadn't got 'em off.'

'Did you notice the size of the scorch marks on the ground, the blackened earth?'

He shrugged again. 'She was burnt. It was nasty. I can't say I remember really looking at the ground beneath her.'

'Who did you speak to once you had found the body?'

He rubbed his head, his frustration becoming ever more visible. 'Two of the lads were here. I went and fetched them. We weren't sure whether it was best to move her body. We were nervous. It ain't something you expect to find!' He took a step back from me and slouched against a heavy wooden cask.

It was only then that I was able to have any real look inside the mill, though my mind was more focused on Miller and his demeanour. When questioning a man, more can be said from his eyes, his tics and twitches, the way he holds his arms or carries himself, than any fine words he may utter. Miller was clearly uncomfortable, nervous, though most people are when speaking to an inspector. More than this, though, I could see he was upset. His eyes grew wider as he spoke about Betsan's body, his words began to shake just slightly. Perhaps finding her, not merely dead but left in such a gruesome fashion, had impacted on a part of him far deeper than the tough, hardy appearance he maintained.

'The lads wanted nothing to do with it. They have their superstitions – most around here do.'

'Of what nature?' I asked firmly.

He huffed. 'No one's told you?'

'I've heard plenty, I would hear it from you, though.'

He shook his head, in irritation it seemed more than anything. 'There's always been rumours of something hiding in these woods. Something dark and evil. It goes back to the ruin of the old fort, down past the Cwm Sior.' He pointed a hand absently. 'Barely anything now, just a few stones and rocks. They call it *Calon Farw*, this thing, whatever it is; when I was a boy my *tadcu* – my grandfather – believed it was real. Said it haunted the place, brought all manner of wickedness at times.'

'But you don't believe any of it?' That was clear to me from the way Miller spoke.

Miller spat on the floor. 'No. It's foolish. The whole thing was nearly forgotten by everyone until a few years back.'

'What brought it back to people's minds?'

He folded his arms and shrugged. 'Who knows – we had a couple of bad harvests, maybe that was it.'

I nodded in silence for a moment. 'Do all your men believe in this evil, this *Calon Farw*?'

Miller threw his hands up in the air. 'I don't know – I think most do. We're simple people here, Mr Inspector, the kind who hold on to our beliefs.' He slunk back into himself. 'Either way, it took some convincing for me to get the boys to help.'

'What did you do?'

He looked down at the floor. 'At first we tried to get the chain off 'er. Bloody thing was wrapped so tight, weren't much we could do with it.'

I was scrawling in my notebook quickly, trying to keep Miller talking whilst he would. 'Did you recognise it – the chain, I mean? Was it something you may use here?'

'Chain's a chain.'

I nodded. 'Then what?'

'Neither the lads wanted to move her. We had a bit of a row, but they were probably right.' He fell silent then and I paused in anticipation, waiting for him to go on. He didn't, though. He stood up straight after a moment and scowled at me, his hard exterior revived. 'This storm is set to get worse and I have work to do.'

As he tried to pass me, I blocked him.

'Did you fetch Vaughn? If so what time?'

He grabbed at me and I shoved him back.

'Answer my question.'

'Edward did! It was me, him and another lad, Will. Edward ran to get Vaughn and me and Will stood around like frightened children until they came back.'

'What time?' I held my ground, though I could see Miller's hands ball into fists as the expression on his face grew deathly.

'Edward left about fifteen minutes after we found her. Was probably half hour till him and the Constable came back. Councillor came down about another half hour later.'

'And there was no one else here the entire time? No one?'

'No,' he growled through gritted teeth. 'Edward got the Constable and then they told the Councillor. That was all that happened, no bloody great lies like you're looking for. If you wan' know what I was doing the night before you can ask my wife, she'll tell you that I was with 'er. That enough – have I told you what you wan' hear?'

He moved towards me again and I didn't stop him. As he wrenched open the door, I tried my luck and asked one final question.

'Did you see anyone, Miller? In the days before the girl was killed. Anyone walking up and down the trail, someone you didn't recognise?'

He turned to me slowly and spoke even more slowly.

'I'm no bloody watchman. Got it? You got ten minutes for your *pictures.*'

He stomped out of the mill and I heard him yell scorn at Lewis still working in the torrent. I had more questions to ask but knew I was more likely to get a right hook than any answers – for now it seemed Miller had said enough.

I pocketed my notebook and set about erecting my camera stand. To my relief, all my equipment was intact and had taken no damage when I dropped it.

The mill mainly comprised one room, consumed mostly by the stone grind and its numerous gears and axles connecting to the water wheel outside. There were many sacks of flour and grain, a workbench stretching much of the far and left wall, littered with tools and equipment that didn't seem out of the ordinary. Lengths of wood and ladders were held in the rafters above; a few chairs and a table were pushed against the far right corner. I quickly opened a small door, nestled just out of sight from where I had questioned Miller. It led to a stone chamber, filled with more large sacks of grain and several dark metal cogs of various sizes. It was all unremarkable.

Nevertheless, I took three photographs in all, moving my camera to different points around the mill's main room. Whilst the exposure was not ideal, I thought it was enough to capture much of the room's contents and detail.

After I had safely tucked my third exposed plate in its black paper pocket, and placed it securely in my case, Miller burst back in from the storm.

'I have more work to do before the day is up.'

He spoke forcefully, and I made no protests. I dismantled all my equipment and awkwardly gathered my damaged case. I thanked Miller, who only stood watching me the whole time. Trying to raise my collar (to what end, for my very skin was soaked to the bone by this point) I made haste from his premises.

18

A Slip of the Tongue – June 22nd, 1904

To my surprise Cummings did what was asked of him, so that when I returned to the Twyn and made my way to the town hall at the base of Britway Road, I caught sight of Constable Vaughn, standing in the relative shelter of the hall's arched entranceway. By now the rain had become even more bitter, biting against the skin in a way more accustomed to deepest winter than late June. I quickened my pace at the sight of lit lanterns and the young Vaughn waving excitedly to me.

He seemed genuinely pleased to see me as I stood next to him, placing a hand upon my shoulder before taking hold of my camera case.

'I d-didn't quite believe it when M-Mr Cummings told me.' He spoke jovially as we walked through the open door. 'You have made quite the recovery, Inspector.'

I coughed violently as I pulled off my heavy coat.

'Not entirely, though I am sure to live.' I was being a little coarse, yet in many ways I felt grateful for the man's welcome, far kindlier than the glares and mistrust I had grown accustomed to since the time of my arrival. I felt in no mood for idle talk however and enquired if there were a fire in the hall. Vaughn led me through a large, stale foyer to a dim antechamber, lit solely by a small hearth with red embers glistening. I knelt beside it and sat in silence for a time as Vaughn spoke of my state of illness.

As I stared into the soft embers, I saw the terrible spectre of the fiery spirit once more, lunging at me in the cellar of All Saints church, eyes hollowed, encased in white flame. I felt a wave of fear pass over me, my chest tightening, my skin turning hot all over as though the fever were taking hold of me again. I closed my eyes, trying to breathe slowly. Was the spectre the result of my illness, an image of my own making? I wished to a god I had no faith in that were so, for the thought of a ghost haunting this place brought all manner of misery and fear into my heart. Horrors began to swirl about me, growing in size and depravity as I was forced ever deeper into a dark void of madness, one I feared I could be lost in for ever.

'I've managed to g-gather twelve or so members of the village, though I don't know how useful th-th-they will be.'

'What?' I asked with a sharp intake of breath as I returned to the room with a start.

Vaughn hesitated, before speaking slowly to me.

'Mr Cummings said you wanted to gather members of the village. I tried the labourers, and f-found one or two, but most are out dealing with the storm. I didn't know where to start but managed to gather twelve persons for now. I thought that w-would be enough this afternoon.'

I nodded as I rubbed at my eyes and continued to take deep, slow breaths.

'You'll have to forgive me, Constable. The illness has not fully passed.' I slouched by the fire, before asking Vaughn where everyone was waiting.

'In the—in the hall. They're not too happy but I'm sure they'll do what they can to help your enquiry.'

I thanked Vaughn and told him I would be a few short

minutes. He left me alone in the room, where I removed my jacket and let my weak body sit lazily about the floor in front of the fire. My hands shook as I held them out before me.

Since the time of this whole affair, I have spent many hours reviewing what notes I made, what scraps of information I obtained and recorded over the course of the enquiry. Like a cipher, these notes at first glance seem random, chaotic. Yet in these pages lie the very keys that unlocked the truth of Betsan's murder. Needless to say, I am grateful for the diligence, what some see as over-zealous manner, in which I carry out my enquiries. *Everything* can be of great relevance and as such, everything should be recorded.

I explain all this to you now to give some indication of how that day in the town hall unfolded. Scanning through my notes, I can see that less and less information was written down as the afternoon wore on. *I did learn* that Betsan was seen the day before her body was found, confirming that her murder took place no more than sixteen hours before she was discovered. Beyond that, much was fruitless, mere hearsay and gossip, to the exception of one slip of the tongue.

I gathered my things on a rickety desk I pulled from the corner of the room, before setting a chair on either side. I set up my camera stand intending to document any scratch marks that may be considered possible defence wounds correlating to the blood found under Betsan's nails. I intended to make each man and woman I questioned show me their arms, as high as the shoulder, as well as the entirety of their faces (removing caps or brushing away hair) and their necks. Such defence wounds could have been exacted on any part of the killer's body, of course, though it was beyond absurdity to carry out *full* examinations of every villager. Nevertheless, I intended to be as thorough as I possibly could from the outset.

It began with the ironmonger, a stout, unshaven man in his early fifties. He had foregone his business that day in light of the storm. He thumbed with his cap and wriggled in his seat. He barely spoke, nerves it seemed holding his tongue.

'You had no idea who she met with, who her friends were if she had any?' This was perhaps the fifth or sixth question I had asked the man.

The ironmonger shook his head fervently. 'No, sir. No. As I say, I really didn't know her.'

'Can you recall the last time that you *personally* saw her?'

Before the last word had even left my mouth, he was shaking his head again.

'Very rarely saw her, sir. Would have been some weeks ago, perhaps longer.'

'Really?' I replied politely. 'In a village as small as this?'

The man nodded. His face was flushed. I folded my arms and leant back a little.

'Need I remind you that omitting evidence to a police enquiry is a criminal offence. Lying to an officer during questioning can result in substantial criminal charges—'

'Please, sir,' the ironmonger near whispered, his hands fidgeting dreadfully quickly with his cap. 'I don't want to lie about any of this – really I don't know—'

'If you don't want to lie, tell me the truth. You claim you hadn't seen the girl for weeks – that to me is unlikely in a village as small as this one.'

I leant over the table. There seemed little point in skirting the matter any longer.

'Are you afraid to talk to me?'

The ironmonger's eyes widened, welling up as though he were close to tears. He squirmed, clearly torn as to what to do or say.

He nodded slowly. 'It's out there. It killed the girl – it'll take any of us if it so chooses. Please, sir—'

'Whatever you fear,' I said, then, sharply and with great authority, 'is a fiction. There is nothing out in those woodlands that will bring any harm to you should you speak to me of the girl's murder. What will be of graver consequence – of *real danger* – will be to allow the true perpetrator of this wicked act to walk free and take another life.'

My sermon did little to rouse the man; it only served to break his resolve so that his head lolled against the little desk and he cried and wailed like a small boy. It was a struggle to coax anything out of him after that. In time, he confirmed seeing Betsan the day before Miller came upon her in the woods. He'd never spoken to her before, having heard unsavoury things of her character. To this I asked him to elaborate and he mumbled something of her promiscuity.

'Is this a widely held belief amongst the village, that she was promiscuous?'

'I believe so,' he said quietly. 'People hear things.'

I asked of any strangers who may have come to him in the days before the murder; to this he said there were none. I then began to ask of his time in the village; had he lived here his whole life, was he married, a family man? He had a wife but said nothing of any children. Could he attest to those in the village; did he believe anyone capable of such a crime? To this he said no one was capable of such a wicked thing.

I asked about the chain in which the body was wrapped – could it have been something taken or bought from him? Like Miller he spoke of the ease of acquiring such a chain, but that he could not recall being asked for one for many months. On and on it went, for I sought to know of his day-to-day dealings and if there was anything out of the ordinary leading up to and after the body was found. What was his business with those in and outside the village? What did he know of Michaelston, for I wanted his take on the abandoned hamlet...

'People felt alone out there. They were afraid of... of, um...' He couldn't speak of the *Calon Farw* then, his lips trembling. 'They just wanted to be more a part of the village. Felt safer that way.'

There were one or two more questions after that, and I closed by asking of his alibi. I decided he had enough of one: staying late at a game of cards, arranged by one of the farmers; rising before dawn to re-shoe some horses of that very same man. A few others had been in attendance that night.

After he had hesitantly shown me his arms, neck and the entirety of his face (revealing nothing that could be considered a defence wound), I thanked him for his time. 'If you strike upon anything, recall something that seemed strange to you, please let me know.'

He nodded his head but remained where he sat. His face had bled of colour. I tried to speak a few words of comfort to him.

'What you have told me today will surely be of the greatest help. Soon the guilty party will be apprehended; this village and those closest by, will be much safer for it.'

'That may be,' the man quivered after a moment. 'But I doubt it.'

He stood from the seat slowly. His hands were shaking as he pulled on his cap.

'I believe something is out there, Mr Bexley, something that took that girl and left her as she was found. You want to believe that a man could do such a thing – I believe different. No man I ever met would want to do such terrible things.'

He turned to walk away but seemed reluctant to do so, as though he were stepping out onto the gallows or before a firing squad.

'We don't talk about it because we know it's there. We know it's real, feel its presence every day.' He glared at me with his red, bloodshot eyes. 'Don't tell me since you've been here you haven't felt it too.'

It took a great effort to stifle a shudder as I thought of all I had seen and heard. Voices in the shadows. Eyes watching in the trees. Betsan's emblazoned corpse, sat up and staring at me in the cellar of All Saints church. Catrin's face twisting and contorting before my very eyes.

I cleared my throat and spoke quietly. 'If you recall anything, please let me know.'

Next came a Mrs Patterson, the wife of the local shopkeeper. She was in her mid-forties, petite, well-dressed, her hair pinned back in such an alarming manner as to pull the skin of her forehead taut and give her eyes the appearance of being for ever opened wide. She spoke candidly when I asked of Betsan's character.

'Her mother.' She wrinkled her nose. 'Having a child at her age; no husband, no father to the girl. It's obscene – *vile*. She used to live in the house by the station you know, till that burnt down. She's a very wealthy woman.'

I thought of the Malthouse, the derelict cottage just up from the station, its roof collapsed, its rotten frame exposed. It seemed much had been left unsaid when I had met with Catrin.

'Burnt down?' I asked. 'When did that happen?'

Mrs Patterson leant closer to me. 'When she was pregnant. She blamed almost everyone in the village, came ranting and raving into the middle of the Twyn. We all knew she did it herself – madwoman! There's no other explanation. Just look at the way she lives her life now, a savage out there. No way to raise a child. We all wonder why she won't leave, why she lurks here. It's no surprise the girl turned out the way she did.'

'Why do you think she stayed here then? Surely if she is a wealthy woman, she could have simply left?'

Mrs Patterson shrugged. 'Who knows what possesses a woman like that?'

I tapped my pencil upon the paper, seeming to look in thought but really letting a rush of dizziness pass me by. I had to give the appearance of good health, even if I was not wholly well.

'You have some sympathies for Betsan then?' I said after a moment.

To this Mrs Patterson shook her head. 'We all must start somewhere, and I admit her start in life was a bad one. Maybe she didn't stand much of a chance of living honestly, wholesome and all. But at some time, we have to take responsibility for what we do. The girl was asking for trouble, the life she led the ... the *carnal desires* she had.'

I shook my head a little. 'You are not the first person in this village who would blame Betsan for her own death and I daresay you will unlikely be the last.'

Mrs Patterson's lips twisted. She took a deep breath and spoke to me in a manner most patronising. 'You don't see other women in this village wandering around in the woods on their own, speaking to strange men, and winding up dead. I would think you had some more sense than to absolve the girl entirely of all her blame.'

'It is not a question of where she walked,' I replied bitingly. 'Or even the manner in which she conducted herself with those in the village. Suffice to say that whether a girl be flirtatious or not, it does not permit a man to rape, defile and butcher her like a mere animal. There is only one criminal in this whole affair and it is not Betsan – a child by all accounts, I remind you.'

I was speaking loudly by the time I finished, though Mrs Patterson seemed wholly unperturbed. She folded her arms slowly, her wide eyes unblinking.

I continued with a little more composure. 'Everyone speaks the same of the girl's ways, that she dallied and so forth.' To this Mrs Patterson scoffed a little. 'But I see no evidence to confirm as much. Can you tell me anything of the *carnal desires*, as you put it, the girl may have had?'

Mrs Patterson rolled her eyes. 'She was a flirt. Men will be men and she liked their attention. Always down by the mill, giggling and running with them. In spite of what you think she was asking for trouble and no one will say otherwise.'

I moved on, for it seemed pointless labouring on this point.

'Did Betsan have any friends that you know of? I haven't seen many other girls of Betsan's age in the village.'

It was the only time Mrs Patterson's demeanour changed. She unfolded her arms, shifted herself in the seat and looked down for a moment whilst she gently laid her hands on her lap.

'I can't say I knew of any friends the girl may have had. I saw her often when she came into the shop. My husband is a kindlier person than I and was willing to serve her. She was never with anyone, though.'

I returned to questions of what Mrs Patterson had seen in the days leading up to the event, though she was quick to give her opinion on the culprit of the crime.

'Mr Cummings spoke of travellers at the town meeting we had and I for one believe him,' she said sharply.

'Mr Cummings is not an investigator,' I replied in similar tone.

We finished on her alibi, to which she could confirm both her and her husband's whereabouts. With little courtesy I made her show me her arms and neck, which she eventually did after numerous huffs and protestations. With not the finest scratch visible, I thanked her for her time, though she left without saying another word to me.

From there I spoke separately to two labourers of the farm south of Michaelston; their answers were simple, and it was clear from their demeanours that neither wanted to talk to me. Whether they actually knew anything of any value was hard to tell. As with the ironmonger, I asked if something was holding them back, perhaps keeping them from speaking openly to me. Did they fear something of which they would not speak? To this, neither man would answer. Neither had a graze upon them.

Then a carpenter by the name of Hennesey, who mumbled in such croaked tones I was barely able to understand him. He spoke minimally, spending slow, painful minutes ruminating on each question I asked. When I began to inspect his arms and neck, he delved into a blow by blow account of each thin scar and healed fracture that he'd received across his hands and wrists over the course of many years.

An elderly couple then, the rather muddled husband a former stationmaster. He wanted to spend more time discussing the poor state of the railway than anything to do with the murder.

And on and on it went for several hours, as each man and woman I questioned grew ever vaguer, plainly wanting nothing more than to be rid of my company. Most it seemed shared in the superstition of the *Calon Farw*, to varying extents perhaps, but fearing it enough to say as little as they could to me. As time passed on I grew unsettled, for each person's account began to blend with another's. Their answers were all so similar.

Betsan had been asking for trouble. No one in the village could have done such a thing. The girl didn't have friends to speak of. The girl was a flirt, a prostitute, in fact. There were travellers in the area – the girl met with them regularly. Nothing but the girl and her mother was out of the ordinary in the village. She was the only person that such a thing could have happened to.

These, of course, were but a small handful of the villagers and perhaps were genuine in all that they knew. But as the hour struck six and I concluded what I believed was my final questioning for the day, I feared that this may be the start of things to come, that all that had already been said would be the entirety of all that I would come to hear.

I slouched in my chair, frustrated, exhausted. My head pounded softly, and I let it slump backwards a little so that I stared up at the hall's dark ceiling. Thunder rumbled outside – I listened to the chatter of rain against a nearby window, what had been a constant during all my questions that day.

'Are you all right, In-inspector?'

I didn't move as Vaughn spoke to me.

'Yes, Constable. Just a little tired.'

He had come in from the hall's foyer and walked over towards me.

'Were you able to learn anything today, something that may help the enquiry?'

I shook my head absently and with a sigh looked upon Vaughn.

'A little, Constable. These were but the first interviews however and I am sure more will come to light in the days ahead.'

I rubbed at my face and eyes, feeling ravaged, and desiring a stiff drink. My eyes felt heavy, my arms limp. I hoped then I would be in a fitter state tomorrow and thought it best to retire for the evening.

'The people of this village, Constable,' I said drearily. 'Have they always held such superstitious views on things? You don't share their belief in this *Calon Farw*, I gather?'

Vaughn shook his head. 'No, sir. It's all ra-rather far-fetched to me, the sort of thing my father would have discouraged when I w-was a l-lad.'

I smiled a little at that. 'He seems like a sensible man, your father.'

Looking up at the dark rafters in the ceiling, I thought of the shadowy corners of Solomon's cellar and the negatives strewn across the stone floor.

'He w-was,' Vaughn murmured. 'He always used to say—'

'My negatives,' I cut in then rudely, sitting straight in the chair and looking at Vaughn. 'Did you see them? Do you have them?'

Vaughn shook his head, what small smile he had quickly fading.

'No-no, sir. I n-never took p-possession of them.'

'Well, who has them then?' I asked bluntly. 'Neither you, Mr Cummings nor the innkeeper claim to have them. Did they simply vanish into thin air?'

'Perhaps they are still in the cellar,' Vaughn replied. I stayed quiet for a moment thinking on the matter.

'Would you mind if I m-m-made my way, Inspector?' Vaughn then said rather timidly. 'I thought it best to forewarn those who will need – who will need to be questioned tomorrow. They may take it better that way than being told first thing in the morning.'

I nodded, for it was a good idea. I impressed upon him that Miller's workers would be best, especially the two who were present when the body was found. Other than them, it seemed irrelevant – most likely everyone would need to be questioned in due course.

Vaughn said he would do his best to speak to all the mill hands that evening. As he bid me goodnight and made his way out of the hall, I gathered up my notebook and thumbed through the pages I had written absently. As I pocketed it and stood to fetch my coat, Vaughn reappeared and called over to me.

'Mrs Shaw has just arrived. I spoke to her earlier and said about the enquiry. Should I tell her to come back tomorrow?'

I sighed again, but sat back down and asked Vaughn to see her in. As she came towards me, carrying a rather large beige umbrella, I signalled to Vaughn he was free to leave, which he did with a brief farewell.

Mrs Shaw sat down rather haphazardly in the seat opposite me. She let out something of a squeak as the seat slid a little from under her, and then smiled awkwardly, before removing a dark bonnet and setting it down clumsily upon the floor.

To my estimation she was in her late fifties. Red-faced, plump, with thinning hazel hair that had visible silver wisps laced through it. She seemed to take care of her appearance, for her clothes were well pressed and neat, the buttoned cloak she wore wet but devoid of even a fleck of dirt. As she removed it, placing it upon the back of her seat, I noted the fine gold brooch she had pinned to her ruffled blouse, its ivory floral centrepiece gleaming in the soft lamp light. It seemed clear to me that she had some wealth, or at least projected thus.

'I appreciate you coming, Mrs Shaw, it is of great help to this miserable affair.'

She smiled a little. 'I'm pleased I can be of any use.'

I took down some basic information: she had lived in Dinas Powys all her life and was widow to a Phillip Shaw, the village's previous Council Treasurer. She had no children nor any immediate family either here or in South Wales. I began then to ask her the very questions I had asked all those that had come before, beginning with Betsan and whether she had known her. After but a few short minutes, it became apparent that Mrs Shaw would be of very little help – she dithered on almost every other word.

'I saw her. From time to time. She... she was a pretty girl. Very fair.'

I nodded and smiled politely. 'But you say you never really spoke to her, nor heard anything of her character – rumours, small talk and the like.'

Mrs Shaw stayed silent, her brow furrowed as she seemed to agonise over the question.

'Well, um. No, not really. Should I have heard anything about her?'

I tried to maintain my now thinning smile. 'No. I'm merely asking if anyone ever said anything of her to you?'

'Oh no,' Mrs Shaw replied, 'I don't like to dabble in gossip. My husband always used to say idle chit chat would spoil our fine community.'

'I suppose that is sound advice. Your husband must have been a well-educated man.'

She burst into life then, clasping her hands together and looking up to the ceiling with a melancholic smile.

'He was, Inspector. Such a fine man. It's been three years now since he passed. Did everything he could for me; doted on me, really. The day we met I felt so blessed – I have a small photo of him here, I carry it around with me always.' She began to rifle at her collar and produced a silver chain and locket which she struggled to unclasp. I told her she need not worry.

'I'm sure he was, Mrs Shaw, but we must press on. Around the time of Betsan's murder, were you aware of anything out of the ordinary that occurred in the village? Even the slightest thing that you may have noticed?'

Like all those I had questioned that day, Mrs Shaw had seen or heard nothing suspicious. She had been present at the meeting Cummings had arranged in the town hall on Tuesday the fourteenth. There he had informed those in attendance of

Vaughn's conclusion that the murder was carried out by some unknown vagrants.

'And you believe that assertion, Mrs Shaw? That someone unknown from outside of the village could have done this?'

She nodded slowly. 'What other explanation could there be? I can't imagine someone in the village doing such a dreadful thing. And before—'

She seemed to catch herself and stopped abruptly.

'Before what?'

She hesitated for what seemed an age, her eyes moving back and forth, as though she were thinking deeply. I stared at her all the while, wondering if she were concealing something from me.

'Before, all this, no one would have thought anything bad could have happened here.'

I rubbed my jaw and paused, a little theatrically perhaps, watching as she shifted nervously in her chair. She didn't say anything more however, and I wondered what on earth she could possibly be hiding.

'If it is true that Betsan were killed by a loner, a gang for that matter, wouldn't you feel unnerved, worried, especially as you are a widow living alone?'

She bit at her lip, her eyes beginning to water at their edges. 'I *am* worried, Inspector. Frightened, in fact. Everyone here is, whether they tell you or not.'

Tears began to roll down her face and she struggled to compose herself. I admit then I felt I had wronged her as she whimpered with every short breath.

'I apologise, Mrs Shaw, that was rude of me. I know you are frightened, and I'll do all I can to put your mind at rest.'

She looked up at me and smiled, her eyes round and wet. I thought it best not to keep her much longer, and after another five minutes, thanked her for her time and assistance. As she stood, she near knocked her chair to the floor.

'I hope I was of some help. If there's anything else I can do—'

'Thank you, Mrs Shaw, but you have been more than helpful.' I pocketed my pencil and notebook, thoughts turning once more to food and rest. Mrs Shaw was speaking to me as she replaced her bonnet and buttoned her cloak. I paid her no real attention, rubbing at the back of my aching neck.

'This has all happened so suddenly, it seems; I used to think of this village as so innocent and quaint. I admit, I did often wonder if *something* could come along and excite us all, but this is not what I ever desired. To be frank, we never thought this would happen a—'

My heart stilled suddenly as my focus returned fully to Mrs Shaw.

'Say that once more. Were you about to say *again* – we never thought this would happen again?'

Her eyes shifted as she bit down on her lip. She tightened the knot of her bonnet quickly and bid me a crisp farewell. I called out to her as I stood and moved around the small desk.

'Mrs Shaw. Mrs Shaw!'

She didn't stop or turn to look at me, moving with great haste out of the hall. I heard the creak of the main door open, before a heavy thud as it was slammed shut by the elements. A draught blew in that extinguished one of the small lamps dotted on the wall.

19

The Scratching in the Ceiling –
June 22nd, 1904

I felt great trepidation as I came back to my room in the inn. The storm made the whole space dark, cast in a peculiar silvery light. I set my camera equipment upon the bed and moved hesitantly to light the lone candle upon the table. For a while I did nothing but stand in the centre of the room and look about me, though my body wanted only to sit and take rest. I blamed my hunger for my decision to leave and return downstairs to the bar, though in my heart I knew it was my fear of the place that drove me out.

Solomon was tending to a few things. The bar was empty; it seemed no one dared venture out on such a torrid night. I asked him quietly for a drink, which he provided without a word. Scotch is not my drink of choice, though it seemed I was having it again that day. It gave me nerve to apologise for the way I had treated the man that morn.

'You're unwell. No one would carry on the way you are.' He spoke sternly but poured me another drink when I had consumed the first. 'You were a madman in your room, in my cellar.'

'You saw the images I developed down there.' I knocked back my second Scotch, and felt the wretched stuff burn down my throat. Solomon laughed dryly.

'What I saw was a man, whites of his eyes burnin' like fire. Skin drenched in sweat, sitting about the floor with strange waters all around, muttering and scratching like he was possessed. I saw nothing in those pictures of yours, but you alone were enough to scare me.'

As I started to ask him to let me return to the cellar to search for my negatives, I stopped myself. Quite suddenly I felt like a fool. Embarrassed, in fact, for how I must have appeared and the damned way I had acted. I felt ashamed in many ways, for in that very moment, all ghosts and spirits and other *unworldly* things I had seen were nothing but symptoms of an illness I had let get the better of me. I realised that the remnants of said illness were now passing, as was all my lunacy. As I tapped my empty glass upon the bar, I struggled to grasp how I had ever thought such things could be real. Even that morning seemed an age past, as though I had been a totally different man. Whether I had been conscious of it or not, the symptoms of my lingering illness had lessened throughout the afternoon. As the day had worn on, I had gradually returned closer to a being of sound mind.

Solomon brought food for me. I thanked him, but he barely spoke and began closing up the inn before I had time to finish. He dimmed all but one lamp and told me he was off to bed. It wasn't long before I followed, the Scotch and my seemingly revived sanity giving me courage enough to enter my room, close the door behind me and sit upon the bed. It was unmade, though the rancid sheets piled upon the floor had been taken away. It mattered little to me, for I lay down gratefully, staring up at the ceiling and thinking of only one thing.

Had Mrs Shaw intended to tell me of other murders?

I tried to recall her words exactly.

We never thought this would happen a—

She'd caught herself at the very last moment. *Again.* Surely what she had meant to say was *again.*

I laboured over what else it could have been:

We never thought this would happen around here.

We never thought this would happen against someone in the village.

I was clutching at straws; why would she stop herself from saying such things? More and more, as the minutes then hours unfurled, I grew certain that she had meant to say *again*, in doing so telling me of other murders. If so, there was no one here I could trust, for all had surely been lying to me, conspiring in mass subterfuge for whatever unknown purpose. I wondered if it was perhaps driven by Cummings, seemingly unhappy with my being here from the very outset. I was so exhausted, my thoughts merely went around and around, going nowhere but back to Mrs Shaw's words and the feeling I had that a grave secret was being kept from me.

I tried then to sleep but to no avail. I moved over to the small writing desk, intending to make some notes in my diary, but that was no good either, for the words would not come to me and I simply began to write a sentence before scribbling it out and starting to write another. In frustration I let my pen fall to the paper and sat staring into the darkness.

Rain chattered. Winds howled.

Something scratched in the ceiling above me.

I looked upwards, my heart jolting a little, for I recalled in a flash the last such time I had heard this scratching, deep in the throes of my fever. I saw myself sat upon the floor, shrieking with torn pages of my diary all about me.

The scratching was faint, coming from right above me. I moved slowly and stepped upon the chair, raising myself so high that I had to bend my neck and shoulders to press my ear against the ceiling. Indeed, I could hear the awful vermin, though they (for I envisaged more than one) moved away quickly, scampering in the direction of my bed.

For a moment or two they seemed to fall silent and I stepped down from the chair with a sigh. I returned to my diary, stubbornly trying to write something of the day. To my great irritation the scratching returned, moving all over the ceiling in successive short bursts.

I threw my pen down, cursed aloud and went back to bed. I pressed my eyes shut and tried to close off the world entirely. I let my mind think of happier things, pictured myself as a boy in London walking through Greenwich Park with my mother, the sun beating down upon us, not a care or concern in either of our hearts and no frets or worries to dampen our smiles or curtail our joy.

The scratching only seemed to get louder, burrowing through the ceiling and into the deepest recesses of my skull. The harder I tried to ignore it, the louder it seemed to get, so that soon I grabbed at the thin pillow and wrapped it around my head in the vain hope of dulling the noise. It did nothing. The scratching seemed to stop and start, stop and start with a constant rhythm. I could only picture beady black eyes and grotesque tails, scampering and fleeting, chewing on splints of wood and for ever hunting measly things to eat. There came more and more of the creatures, running over from other corners of the loft space, meeting at a point right above my head and joining with the incessant, maddening noise, so that I started humming a tune and tried to focus on some other, kindlier sound.

At last, as it all seemed to reach a dreadful crescendo, I groaned and cursed again (vile language, I must admit), throwing myself from the bed, marching to the door and flinging it open with some force. I stepped into the darkness, before returning and fetching the small candle.

The scratching seemed to follow me as I moved towards Solomon's door; I intended on waking him. I stopped myself as I raised my hand to knock. It seemed unfair to rouse the man at such a late hour. I looked instead toward the ceiling, assuming then that there must be a hatch or other means of entry to the loft space above.

There was nothing in the short hallway. I sighed a little despondently, guessing then that any entrance to the loft would likely be in Solomon's room. I meant to return to bed, but the scratching stopped me before I could shut myself in my chamber.

In the shadows across the hallway, I eyed the door of the third room. I recalled the argument I had heard on the day of my arrival, the assumption I had made that the room must have been occupied by guests or even Solomon's family. The man had never mentioned what was in there.

I crept across the landing toward the door and pressed an ear against it. I heard nothing stir within, though the scratching above seemed to grow even louder. Tentatively I laid a hand upon the doorknob and turned it slowly. With a gentle shove the door opened, and I stepped into the room, my candle held out before me.

It was smaller than mine, completely empty and no windows were fitted in the walls. Consequently, the air felt close and stale; in the far-left corner I noticed damp coming from the ceiling. A small hatchway was fitted there, a pull string hanging limply from it.

It was plain to see that the room had been empty since before my arrival. Whatever I thought I had heard was surely a result of the illness, perhaps even the first warnings of the mania to come.

I stepped over toward the hatch and stretched my arm up to try reaching the pull string. I was some inches too short and with little dignity (for I was still in my undergarments at this point) leapt up once and then twice, upon which I took hold the string and pulled open the hatchway. A thin wooden ladder extended and clattered to the floor, near hitting me where I stood. I winced at the sound and listened for any signs of Solomon waking. All I heard was the incessant scratching.

I stepped awkwardly up the wooden rungs, being sure to hold my candle firmly. It flickered as I reached the hatchway and I felt a cool breeze against my exposed skin. I paused momentarily, thinking of the vile vermin that I would surely find. I had no real plan for dispersing them but thought to gaze upon their number first.

I gingerly immersed myself in the darkness and looked about me. The loft was just high enough to stand in, though the warped and misshapen rafters hung low in places, so that one would have to crouch to get under. The place was filthy, the rickety slats of the floor uneven, creaking at every minor movement. The smell of mildew was palpable, the howling wind and driving rain outside seeming to shake the very roof. Indeed, a tile had come loose just above the open hatchway. It exposed the dark night and allowed rain to drip and trickle, pooling just beside where I stood and no doubt causing the damp in the empty room below.

I saw no signs of rats.

I stood in one corner of the loft space, the exterior walls of the building behind and to the right of me. The candle I held provided little more than a foot of light; I fumbled my hand about on the floor, grimly feeling for any droppings. There were none and suspecting that the rats had fled at the sight of me, moved forwards in search of where they hid.

I heard no sounds of scratching.

There was nothing but paper-thick cobwebs hanging all around. These I cast my arm through, though on more than one occasion I felt the spindly legs of spiders crawl across my hand.

My bare feet trod on damp wood in places, where more of the elements had seeped in through the cracks in the roof. The space seemed vast, for the depth of darkness made it so.

I recalled the cellar beneath All Saints church. It stopped me in my tracks, for then I felt more than just fear of hidden vermin. I took a few deep breaths, convincing myself that what I had seen in that dreadful place was nothing but fantasy, invention of the fever, unreal, no matter how real it had seemed. It gave me confidence enough to continue onwards, though I moved the little candle more frantically as I swept my eyes about the loft space.

I grew more confused for nothing stirred around me.

As I came towards the farthest wall I spotted some shapes in the gloom; a few crates and small wooden boxes. These looked aged, tatty and broken. I knelt to have a look inside, though most contained nothing but rotten papers and broken glass.

I shook my head, holding my breath for a moment to listen. Not a peep, nor even a small squeak or natter. I moved a little along the wall, feeling with my hands for any breaks in the masonry where the horde of scurrying vermin could have escaped. Nothing – not even the smallest crack through which a field mouse could squeeze.

My heart began to race a little faster. If not rats, what had caused the dreadful scratching? It was surely no creation of the fever, for that was passing, its effects all but gone. The noise had seemed so real, being so loud just moments before. Yet so had the argument in the empty room when I first heard it, and the dreadful natter of the claws that had burrowed into the flesh below my left shoulder blade.

I looked about me in the dark and the silence for a spectre hiding, a dreadful figure with hollowed eyes waiting to strike.

The candle tremored in my hand. The loft space groaned and creaked from the wind outside.

Nothing came. All was still.

I wanted to believe my tiredness was getting the better of me, though my heart still fluttered, and my mind could not fathom what had brought me up here. I decided to return downstairs; all perhaps would make sense in the morning. I moved back towards the open hatchway, swinging my candle slowly as I did, taking a few short steps to inspect one final corner of the attic. Something caught my eye, barely visible from where I stood.

Here, the roof sloped down considerably, so that as I moved towards the corner I had to drop down onto my haunches and then crawl a short distance on my hands and knees. A dusky sheet had been placed loosely across a few misshapen items. Melted wax had pooled in two places on the floorboards.

With my free hand I pulled the sheet away. I couldn't quite understand what I found at first.

What took my attention were two wooden soldiers at the top of several crates, stacked irregularly. One red, one blue, their paint chipped all over. Below these were more items clearly belonging to children. Two pairs of finely made boys' trousers, a brown cap and two small shirts, 'dressed' as it were, on two very large, empty glass bottles. Between the bottles were two pairs of shoes, arranged neatly in a single line. These were surrounded by five half-used candles, and before these two small wooden plaques. There were names inscribed onto them – Evan and Peter.

'What in God's name—' was all I could whisper. I moved my light about, finding a few other trinkets and items stacked in this 'shrine' (for no other word described it better). Someone had taken great care in arranging it.

So focused was I on all this, I paid no credence to anything else.

Something was watching me, but its creeping steps across the floorboards went unnoticed. It moved so slowly, ducking below the rafters and edging around the loft space so that soon it stood at my very back. It drifted silently through heavy cobwebs, its hands reaching out to me as it drew ever closer.

'What is all this?' I murmured, taking the two soldiers in hand and shifting backwards to stand.

In the corner of my eye I noticed warm light shining upwards from the open hatchway at the far end of the loft. I scanned the room in that direction but saw no one. Only when I heard the last few footfalls approaching me from behind did I turn in quite the panic, spinning and extinguishing the little candle as I did.

In the darkness I tried not to scream. A match was struck close to my face.

'Inspector,' Solomon muttered, ducking under the low roof. 'What are you doing up here?'

20

One Man's Grief – June 22nd, 1904

We sat in the bar once more, though Solomon had only lit a few candles, spaced out across some of the tables. The two wooden soldiers sat between us. Solomon was sipping on what I thought was brandy, a few fat tears rolling from his sad eyes. He looked quite pitiful, his large body hunched forwards, meaty hands clasping the small glass, what little hair he had sticking unkempt in all directions.

He had near run from the loft upon finding me and seeing what I had found. I'd scrambled after him, thinking in an instant that he wished to flee me. But I'd found him at the bottom of the narrow ladder, his head lolled against it. He had been sobbing quietly and didn't meet my gaze as I looked down upon him from above.

'My children,' was all he'd whimpered repeatedly, though in that moment I didn't fully understand. I'd returned to the shrine and gathered a few of the items, before easing myself down from the loft and coaxing Solomon to the bar downstairs.

He was regaining some of his composure, his breathing becoming steadier. I tapped my finger lightly against the table, thinking where best to begin.

'These were your children's?' I asked. He nodded slowly. 'They have, um … passed, I presume?' I felt quite a stab of guilt as he slowly nodded once more. 'May I ask how?'

He fell silent again for quite some time, taking one or two small sips of his drink before wiping his eyes with the back of his hand.

'Wife died in childbirth. She was a good woman, would have been a good mother. The boys were all I had.' He emptied the remainder of his glass and hit it down hard on the table. 'We found 'em in the woods. Some bastard had done away with 'em – cut their—' He ran a finger along his throat before cradling his head. 'I didn't want to look upon this anymore – their toys, their clothes. But I couldn't be rid of it. For so long I had left their room as it was, but in time I couldn't bear to look at it all without them there.'

I sat in complete shock. Words wouldn't come to me.

More murders in the village! It was beyond all belief. Even with what Mrs Shaw had said (or not said, more to the point), I don't think I truly believed it possible. How could it be? Why would it be kept such a secret?

'Why on earth would you not tell me of this, man?' I asked dumbfounded.

'I wanted to,' he replied, his voice breaking, his words choked with sorrow. 'So many times, I wanted to. But Mr Cummings – some of the others – they begged me not to. They were afraid you may awaken *it*, that evil spirit they think is out there! I just want to forget – some days I wish I were never born.' He began sobbing loudly once more.

As thoughts dashed through my mind I moved quite mechanically, heading back to my room to fetch my notepad. When I returned, I barely paused before rattling off questions in as calm a manner as I could maintain.

'This is hard, Solomon, but you need to tell me everything – when did this happen?'

He rubbed at his eyes. 'Five years ago this summer. Beginning of this month. I moved their things I wished to keep in the loft about three years ago. I go up there each year on the day it, the day it—' He stopped, his lips trembling.

I jotted this down frantically. 'Their names, Evan and Peter?'

He nodded. 'Evan was the wife's father so one of 'em had to have it. Hated it myself.'

'How old were they?' He replied that they had been five. 'Why were they out by the woods – had you lost them, were you with them?'

He shook his head and hit his hand down on the table thrice as he spoke. 'They were just *playing*. They had no school and were just off playing, what children should do, what they should have done...'

He stood and began to pace, raving, moving his heavy frame around quickly. I wished only to calm him down.

'What happened when they were found – do you recall who found them?'

'No. The Constable came to tell me.'

'And do you recall the time of day?'

He said nothing to that. 'They put 'em in the hall, laid out on the floor. Brown sacks on 'em. Just lying there.'

'Did Vaughn carry out an enquiry? Were there any suspects?'

'There was nothing. No one knew anything – I don't think anyone here could have done it. Why would they?'

He looked at me with desperate eyes, slumping back into his chair and drinking a full glass of brandy with shaking hands. 'When word of Betsan's death came it brought all the horror back to me. You can't know, you just can't know.'

He continued to drink, even after his tears had passed and

his hands had ceased to shake. I thought best to wait for him to speak. The clock on the wall told me it was nearly two in the morning.

'The Constable did what he could. I know he did, Inspector.'

'Call me Thomas,' I said then, trying to ease him more.

'It was my fault. I didn't think of what sick bastard could be hiding out there. Watching 'em.' He took another swig. 'When the Constable told me he had no suspects, that it was no one of the village, that no one 'ere was so full of evil to kill two little children, I believed him. I couldn't imagine any here, who I lived with, who I trusted, being so cruel.'

'Where were they found?'

He didn't answer me. 'I wanted so bad to find the man. I tell you now, Insp— *Thomas*, that I would have wrung his neck and tor' it clean away.'

'I need to know where the children were found, though, Solomon. It's relevant to all this.'

He nodded absently. 'Beyond the Cwm Sior, near up by Michaelston. They were left in a ditch; whoever done it hadn't even bothered to cover 'em up much.' His words were beginning to slur. 'I remember now, some farmer found 'em. That's what Vaughn said, at least.'

I felt uneasy in that moment but knew I had to ask the question.

'I'm sorry, Solomon, but I need to know. Where were you the night of Betsan's murder. Can you tell me?'

He nodded. 'You don't need to be sorry. I'm not sure you'll find the scum who did what they did to her, but I know you'll do your best to look. I was here, in the inn.' He pointed around the room, slumping a little on the table. 'The lads from the mill, the farm, place was full up till nine. They all went around then, wasn't a rowdy night. I was in bed not long after, had a few barrels coming next morning, though there was so much commotion that day it didn't really happen.'

'To clarify, you were nowhere near the woodlands all day? You were here and went to bed around nine.'

He shrugged. 'I had a few things to do in the village. But no, not the woods or the mill. I got no reason to go down there. I stay in the village and sometimes go to the city, but not much lately. I was here, asleep through the night. Ask those who live around, they would've seen the place locked up if they'd looked.'

I nodded intending to ask if Solomon could specify the men in the bar, their state of drunkenness as well. He spoke before I could.

'Nobody wanted to send their children away but they all did. Too afraid. Thought their little 'uns would be next.'

I stopped writing mid-sentence. 'What?'

He looked up at me wide-eyed, though his eyes were now glossed over.

'You didn't know?' I asked again what he meant. 'You haven't noticed? There's no children in the village. Not one. Everyone sent 'em off, as far from this place as they could get 'em. Off with family, one or two off with other families. Anything really – that's how scared everyone was.'

I thought about the time since my arrival, realising that Solomon was right. I hadn't seen a single child – not on the common, or on the Twyn. I'd never heard the school bell, nor seen a schoolmaster, nor a mother scold her son or straighten her daughter's dress. None of the villagers I had questioned had said anything of having children; I had seen no one of Betsan's age or younger. I had made no sight of children at play or caught the sound of innocent laughter. So obvious now, yet seemingly so easily missed.

'I can't believe this,' I muttered to myself more than to Solomon.

'Why on earth would Vaughn, would Cummings keep this from me? Why the village – you are the only person to tell me.'

Solomon was now clearly drunk. He shrugged and hit the bottle clumsily, spilling the last dregs of brandy across the table.

'You'd have to ask Mr Cummings – he made it plain in our town meeting that we should try not to speak with you. Some will tell you they didn't want you prying into their business – there's a few round here like that. Most I reckon are just afraid, afraid of that demon, that Calon—' He waved his hand absently, smiling drunkenly. 'All the fears, all the rumours about that bloody thing started when my boys were killed. I had near the whole village knocking down the door of the inn, either trying to offer sympathies or bless my spirit.'

His face fell, his eyes darkened. He slouched forwards onto his elbows and looked towards the door in panic.

'It'll all happen again. The well-wishers with their dumb stares, the preaching fools with their grave tidings. Some thought it was down to me you know, that my boys died to right some wrong I had committed.'

He reached for my arm then with sudden speed.

'Please don't tell 'em it was me that spoke to you. They'll blame me for anything else that happens here – they'll stop coming in here, I'll lose the place!'

He was getting quite hysterical and I hushed him gently, assuring him that I would be discreet in the matter.

'Last thing I need,' he muttered manically. 'Last thing in the world is for all this village to blame me for a demon killing people in the night.'

'There is no demon,' I said with quiet words of rage, 'or beast hiding in the woods, killing children and young women. This village has a killer, one who struck five years ago and has only now regained their thirst for blood.'

*

I helped Solomon to his room at around quarter to three. I was tired but still in shock, enraged by all I had learnt. It was all I could do not to fetch my coat and confront Cummings at his estate. I brooded instead, having a drink alone in the bar. It did nothing to calm me.

I shan't express in full the fury I felt, for words alone would do it no justice. Never in the years of my work had an omission of such gravity, a secret so widely kept, been unveiled to me. Graver and graver ideas swirled in my mind, fuelled by my exhaustion and anger. I was soon ready to drag Cummings and Vaughn to the middle of the common and give both a thorough thrashing. They, in my mind, were the perpetrators of this insanity, the mass of untruths and lies I had been fed since my arrival.

I poured myself another drink, moved then to do something of use, if only to distract myself for a short while. It occurred to me that my time would be better spent doing some productive work. Despite my reservations the previous morning, I decided to develop the dry plates I had exposed at the mill.

I opened the hatch behind the bar and stepped down into Solomon's cellar. It occurred to me that I should first search for my missing negatives, though after a short look with a single candle in hand, I decided they were not there. In spite of my revived state I had no great desire to remain in that cold, gloomy place, and returned up the small rung of steps. With only myself in the bar I could dim what little light there was to carry out my development. This I did slowly and pragmatically, boiling water in Solomon's tiny scullery, inviting myself to use what tins and ladles I found useful. I combined my chemicals slowly and took adequate time to wash the dry plates one by one.

I cannot pretend as I stared down at the first plate, the dark light of the mill emerging before any finer details, that I felt no trepidation or nervousness. I had near vanquished the remnants of my fever and all but a few lingering thoughts and fears of the paranormal with it. Yet fear is the very thing I felt as the full image became plain to me.

Would the girl's spectre look back at me, hiding behind the grindstone or crouching below the workbench? Would she be her kinder self, or the monster in flames? Would the sight of her push me back down a pit of corruption, where all my world was thrown into peril, smashed to pieces and reshaped as something far uglier and more bizarre?

The fear was fleeting. I saw nothing but the inside of the mill in my first plate, and nothing more remarkable than that in the second and third. I spent perhaps forty-five minutes examining the images, though nothing obvious leapt out at me. All was quite mundane, though my development was excellent. I saw in great detail even the clutter of the tools and other items strewn across the workbench: hammers, saws, spanners and bolts, paint tins stacked, and dirtied brushes stood upright in a glass jar. A few chewed pieces of wood, off-cuttings from longer lengths of timber, no doubt. Nothing out of the ordinary; nothing that would aid my enquiry.

At least that's what I thought. I have only bothered to mention in brief the development of these few plates for the simple fact that they played a much larger role in this whole affair than I could have known then. As I have already said, I am grateful for my diligence. It's what leads me to killers.

21

An Unknown Engagement –
June 23rd, 1904

Vaughn cowered from me as my voice reached fever pitch.

'Are you mad? When exactly did you lose all sense?' I was so enraged then I could have swung for him. 'To have the innkeeper tell me of other murders and not the Constable? Does that seem reasonable to you?'

Vaughn edged away from me a little.

'W-we... We-we... We thought the murders were unconnected—'

I knocked over a chair beside him that crashed against the floor of the town hall.

'Madness! Utter madness! *We* is you and Cummings, I assume? What reason did you have to conceal this from me?' I thrust a hand in the rough direction of the inn. 'Solomon was torn up last night as he told me. Can you imagine how hard he's found all this?'

Vaughn's brow furrowed. 'It a-affected us all badly,' he muttered sheepishly.

'Like hell it did! You're aware you've broken the law, yes – withholding evidence relevant to an enquiry?'

The Constable seemed to grow smaller then, stammering uncontrollably whilst shaking his head.

'I-I-I d-did an enqu-quiry. I looked f-for motive, for alibis.'

'And let me guess,' I scorned, any sympathies I had for the young man gone completely, 'you concluded someone outside the village committed the crime. Vagrants? Gypsies? Jack the Ripper retired to the damned Welsh coast!'

I fell silent then and walked across the hall. Vaughn was muttering, explaining what he had done at the time, the work he had carried out. I rubbed at my eyes, still tired, for I had not slept even after developing the photographs from the mill. In spite of this, I was more like the man I had been on my arrival, now growing ever more rejuvenated from the passing of the fever.

'The woodlands, there are – are so many w-ways to reach them. It made sense, such sense that it was someone passing through, an outsider.'

Vaughn was now bumbling, and I was doing all I could to calm myself. We stood in silence for quite some time before I collected the chair from the floor.

'Did it occur to you,' I sighed, 'that these crimes were connected? That the killer could be the same man?' Vaughn said nothing. 'Did you seek assistance at the time, the Constabulary in Glamorgan, or Cardiff for that matter?'

Vaughn only shook his head. 'It didn't seem necessary. W-we – Mr Cummings and I – were ad-adamant the murders of the twins were committed by a loner, someone passing through. We-we're remote out here, I-Inspector – terrible things like this d-do happen in remote places. Wh-what good could come from bringing in m-more police?'

I nodded, exasperated. 'Back then maybe nothing, but when Betsan's body was discovered you surely must have thought otherwise. It should have seemed common sense to tell *me*. Did Cummings want you to keep this quiet? The whole village, I presume.'

'P-people were scared when the t-twins were found. After

th-the rest of the children were s-s-sent away, we barely had any contact with th-th-the outside world for months! It n-near destroyed us – the sus-suspicions, the doubts. The f-f-fear – talk of the Ca-Calon, Calon.' He stopped to compose himself, his hand (tremoring ever so slightly) rubbing nervously at the corner of his eye. 'So many people believe in that *damned* thing. They tr-truly think it will come for them if they s-speak ill of it. In all the commotion after Betsan's body was found, Mr Cummings and some others on the council decided it best we-we hold back on telling you of the previous murders—'

'Utter madness,' I muttered sharply.

'Mr Cummings assured us all that Betsan's killer would not be a local man. I-I believe that to be true as well. He said t-telling you of the previous murders would o-only serve to dig up the past – you would pry into everyone's lives, bring more police here, upheave the whole village.' He rubbed at his brow, his skin now so drained of colour it seemed to blend with the stormy skies shining through the window behind him. 'I-I had no intention of misleading you, Inspector. I assure you.'

I looked squarely at him, until he turned his gaze from mine. I managed to quell my anger momentarily to speak slowly.

'Regardless of your intentions, Constable, you *have* misled me. And this enquiry. You've failed at your duty to these people, to the title you wear.' I could not contain myself, for my frustration and scorn took hold of me once more. 'Have no doubts that when all of this is done, I will work tirelessly to ensure you are dismissed as a Constable. I may act to bring charges against you and I do not say that lightly. Your actions from now will determine my own in due course.'

The young man was crestfallen. He nodded just a little, looking down at his uniform. I moved to step away from him but turned back, thrusting a finger at his chest.

'I still need help. A killer is out there. Your redemption may lie in his capture. If there are any secrets you still keep, tell me now.'

He looked up at me, rubbing at his eyes before near whispering that there was nothing else to tell. At this I nodded.

'Find Mr Cummings, tell him that I would speak with him presently. I will question those you have already beckoned here. You informed members of the village last night, yes? Miller's men as well?'

He replied that he had only tracked down a few.

'Fine. Then find the rest. They shan't be working with this storm still raging on so have no excuse not to answer me. Get Edward and Will; they were present when Miller found the body.'

Vaughn said nothing but began to leave the hall.

'And the tall brother,' I called after him. 'Geraint Davey. Make sure he comes as well.'

Within an hour of Vaughn leaving, I had interviewed three further members of the village. They maintained the same degree of reservation as most others I had already spoken to, providing as little information as possible to each question I posed them. I was far more probing, and had even begun asking about the previous murders. This took the interviewees by surprise, for they looked at me quizzically, each sharing the same expression, as though dumbfounded by my strange query. In reality it was plain to see the cogs move behind their eyes, as they hurriedly tried to consider how much I possibly knew.

It was the Postmaster, Jacob Clyde, with whom I lost my patience.

'Murders? In the village?'

'Look,' I barked, silencing the quiet whispers of those who had been gathered and were now waiting in the hall. 'I know it all. I know of the murdered twins, how they were butchered in the woodlands five years previous.' I looked then past the Postmaster's shoulder at all those who looked back at me. 'Let us not pretend anymore for it is both a waste of time and contemptible. Irrespective of what you may fear or what Mr Cummings or whomever else told you.' I turned my focus back to Clyde, though spoke loud enough for all to hear. 'Do you want to enlighten me as to what you know, or shall I consider your silence suspicious?'

His eyes widened and his whole face began to twitch. He tried to smile but was only capable of forcing a ghastly, dread-filled grimace.

'Yes, I recall those murders now.'

Clyde knew nothing of any real worth. Some of those that followed spoke briefly of Vaughn's previous enquiry, but most were too terrified to answer any of my questions at great length. One man had the audacity to ask if Mr Cummings would be happy discussing the matter. All of these were unworthy suspects, for none had any apparent motive, or marks or abrasions that resembled anything like defence wounds. All had reasonable alibis, which was of no great surprise, as most were husbands and wives, hard-working, simple, God-fearing, content with their quiet lot in life.

To those of parenting age I asked of children. It was an un-pleasant subject that struck nerves, for all had sent their sons and daughters away, some as young as three years of age. Most had gone to relatives, far flung across the country. In two instances, children had been sent into the care of guardians, so desperate were their parents to ensure their safekeeping. It was these people's indignation I incurred the most; my questions rubbed salt into unhealed wounds.

Few, if any, spoke highly of Betsan when asked and I could

not fully understand why. It seemed only rumours had caused such low opinions of the young woman. Many considered her an innocent free spirit in her youth, corrupted by the lack of real parents, or any sense of morality. None spoke of Betsan's mother Catrin, refusing, as though it would soil them somehow. When, on one occasion, I asked about this, I garnered that many held the opinion that Catrin was, in some way, connected to the dreaded *Calon Farw*.

Midday rolled by, as did the thunder, for the storm had not abated. Those waiting were sodden, adding to their displeasure. The numbers dwindled in the early afternoon, before labourers from the mill began to enter in a steady fashion, clad in their shabby jackets and trousers, caps pulled low, dark, piercing eyes watching me as they waited.

When the time came, I called over to these men, who had congregated together and begun smoking and speaking amongst themselves. I asked for Edward and Will, and two of the lads, both around the age of twenty, lifted their hands casually. I spoke to each separately, taking their account of what transpired after Miller had found Betsan's body. Edward, who had run from the woodlands and raised the alarm with Vaughn, gave a frank, dare I say, thorough statement. He seemed wiser than his years, well-spoken and articulate. He explained quite plainly his fear upon seeing the body; there was no shame in that. He had run without any real thought, claiming it had been the right thing to do.

'Most here believe something dwells within the woodlands,' I asked him flatly. 'That *it* – be it spirit, demon or monster – killed the girl and left her in the state you men found her. Do you share that opinion?'

He shrugged. 'I'm not arrogant enough to claim I know every-thing of this world.'

I smiled thinly at that; a good answer if any were ever given.

'Did you speak to Betsan much or know her personally?'

'Not personally,' he remarked, rather guardedly. 'She was often at the mill, though.'

'There have been claims she may have grown *close* with some of the men.'

He seemed to take my meaning. 'I know I never did, and it's not my place to speak for others.'

'That may be,' I replied, 'but it is imperative to this enquiry that you tell me.'

He scratched his chin, before looking briefly over his shoulder at the group across the hall.

'Yes,' he said as he turned back to me. 'I know some became *close* with her, as you put it.'

This was something of a breakthrough, for there was finally some weight to the rumours of Betsan's dalliances.

'Who?' was all I asked.

'It's not my place.'

'Who?' I pressed him.

With a sigh and another brief glance behind him, Edward rubbed his forehead, leaning into me a little.

'Speak to Geraint, I'm not sure there was anyone else,' he whispered.

I nodded. As I glanced over Edward's shoulder, I could see Geraint Davey wasn't in attendance; he would have stood head and shoulders above those in the hall. Vaughn must still have been looking for him.

I questioned Edward for another ten minutes, before checking his arms. He had a long, slender abrasion running from the base of his neck, and revealed more of it across his right shoulder.

'Bloody barbed wire farmers are sticking up. Tried climbing through a gap and got caught.'

It seemed a reasonable explanation, though I dared not take

any chances. With all the secrets and lies of the village, I was accepting no one at face value.

'I'll need to photograph it for the enquiry. Stand here, please.'

Edward grumbled as I made him stand sideways on before the camera, though acquiesced as I told him to reveal the abrasion in full. I only took one picture, though it would be more than enough. When I was satisfied I told him he was free to leave before thanking him for his time. He looked at me a little aggrieved and took a step away, before coming back and leaning in close.

'You shan't tell Geraint what I told you?'

I merely shook my head, though a look of disappointment remained on his face. He walked over to the group of men, spoke to them a little, before leaving the hall.

I mused on the day of my arrival, recalling Geraint and his brother passing by as I had made my examination of the scene.

Great shame about the young woman, Inspector.

It was apparent then that he had meant what he said, for his tone was disheartened, his expression one of melancholy. It was a priority that I spoke with him, and as I continued questioning the mill hands one by one, I regularly looked over towards the door of the hall, waiting for any sign of Geraint's arrival.

The hours passed. Some of the men spoke poorly of Betsan, though with the knowledge I now had, I wondered if their words were driven by some spite and envy; I asked each one if they had made advances on the girl. To this I received bitter laughs, sarcastic remarks and words of disdain. Each man was clearly bluffing, for it was obvious that Betsan had rejected them in some fashion. I took another two pictures of potential defence wounds inflicted by Betsan at the time of her attack, though as with Edward, both men provided very reasonable explanations.

Soon I began to worry that Geraint would not show, envisaging then that upon speaking to Constable Vaughn, he had tried to flee the village. More and more I wondered if he was the guilty man, and as I noted the time at four o'clock, I was almost certain of it. With only a handful of the mill workers left, I debated abandoning my questions to go in search of him. As I became set on this notion, concluding a round of questions and rising from my chair to speak to those left waiting, I heard the door of the hall open. In stepped a drenched Constable Vaughn, followed by a downtrodden Geraint Davey.

I returned to my seat, gesturing subtly to Vaughn. He stood close to the door, watching those who remained. They were quiet now, a small pile of cigarette ends stubbed out on the floor.

I thought best to leave Geraint last, and whilst I shouldn't like to admit that I rushed my questioning of the other men, I certainly did. I caught his eye on more than one occasion. He was clearly nervous.

The hall was empty, with the exception of Geraint, Vaughn and myself. Vaughn had pulled up a seat and sat close by, leaning against the wall with his arms folded. Geraint sat opposite me, his tanned forearms resting on the desk, his hands clasped.

'What's all this about?' He had dried off somewhat in the time since he had arrived, though as he spoke, a single fat drop of rainwater fell from his hair onto the table.

I thought how best to start, whether delicately or otherwise. I chose the latter. 'Betsan, of course. Her murder. You were intimate with her.'

He looked at me, shocked. 'You couldn't know that.'

I concurred. 'I couldn't know that for certain, but the way you spoke to me briefly down in the woodland suggested it. Some today have hinted at it.'

He remained silent but began cracking his knuckles.

'Intimacy is a broad term,' I continued, 'meaning all sorts of things. Either you were together, courting as it were.' He scoffed a little at that. 'Or it was something more salacious. Most in the town agree that Betsan was promiscuous.'

'They're bloody liars,' he snapped back at me.

'Then tell me the truth, now is your chance.'

He shook his head a little, looking down at his hands. There was an awkward smile, a brief stifling, before he broke down entirely and burst into tears. It took me quite by surprise, and I glanced over at Vaughn, who had sat up fully in his chair. He too seemed quite taken aback.

'She meant the world to me,' Geraint wept, running his hands through his damp hair. 'She didn't deserve any of it, what was done to her.'

His tears began to flow more heavily, his soft whimpers echoing around the hall. I tried to maintain my cold demeanour, though this reaction was far removed from what I had expected.

'You need to tell me everything,' I finally said, tapping my hand lightly on the table.

It took him quite some time to bring himself under control, though even then he seemed fragile, ready to break down again at any moment.

'What do you want to know?' he snivelled after a few minutes.

'You and Betsan, when did it start?'

He shrugged. 'About six months ago. We'd spoken before then, only a little. I started talking to her one day up on the common. It all began from there.'

'You were courting then, a fair description?'

He nodded. 'She'd come down and see me when she could. She used to hang around a lot, would talk to the boys so it didn't seem like she was just there for me. Some of them had eyes on her, got salty when she turned them down.'

'So you hadn't told anyone then?'

'No. She was scared of her mother, thought it would get back to her. I didn't care what anyone thought; it didn't matter to me.'

'Why was she so fearful of her mother?'

Geraint laughed dryly. 'Have you met her?'

I nodded, recalling some of my addled conversation with Catrin. 'I have.'

'Then you know how mad she is – she raised her own daughter in the middle of a marsh, for Christ's sake.' He pulled out a packet of cigarettes from his pocket, fumbling to take hold of one. 'She never wanted Betsan with a man, never! Used to beat her when she was a child, told her she had to be her own woman when she grew up.' After a moment he tossed the pack onto the table. 'Betsan was worried she may kick her out of the house, or worse.'

'Worse?' I asked slowly. 'Was Betsan in fear of her life with Catrin?'

Geraint shook his head and waved a hand away. 'I don't know – some days I think Betsan would get upset, is all. Perhaps she made things with Catrin seem worse than they really were. She always asked if she could come live with me but that's not possible with my brother...'

He trailed off then, snatching a cigarette quickly. I shared a brief glance with Vaughn as Geraint struck a match upon the table.

Could Catrin have played a part in the murder? Could she have found out about Geraint and seen to her own daughter's death?

I paused for just a moment. 'So, what was your intention? Had you talked of any plans with her?'

'We wanted to leave. Head to Cardiff, maybe London.'

'What stopped you?'

'Money, of course, I'm not a rich man. I couldn't just take her away. Then there's Lewis, he needs help. I couldn't leave without him.'

I nodded, watching Geraint as he took a heavy drag on his cigarette.

'So Betsan was afraid of her mother, wanted to get away from her – this village, really – but couldn't. How did that make her feel? So far, I've gathered that Betsan had very few friends, if any. You were probably the only person here she really confided in.'

'She didn't have friends,' Geraint replied simply. 'I think everyone her age got sent away when those two young 'uns were killed five years ago.'

I was taken aback. 'You're willing to talk about those murders?'

'I wasn't going to talk about *any* murders. Had a feeling you might try and blame me for Betsan's death once you found out we were close.'

I said nothing of the last remark. 'Do you want to tell me anything about the murders of the twins?'

Geraint shrugged. 'Changed this place. It's never been as kind as it once was. Now with Betsan…' His hand shook as he took another drag.

'The Constable believes the murders of the children were committed by a vagrant, an individual who happened upon them in the woodlands. Their father thinks the same.'

'You've spoken to the twins' father?' Geraint was obscured for an instant by a thick cloud of blue-grey smoke. I nodded; he stared into space for a moment or two. 'I would have believed that story before. Now with Betsan.'

His cigarette had burnt down to a slender nub, though his fingers held firm to it as the glowing ends of charred ash burnt against his skin. I thought how to go on.

'Catrin told me Betsan was bringing money home with her

recently.' I could barely remember the conversation but knew what I said to be true. 'Were you giving it to her?'

'I gave her a little,' Geraint said vacantly. 'Odd bob here and there.'

'The mother implied Betsan was bringing home quite a bit more than that, with some regularity in recent weeks.' I coughed, knowing there was no easy way to say what needed to be said. 'There are rumours of possible prostitution—'

It was all I was able to say. Geraint stood suddenly and kicked his chair before moving over to the wall opposite Vaughn. He leant his head against it. Vaughn and I shared wary glances, before turning back to Geraint, who sunk to the floor. He was nothing of the man I had watched brawling outside the inn. No more a towering thug, now a heartbroken wreck, tears flooding from his eyes once more.

'I need to know, Geraint,' I called over to him. 'If travellers were camped just outside the village, I have to be sure that Betsan wasn't visiting them to sell herself.'

His head had been in his arms but now he raised it, looking straight at me, as though my words, my very insinuation, had physically hurt him. He sniffed loudly.

'She loved me, Inspector. And I loved her. She wasn't visiting any *travellers* – I never saw no sight of them anywhere near the mill and I know that's not what she was doing.'

He wailed more than spoke, but I needed to get to the bottom of the matter.

'If you were not giving her money – and if a group of travellers weren't – where would such money be coming from?'

I feared I had pushed the man too far for he wouldn't answer, nor did he speak for another five minutes or so, his sobs bellowing by comparison to the storm's meagre thunder. Vaughn left his seat and stepped over towards me, though neither of us conferred or uttered a word.

Finally, Geraint looked over towards the pair of us. 'She started talking about the General,' was all he could whimper.

'The General?' I asked with some confusion. 'General James, on the mount?'

Geraint nodded. 'She'd been speaking with him. I don't know when it started. She told me he wanted to see her.'

At this I rose from my chair. 'What were they speaking of?'

Geraint rubbed his eyes and muttered something under his breath. I told him to speak and he did so quietly.

'About three weeks ago she got excited. Talked about something wonderful, something for the both of us. She wouldn't say what, kept telling me it was a surprise.'

I noted this down, as Vaughn began talking, asking Geraint why he had not spoken of this before. I interrupted him as he quickly became more animated with Geraint. He was over-zealous, perhaps trying to right his wrongs, those he had admitted to me that morning.

I stood in silence for a moment, thinking. What on earth could Betsan have had to do with the General? Whatever his sudden interest with her, I was certain it was linked to the murder.

'Where were you on the day prior to the murder and during the night it took place, Geraint? Did you see Betsan at all?'

He was looking at Vaughn angrily, turning to me slowly before he spoke.

'Yes, I saw her.'

'When?'

'In the evening, after I'd been working. I met her down past the mill, at the old fort around the Cwm Sior.'

'What time?' I was stern with him then.

'Seven, maybe a bit later. She was all excited again, talking 'bout the General. I kept asking what her secret was, and when she wouldn't tell me, I got angry.' He pointed a finger at me. 'Before you get any ideas, I wouldn't tell you this if I thought you might pin it all on me.'

I began putting on my coat. 'So keep talking and make sure it is the truth.'

'We rowed. I told her I didn't trust the General, that he just wanted something from her, that he was a blithering fool. She got upset. Ran away from me before I could stop her.'

I stepped over to him at quite a stride, pocketing my notebook as I went.

'You realise that so far you are the last man to see her alive? You've told us you argued with her.'

As I came close to him he looked up at me furiously.

'Why would I tell you then? What good would it do me?'

'It's a ruse, to rule yourself out. You tell me part of the truth to conceal the entirety of it. It's why you didn't tell me this sooner and why you never reached out to the Glamorgan Constabulary when Betsan was killed. Show me your arms.'

He looked from me to Vaughn in total amazement. 'You can't be serious?'

'Why didn't you come to me sooner then?'

'For this reason,' he cried. 'You'll blame her death on me.'

'Your sleeves, roll them up.'

He began to stand and I held him down by the shoulder, calling over to Vaughn, who whisked across the room to my side.

'You're a prime suspect, don't make this more difficult than it needs to be.'

After a little more jostling, he yielded, shaking his head with incredulity, before shrugging off his coat and going so far as to unbutton and remove his shirt.

There was a thin gash across his upper arm, healing over but still visible. Upon closer inspection I saw an even thinner mark just below.

'How did you get those?'

'For God's sake, I can't know how I get every mark and scratch as I work.' He leant his head back against the wall as his eyes began to well up once more. 'This is insanity. I didn't do it! I didn't tell anyone 'cause you'd pin it all on me!'

'We'll need to document those. I'll see to it later.' I turned to Vaughn. 'Make sure he doesn't leave; use what means you see fit.'

Vaughn hesitated. 'Um. I don't ... Um—'

'You have shackles, yes?' Vaughn nodded. 'If you need to, use them.'

'Where are you going?'

'To speak to the General. To get to the bottom of this.'

I began to leave the hall, walking brazenly. Neither man said anything to me, and as I came into the small foyer, I pulled up the collar of my coat, preparing for the dreadful weather outside.

I felt a stab of pain in my left temple. An image came with it, the image from one of my negatives. I saw Betsan's body at rest in the cellar of All Saints church. The cracks of burnt flesh glowing like cinders. Flowing hair like lightning streaks. The dreadful spectre lurking in the background – though this is not what I focused on.

I saw the ring upon Betsan's left hand, the fourth finger, glowing brighter than all else in the image. A ring that hadn't been on the body, that hadn't been found at the scene. A ring that up to this point I had no thought or recollection of, for down in the cellar of the inn and in the darkness of my chamber the fever had gripped me so terribly.

I tried to dismiss the thought as I recoiled from the pain in my head. The image remained though. I didn't want to think of it, or even acknowledge it. To do so would mean acknowledging all else in those negatives, that which I now considered sheer madness, for I would find myself returning to a realm of ghosts and hauntings.

I moved in a haze as I carried on leaving, going so far as to open the main door of the hall to the world outside. A cool breeze struck me as thick sheets of rain distorted all sight of the village.

Still the thought lingered. I could not escape the image.

I found myself returning into the hall with a perplexed Geraint and Vaughn looking at me.

'You asked her to wed you, didn't you?'

Geraint remained frozen where he was.

'Yes, though we used to laugh and say we were already married. I never told you that.'

'And a ring, you gave her a ring, a thin one. She wore it as a sign of your engagement.'

He nodded slowly. 'Just a piece of tin really. It was all I could afford to give her. She could only wear it when we were together though. How could you—'

'Do you have it?'

'No, I don't know what became of it.'

I felt my stomach lurch; the heat of panic and fear washed over me like needles pushed into my skin. It was real – the ring from the negative was real. And perhaps, so too, was everything else.

22

The Truth from General James – June 23rd, 1904

I stood outside the hall, deciding which way was best to head to the General's estate on the mount. I elected to walk across the Twyn, though with one final glance up Britway Road, I caught sight of a garish blue coat moving towards me through the rain. The figure in question walked with a dark umbrella; it didn't take me long to recognise the man as Cummings. I didn't wait for him, instead moving up the slope of the road, meeting him some thirty yards away from the town hall.

My anger got the better of me. This was in part due to Vaughn, and what he had told me of the previous murders. More so it was caused by the shimmering ring in the picture, that which I now knew was real. I was shaken badly.

I grabbed Cummings and he tumbled to the ground.

'What the hell are you doing!' He was yelling at me, and began to bat away at my arms and face.

'You kept the murders from me – Evan and Peter five years ago. You lied from the start. You're a blackguard, a villain!'

I hauled him up from the floor, though he pushed me away. He'd dropped his umbrella and swept it up quickly. Purple veins throbbed from his temples; his face darkened as he stepped back from me.

'Solomon told me everything last night. You told him – this village! – to stay silent, after all he—'

'It was not for you to know,' Cummings howled over the rain. 'I kept it from you to protect these people.'

'In what way? Tell me with all good conscience how you did this for them?'

He tried to walk past me and I grabbed at him again.

'People are frightened, they have been for years now. All this nonsense about spirits and monsters – in spite of it all we were coming to terms with the death of those children and things were returning to how they once were. We did our duty to them – then that girl winds up dead! I had to keep this village from tearing itself apart and the last thing I needed was some … some … London-born Inspector coming and accusing everyone of crimes they didn't commit. We have our ways of dealing with these things. I had no desire for your being here and—'

'Dealing with these things?' I interrupted him. 'You have dealt with nothing – a killer still roams free. What reasoning could have possessed you not to reach out all those years ago, to keep the murders of two children a secret from me?'

'My reasoning is my own. I told you, we did an investigation, we made our conclusions. What happened to those children was tragic, horrible. But it happens – and whether you agree or not, that girl was asking for trouble! Who's to say there's a great conspiracy here, a killer in hiding? You cannot entertain the possibility that both murders were unconnected and will go as far as you can, destroying everyone's lives, just to place the blame on someone's shoulders!'

A flash of lightning burst overhead. Both Cummings and I leapt in surprise. The barrage of rain beat down upon us, as a blast of thunder, like a hundred cannons firing at once, erupted, as though they were beside us. The most unnatural of storms;

we both stared pensively up at the sky. As Cummings muttered some foulness under his breath and tried to walk away, I reached out and took hold of his arm.

'You have much to answer for, Councilman, and I shan't let you out of my sight. You're coming with me.'

'I'm going nowhere with you.' He tried to pull his arm away but I gripped him tighter.

'I'm going to speak with the General, and you're coming with me. I'm not finished with you yet.'

'What do you want with the General? You spoke with him upon your arrival.'

I let go of his arm but did not answer his question.

'Lead on, Councilman. Or like the young Constable, I'll see to it that charges are brought against you when all this is through.'

He looked at me outraged, though I didn't let him speak, instead shoving him roughly down the road. We marched together through the Twyn, as another blaze of lightning illuminated the terraced houses and small shops. All were closed up, with not a sign of life or movement inside.

Cummings growled at me as we walked, though I paid no attention. By the time we had climbed the small incline and come to the black iron gates of the General's estate, he had become quite volatile. He jabbered at me, ranted as I pushed against the gold insignia at the centre of the gates and stepped along the gravel path of the General's drive. The place was entirely different from my previous visit, for the blooms of flowers were beaten and dishevelled by the ferocious storm. The three-tiered fountain was overflowing, the cherub adorning its peak seeming to sneer at us.

Stepping through the marble pillars to the front door, I took hold of the gold bell chain and pulled repeatedly. Cummings tried to yank the damn thing off me.

'You cannot simply come to the General this way!' he said as he gave up trying.

I continued to ignore him.

'Whatever you think you know is likely a falsehood. And the General – you've met him. He can say anything, he's mad, completely mad.'

Just then, a large metal bolt was shifted, and the front door opened slowly. To my surprise, a rifle barrel was thrust in my face.

'I don't know what you think you're doing but clear off! You want trouble, I'll give it.' The voice was as steady as the gun barrel, though the figure remained obscured by the front door. I took a small step backwards, my eyes fixed on the gleaming muzzle.

'This is Bexley,' I announced. 'I'm here to speak with the General.'

The gun remained where it was, though the housekeeper emerged slowly, looking from me to Cummings.

'What is this? I thought you ruffians, burglars.'

Cummings spoke up from beside me. 'Harriet, this is not my doing. The Inspector here is raving – he manhandled me here.'

The rifle was still pointed right at me. 'I'd appreciate you lowering that.'

The housekeeper, Harriet, held it steady.

'This is not the way things are done here, Inspector, *or whatever you are*. Even if the gates of Hell have ripped open on the other side of the village green, you do not rattle and smash on the door of the Lord of the Manor!'

'He is quite insane, Harriet – his fever no doubt remains—'

I shoved Cummings to one side. 'I'll speak with the General now. It is imperative to my enquiry.'

'You spoke with him previously,' the housekeeper remarked

calmly. 'And he had nothing to say to you then. He is not a well man.'

The door began to close as the rifle was lowered. I put a hand against it, at which the housekeeper exclaimed.

'He was meeting the girl,' I called through the door. 'I must know for what purpose. If not, the General shall be considered suspect and this storm will not last for ever. Would you care for the whole Constabulary beating down your door and searching every inch of this manor?'

To that the housekeeper said nothing, though I heard her sigh and groan a little. The door swung open then. She kept hold of her rifle as I and a waffling Cummings stepped inside.

'He is bullying you, Harriet. You can't let it stand.'

The housekeeper only spoke to me. 'He had no part in that girl's death you know. There is not a scrap of malice in him.'

I began walking through the greeting hall towards the flight of stairs leading to the upper landing. The housekeeper scurried after me quickly and took hold of my arm.

'Believe me – none of this was his doing.' Her eyes were pleading.

I shrugged. 'Then he can tell me that for himself.' I began skipping up the stairway, the housekeeper followed after. I called down to Cummings, still standing by the door.

'I would have you up here too.'

'I need a minute.' He closed the front door with a thud, before walking out of sight into one of the downstairs rooms. I didn't push the point and let the housekeeper, rifle still in hand, lead me along the upstairs corridor toward the door of the General's study. Rain cascaded down the two large windows that looked out onto the gardens – the horizon was consumed by deathly black clouds.

'When did the General first make contact with Betsan?' I

asked as we came to the end of the corridor. 'I assume that he sent you to invite her here.'

The housekeeper went to knock against the heavy wooden door but stopped herself, turning to me and muttering softly.

'He first asked over six months ago. The state of his mind, I thought nothing of it. But then he would come back to it – *to her* – again and again. I thought if she came here once he may forget about her in time. His memory slips so much, and he gets so confused, it can be days before he speaks of her—'

'But he always comes back to her,' I said gravely. 'When did she first come?'

'A little over three months ago. She didn't come back for some time after that first visit. Then it was once a week, twice. More frequent than that recently.'

'What did they talk about?'

The housekeeper shook her head. 'I never sat in with them, nor asked the girl what the General wanted with her. It's not my place.'

'You truly expect me to believe you know nothing of what they discussed, that you never overheard anything, or that the General never admitted something to you in his confused state?' She only nodded. 'Your duty was to tell me that that girl was coming here if nothing more.'

'My duty is to serve General James and safeguard his well-being,' she said stoically. 'That is my priority. Do not mistake me for some meddler—'

'Fine.' I was growing impatient. 'When did Betsan last come here?'

The housekeeper hesitated. 'The day before her body was found. She was excited, happy when she left.'

'Open the door,' was all I replied. The housekeeper faltered a moment, before giving a quick, sharp knock on the door. There came a dry bark in response, and I stepped inside. The General, unseen in his high-backed leather chair, grumbled quietly.

'W-what's the meaning of this? I thought I heard a commotion. What are you doing, Harriet?'

The housekeeper came into the room behind me and began to talk, though I strode to the side of the General, looking down onto his withered, cantankerous frame. His thin grey head tipped up towards me, his vacant eyes squinting. He smiled a dreadful toothless smile.

'Have we met ol' boy? Don't think we have.' He leant over his chair a little and waved a scrawny arm at the housekeeper. 'We have a guest, woman – fetch the brandy. And why are you carrying a rifle? Hunting season again?'

He began to laugh his dreadful laugh and I pulled up the leather chair opposite him. He smiled as he turned back to me, a little vacant, as though he were looking straight through me.

'General, I have to ask you about Betsan, Betsan Tilny.'

'How is she?' He beamed, before pulling a half-burnt cigar out from under his seat and patting slowly on his chest. 'Damned matches. Harriet! Harriet! I need matches.' He craned his neck and looked behind him. 'What are you standing like that for?'

I glanced over toward the housekeeper. She looked from the General to me and shook her head a little. She walked across the room to the General's writing desk, clattering the rifle onto it, before opening and searching through drawers.

'Make sure to clean that when you're done. Bloody Zulus don't sit around and wait whilst we clean our guns.' He turned back to me, rolling his eyes. 'Bloody hot out there, old chap – they're brave, fearless, those Zulus.'

'I need to talk with you, General.' I spoke a little desperately as the General leant back in his seat. 'About Betsan. You had been seeing her recently?'

'What are you talking about?'

The housekeeper stepped over and thrust a small box of matches into the General's hand. Without a word of thanks, he took them, though spilt half a dozen onto the floor as he did. He fumbled to strike one and I moved to grab a match and light it for him.

'Betsan Tilny,' I repeated slowly as I held the little flame to the tip of the General's cigar. 'You were seeing her recently.'

He stared at me, puffing on his cigar with thin wheezing breaths as wisps of smoke swirled about his face.

'Rainy season did nothing for the heat. Rain far worse than this.' His words were slurred and mumbled.

I glanced at the housekeeper standing just behind the General. She could only shrug at me. I thought with some deflation that I'd learn nothing from the old man in his present state.

He hacked and coughed, writhing a little in his chair. 'Fine girl,' he said after a moment. 'Fine girl. Pretty young thing.'

I leant forwards excitedly. 'Who, General? Who?'

He frowned at me. 'Betsan, of course. Lovely girl. If you stay long enough, you may meet her. Is she coming today, Harriet?'

The housekeeper said nothing.

'Lovely girl; very talkative,' the General chortled. 'Loves hearing my old war stories.'

I spoke quickly, afraid that the General may lapse and lose all knowledge of what we were discussing. 'Why did you invite her here, was there a reason?'

He sucked on his cigar. 'Well, I felt I owed it to her. You're a man like any other, we all do things we shouldn't, y'know. Miriam, now she took it badly, but uh, like any good wife she stuck by me.'

The General took a long drag on his cigar. I looked up at the housekeeper, shaking my head in bemusement.

'Miriam was the General's wife; died ten years ago, just before I arrived.'

The General didn't seem to notice. 'She was worried of the scandal, mind – my age and all. Would have been quite the story, really. She wanted to maintain appearances.'

I couldn't understand what he meant. 'Your age, General?'

'Well, of course,' he smiled. 'Old dog, I admit. Mind Catrin, she was old herself, forties and all.'

I started to realise what the General was saying, though it seemed completely absurd.

'General, are you ... are you saying you had an affair with Betsan's mother?'

He thumbed at his cigar, the bones of his hands clicking as he did.

'Briefly, chap, briefly. Catrin's father was a wealthy man, had bought up the land over, over ...' He waved a hand absently. 'When he died suddenly, he left her everything. She lived in a little cottage just by the railroad station. What was it, Harriet, the malt-something or other?'

'The Malthouse Cottage,' I cut in. 'It burnt down when Catrin was pregnant.'

The General nodded. 'Are we having tea at any point, Harriet, or should we go straight for brandy? Do you drink brandy, old boy?'

I ignored him. 'General, were you Betsan's father.' He was looking about the room and I feared now that I was losing him. I leant a hand over and placed it on his knee; it was like placing a hand on a clothed skeleton. 'We have to know.'

He didn't look at me, staring instead at the large painting on the wall above the mantel.

'Miriam wouldn't let me have anything to do with Catrin or the child. Tell you the truth, I always had a suspicion she caused the fire, wanted Catrin gone from here!' He shook his head, his vacant expression changing for just a moment. His eyes grew melancholic, his smile twisting to something filled with sadness, perhaps shame.

'I think that hurt Catrin badly; she loved Dinas Powys, her home. She didn't want to leave here, nor I for that matter. Something snapped inside her, corrupted her, pushed her out to that little hovel she stays in.' He looked squarely at me then and nodded as he spoke. 'I regret it all, of course; I wanted to make amends in some small way. You know how it is; when you get older you think of all the wrong you've done.'

'That's why you asked Betsan here, then? You told her everything.'

He continued to nod. 'Yes. Of course.' His eyes began to glaze over. 'Bob wasn't happy when I told him. Was more than a little annoyed.'

He'd lost me again. The housekeeper, Harriet, was rubbing her face with her hand. She looked pale, shocked.

'Who's Bob?' I asked the General.

'Have you not met him? Gosh, seems strange, he looks to puff out his chest and march about the place like *he* was the Lord,' the General quipped. 'Once it annoyed me, but now it's quite amusing. Bit of a fool, mind.'

'Cummings, you're talking about Robert Cummings?'

The General leapt a little in his chair. 'You *have* met him then.'

'This is madness,' Harriet muttered. She was not wrong in that.

'Why would Robert – Bob – be annoyed at you meeting Betsan?'

The General barked with laughter and weakly hit a hand across his leg.

'Well, the money of course! It was going to be his when I died, my not having any children supposedly. But Betsan changed all that. I wanted her to have it, my estate and everything.' He laughed and kept rambling. I leapt from my chair and began charging out of the room.

'I knew nothing of this, Inspector,' Harriet yelled after me. 'For God's sake, I knew nothing!'

I was thundering down the short corridor. When I came to the landing I yelled down for Cummings. There came no reply, and I noticed the front door was wide open. I near fell down the stairs, glanced in one or two of the rooms but made no sight of the man. He had fled the manor, disappeared into the furore of the storm.

23

A Fall from Grace – June 23rd, 1904

I ran as fast as I could across the common, now waterlogged and soft underfoot. I didn't skirt the large, muddy puddles that had formed, splashing through them with little care. As I came upon Cummings' estate, I could tell in an instant that he wasn't there. Nonetheless, I scrambled over a high wall to gain access to his rear garden and make certain. The entire house seemed dark and vacant.

I headed then to the town hall, speeding down Britway Road. A river of rainwater flowed with me, interweaving and rippling over the compacted chalk and dirt. A few lights were plain to see in some of the homes I passed, and midway down the road I skirted a slender, elderly man who I had interviewed that very morn. He goaded me with some sarcastic remark that I barely noticed.

I ran faster in sight of the hall, and when I came upon it, near smashed the doors away from their hinges. I panted and wretched, finding Vaughn and Geraint in the exact spot I had left them. Both men were smoking, though Geraint seemed as emotional as he had been when last I saw him.

Before Vaughn could speak I rushed over to him.

'Cummings. Cummings has run. He … he—' I had to catch my breath and bent over double. I managed to wheeze out my words. 'He has a motive, a grave motive. I think he saw to Betsan's death.'

I breathed in heavily, dark spots forming at the edges of my eyes. When I hauled myself upright, I looked down at Geraint, still slouched upon the floor.

'You have to stay here. You're still the last known man to see her alive.'

'He, Mr Cummings. He d-did not kill her, Inspector,' Vaughn said to me quietly.

I turned to him and placed a hand upon his shoulder.

'Whatever loyalties you have towards him do not matter now. You must help me apprehend him. Where would he go – he is not at his house.'

'I-I-I know he didn't k-kill her, Inspector.'

I shook my head at the young man, my frustration bubbling for we were wasting time.

'I lied to you this morning when I said I had no m-more secrets.' Vaughn stepped away from me a little. 'I s-swear I know not of any motive you speak, but I know he did not kill Betsan.'

I lunged at him as I regained some of my stamina. I pinned him to the wall, at which Geraint leapt up and split us both apart. As I cursed and bellowed at Vaughn, he tried to speak over me.

'I'll help you find him,' he yelled desperately, his whole body shaking. 'I know where he may have got to. When w-we find him, I'll confess all to you, as will he.'

I barged Geraint away with strength I did not know I possessed. Grabbing Vaughn again I grappled him away from the wall and shoved him towards the door.

'Where would he go? Show me!'

'H-h-he has a s-small stable further along the common road. If he's trying to run, he'll fetch his h-horse.'

I pushed Vaughn again and together we left the hall, moving as fast as we could through the wind and rain to return up the hill. My lungs screamed, my legs weak, barely able to carry me. I had to stop at one point, to which Vaughn showed real concern. I batted him away, for I wanted nothing from him then. I pushed on stubbornly, and after a few minutes I was outside Cummings' house once more.

There I could not go any further and halted in the middle of the road.

'Where … where is his stable?'

Vaughn pointed further ahead. 'About half a mile. The road goes a little f-f-further than that. It would be far too – too treacherous for him to ride that way.'

I couldn't reply, breathing too heavily. The wind seemed to suck the air from my lungs and I moved myself over to the front wall of Cummings' garden to lean against it. I stayed there for over a minute, before gingerly continuing along.

'He had a start on me,' I said hoarsely. 'He could have already fled the village, even in this frightful storm.'

Just then, as if planned, a purple streak of light cracked the sky asunder. Once, twice, then thrice; the flashes of lightning brightened the world for an instant. I spoke over the cacophony of thunder.

'We must be certain he has left the stable!' I said bitterly.

We soldiered onward, along the length of the common for another few hundred yards. Blighted by the elements, it seemed the longest few hundred yards I had ever walked.

Vaughn stopped me then, pulling me close to speak clearly in my ear. 'This is no mere storm, Inspector. D'you really th-think he's tried to flee?'

I carried on without replying. Vaughn scampered after me, though we walked no more than four or five paces. Above the wind and rain, I began to hear a faint rhythm, quickly growing louder. I withdrew my Enfield from my coat pocket, for then I knew the approaching sound was a horse charging in our direction. Sure enough, a shape began to emerge in the haze.

'You cannot mean to shoot him, Inspector?' Vaughn sounded desperate.

'If he does not halt on the road.' I moved a little to my right and pulled back the hammer of my gun.

Cummings fast approached, and I could see him now clearly, clad in riding boots and gloves, clinging to the reins and jockeying his horse along the road. His brown stallion moved at pace, and whether he saw me or Vaughn, it didn't seem to matter.

Vaughn foolishly began waving his arms. I, in turn, raised my gun.

'Stop! For God's sake, s-stop!' The young man seemed genuinely terrified.

As he came within fifty yards of us, it was clear that Cummings had no intention of slowing. He yipped the horse onwards, whipping at its hind with his riding crop. It seems so clichéd in moments such as these, but all things then seemed to slow around me. Vaughn began to run to his left out of the road; I altered my stance and took hold of the Enfield with both hands. Thick drops beat across the barrel as I trained my sights and made ready to fire.

Lightning crashed, striking against a tree on the opposite side of the common. I flinched, as did Vaughn. Within ten yards of us, Cummings' horse skidded to a halt. It brayed as he tried to bring it to heel, before it reared frantically and threw him off the saddle. He fell dreadfully, landing on his back with his left knee and shin buckling under him. He cried out in anguish, though was very lucky, for his horse beat and trampled the floor beside him, before bolting back in the direction of the stable.

Vaughn ran to Cummings' side; I walked over slowly, my gun still in hand. The man was screaming on the floor, trying to shift and move his leg. It was clearly broken, and he clutched his knee as he writhed, mud covering much of him.

'It's broken,' he yelled, clenching his eyes shut. 'My bloody leg is broken.'

I had no sympathies. 'It is the least of your worries. Get him up, Vaughn.'

Cummings protested, as did Vaughn. I had no patience for either of their complaints and knelt down, threading an arm beneath Cummings and pulling him upward. He screamed at me, though I did not pause, moving the man awkwardly and with no care. Seeing this, Vaughn took Cummings' other arm and wrapped it around his shoulder. As we began to move, Cummings was made to hobble with great difficulty, flinching and moaning with every step. He yelled all manner of insults my way, though it only made me move him quicker.

'We're going to the hall,' I said coolly. 'You're both going to tell me everything you know.'

Geraint had gone. I cursed under my breath. By now it was approaching evening and the day was taking a toll on me. We shuffled over to a few seats and there I dropped Cummings clumsily into one. He screamed out again for his useless leg jolted against the floor.

'Bastard!' He pushed Vaughn away and returned his attention to his leg. My gun was still in hand, and in quite a rash move, I aimed it straight at Cummings. Vaughn stammered uncontrollably.

'Sit down!' I shouted, at which he did, his hands raised a little.

I moved about then, before replacing my gun for my note-book and pencil. I still had duties, murders to get to the bottom of. Nothing would be resolved if I let my anger take hold of me.

'Start from the beginning, five years ago.'

Cummings scoffed. 'I told you of all this. The lad here did too, no doubt.'

'You lie. You say your reasons for not alerting the Constabulary were in the interests of the village, that you carried out an enquiry, that you did your *duty*. *That* is weak reasoning if any, I know there was something else to it. Tell me.'

Cummings only shook his head, avoiding eye contact with me.

'You are my top suspect for the murder of Betsan Tilny. You've colluded with another to have her killed so you could be the beneficiary of the General's estate. Tell me that is not true.'

'It is not,' Cummings replied savagely, his face gnarled and twisted. 'I had nothing to do with the girl's murder.'

'Then what of the children's murders five years ago. What part did you have in that?'

'I had nothing to do with it,' he snapped.

'You made a hurried investigation back then to sweep every-thing under the carpet, ensured no one from the surrounding Constabularies was informed and now claim to have had no part in these murders – so tell me the truth!'

Cummings started to speak but stopped himself. He was shaking, his jaw clamped shut. Rainwater and sweat dripped down from his forehead to his jowls. With his dreadful blue coat open, I could see a fine three-piece suit, in the style he wore at all times, torn and tatty now – like every other façade he tried to maintain.

'Fine,' I said crisply, thrusting my hand in my pocket and

gripping my gun. 'Until you are willing to divulge what you are so clearly holding back you will be considered the leading suspect.' I looked at Vaughn. 'I'll assume for now that you are his accomplice in all this, so you'll both need to be held until I can send for the Glamorgan Constabulary.'

Vaughn rose a little in his chair, reaching out to me, pleading. I pulled the gun quickly and barked at him to sit back down. Cummings jolted in his seat and cried out once more.

'You're both under arrest for the murder of Betsan Tilny. Throw me your shackles.' I was aiming the gun at Vaughn then, who only quivered in his seat.

'Just tell him,' Vaughn near whispered.

Cummings remained silent for a moment. He turned to Vaughn beside him for some sort of support. The young man could only look down at the floor.

'When the children were killed,' Cummings began slowly, 'I feared ... I feared an investigation might pry into some ... business dealings I and others had undertaken.' He inadvertently moved his leg and groaned.

'Business dealings,' I said. 'What kind of business dealings?'

He was rubbing his knee. 'The kind that are not strictly legal.'

I shook my head in total disbelief. I'd like to say I was surprised, but nothing of this village and its secrets seemed to shock me anymore. The man had let a killer walk free to save his own skin – in my eyes then he was as culpable as the murderer.

Cummings explained in brief his illicit dealings. Fraudulent transactions in the purchase of property. Bribery to Glamorgan and Cardiff officials in the pursuit of land ownership. Tax evasion. The opening of multiple fraudulent lines of credit. He was the owner of the Mill Road properties: the new red-bricked houses of which I'd taken note on my first day (they had been built with no due diligence in respect of the land, and were overvalued prior to any sales). Embezzlement of funds entrusted to him by General James and the local council. On and on it went for the list in his serpentine business stretched back many years.

'Who else was involved?' I interrupted sharply at one point. By now I had put my gun away again and was scribbling details down in my notebook.

'It was mostly my doing—'

'But who else was involved?' I asked with greater force.

Cummings clenched his fist and spoke through gritted teeth. 'Myself and a man called Phillip Shaw started the whole thing, really, when the General first began showing signs of his *illness.*'

I thought of the dithering Mrs Shaw, the woman who had nearly told me of the previous murders. She'd said her husband was formerly Treasurer of the Village council. This I confirmed with Cummings.

'He passed away three years ago,' Cummings muttered bitterly.

'His wife told me,' I replied.

He shook his head despondently. 'She never could keep her mouth shut.'

'Who else?'

Cummings fidgeted and wriggled. 'Some other members of the council, Patterson, the shopkeeper.'

I recalled my conversation with Mrs Patterson, the shop-keeper's wife, that previous day.

'His wife holds you in high esteem – does she have something to do with all this as well?'

Cummings looked at me viciously then, stabbing a finger out towards me.

'Margaret has nothing to do with this!'

I had clearly struck a nerve. 'Are you and Margaret close?'

'Whether we are or not is of no concern to you,' Cummings snarled defensively. 'This has nothing to do with anything.'

'I'll assume that is a yes. Is your good relationship one of *public* knowledge?' I took some pleasure in seeing the scorn wash over Cummings' face. He clearly wished to yell all manner of foulness at me then.

'Who else?' I growled.

'The lad here's father,' Cummings pronounced, nudging Vaughn next to him. Vaughn was still staring down at the floor, though he closed his eyes at the mention of his father.

'He wasn't much involved before his death,' Cummings continued. 'Johnathon Miller more recently, when he needed help with the farm.'

I thought back to my conversation with Miller that previous morn.

Mr Cummings has been very good in assisting with getting the work completed. He's a good man, the Councillor.

A dreadful idea struck me then.

'Did Miller really find the girl's body that morning?'

'Of course he did,' Cummings blurted.

'Yet he, and all those involved in your illicit business, sought to keep the previous murders quiet and withhold as much information from me as possible.'

To that Cummings said nothing. Things were beginning to make sense to me.

'That's a good handful of people in this village who were involved, many I have spoken to. It was in their interest to conceal the previous murders – they didn't want to draw attention to their financial crimes. Even then though they likely needed some convincing to stay quiet.'

Cummings moved to stand, as if forgetting his leg was broken. 'Not everything I, or anyone else, did was for profit, Inspector,' he groaned. 'And what good would come from dragging up the past, destroying the work we have done for this village, just for you to draw a blank, to make the same conclusions we did all those years ago?'

'Did you try to hamper any of Vaughn's enquiry five years ago?' I asked plainly, turning then to Vaughn. 'Did you actually carry out one or has that all been lies as well?'

'We were horrified,' Cummings cried with volume. 'I helped Vaughn here carry out whatever investigation he saw fit – there were no suspects then and it was well within reason that the murders were committed by someone unknown. Anyone can pass through those woodlands, anyone!'

Vaughn was tapping his leg nervously. His lips were pursed together tightly – he was panicking, the stress and reality of it all now impressing upon him. I doubted then he would be able to speak.

'So your business – what you feared the Constabulary may unearth – played no part in your failure to alert them to the murders?'

Cummings rubbed his eyes. 'It was a concern, of course, but I was satisfied enough by Vaughn's conclusion.' I laughed bitterly at that. 'What point was there,' Cummings continued, 'of kicking up all manner of fuss when we had determined what had happened to those poor children?'

'Ha! You determined nothing. You merely wanted to hold onto your ill-gotten gains. What then of Betsan's murder? You've made it quite plain that you had no desire for my being here, wanted me gone as soon as I arrived.' At this, Cummings turned away from me. 'The two of you have stuck steadfast to the preposterous notion that two separate incidences of murder were carried out by some random, unknown assailant. Unless of course it was the bloody spirit, the *Calon Farw* demon!'

I was being facetious, though talk of spirits made me think of Betsan, and of her ring. It jarred with me, struck me so that I stopped dead for a moment where I stood. In quieter tones I continued.

'Do people truly believe in that thing or is that all lies and deceit as well?'

'Most people are afraid of it,' Cummings grumbled. 'They wanted nothing to do with you for fear of what it may do to them.'

'I imagine you did little to quell the rumours of such a terrible creature, though. It was in your interest that people stayed quiet around me.'

Cummings only glared at me in silence.

I had been pacing before the two men, though the energy, the rage I had felt upon our arrival had dissipated somewhat. I wiped my brow, stood for a time in silence to contemplate what I had heard so far. It was salacious, damning, confessions of conniving crimes and withholding of pertinent evidence. And yet it proved nothing of Cummings' innocence in the matter of Betsan's death, in spite of the young Constable's assertion that the Councilman had nothing to do with her murder. There was clearly more to be told.

I stepped over and stood just before the two men.

'You, Councilman, have a strong enough motive to put you before a jury for murder, never mind any of your contemptible embezzlement. Up till now you have given me no reason to rule you out as a suspect for Betsan's death.'

Cummings began to squabble with me, insisting he hadn't killed Betsan. To my surprise Vaughn cut in, unable to sit silent anymore.

'T-tell him, Mr Cummings.' To this Cummings hissed, at which Vaughn turned upon him and shook him by the arm. 'For

God's s-sake, tell him! We're both already damned for what we did.'

'What?' I exclaimed. 'What else did you do?'

'The b-b-body.'

'Shut up, boy!' Cummings groaned in agony as he lurched his leg to the side.

I implored them both speak. Vaughn stammered as Cummings tried in vain to silence him, and we all began to shout and yell over each other until at last Cummings raised his hands in surrender.

'All right. All right, here it is.' He shook his head, muttered to himself for a moment and fidgeted with his hands as he looked about the room.

'The night that *girl* was killed, I couldn't sleep. It was stifling and clammy and I took to the common for a breath of air.' He looked at me in the eye for a moment but seemed incapable of holding my gaze. He spoke on hesitantly. 'We had had a council meeting that had gone on late and I suppose my mind was still mulling things over. There were numerous people in attendance, should you need to corroborate my whereabouts.'

'When did it finish?' I asked bluntly.

'Around half past ten, perhaps later. After spending hours lying awake I intended to circle the cricket field on the common but barely made ground from my house.' He paused, looking down now towards my feet, his mouth agape as if he were staring at something in amazement. 'There was a clump, a strange shape, piled on the floor in the darkness.'

He broke off until I ordered he speak on. His words were hushed, shaky.

'I approached it with no real thought. Even as I stood over it in the gloom, I couldn't understand what it was. It was only when I knelt down and rolled it over that I screamed in terror and fell backwards from it.' He pulled his arms close around him, rubbing nervously at his shoulders. 'It was the girl's body. Bound in chain, burnt.'

I became motionless, unable to move. Like a burst dam Cummings began to tell me everything as fast as he could. How he had looked about for some minutes, seeking to alert someone. How he had thought of his motive, his potential implication in Betsan's death. How in a moment of panic he had begun to drag the girl's body the short distance to his house. How there, realising the hour was approaching four and wary of being seen in daylight, he had run quickly through the village, rousing Vaughn and bringing him back to his residence.

'He didn't t-tell me what was happening when he woke me,' Vaughn moaned. 'I swear I w-went with him in good faith.'

'And what did you do then?' I asked Vaughn quietly. 'When he showed you Betsan's body, what was your first thought?'

'I -I wanted help but, but Mr Cummings … Mr Cummings.'

'You played your part in this, boy,' Cummings interjected with a sudden burst of anger. 'Don't try to blame all this on me.'

'You said things to me,' Vaughn blurted. 'Y-you said it was in our interest to move the body. You said w-we had to make it look like the last, th-that if we d-did, it would not reflect badly on us. You said another killing down the woods could not be blamed on us, would mean we h-had not failed in our duties with the previous murders.' He thrust his hands out to me then. 'You must understand, Mr Cummings has been good to me since my father's passing and I wanted to do right by him. I knew nothing of the General's money, I only feared what would happen to him, to ourselves. I panicked – I panicked!'

'So you helped him move the body,' I said grimly, for I did not need to ask.

Cummings nodded his head. 'We took it down by the mill. By then it was nearly dawn and we headed to the woods via the back of my estate. There are many ways to get to the Cwm Sior and we followed a little-used path. We put her by the mill, so she was obvious, so that no one would suspect she had been anywhere else.'

'And you tried to stage it, no doubt?' I was pacing again now, feeling I must admit, a little light-headed. What I was hearing was unbelievable; I was struggling to come to terms with it.

'W-w-well, we barely had time. We put the body there and heard someone coming. We fled before we could do much else.'

'But the burn marks upon the floor—' It dawned on me then. The blackened earth at the scene upon my arrival. I'd thought it madness, presumed it some symptom of the fever, a delusion of my own making. The charcoal had felt warm to the touch, as if the earth had only just been scorched.

'The day I arrived, you burnt the soil where you'd laid the body. You did so I would think she was killed by there.'

'We thought you'd agree with our story,' Cummings said in an exhausted manner. 'There had been some rumours about travellers in the area and we just thought it made such sense. I imagined your being here was merely a formality, that you'd be a day or two at most. And then you said you wanted to see where she was found, and, and . . . I got scared, we both did. Burning the ground just fitted in with our theory that the travellers did it. I swear to you I – we – had every intention of seeking out the guilty party upon your leaving.'

Both men nodded and began talking on. I turned away, took a few steady breaths before I could take no more and saw only red before my eyes. I don't regret what I did, for no honest man could hold himself after hearing of such treachery.

I turned, grabbed up Cummings from his seat and struck

him hard in the jaw. He crumpled to the floor with a whimper. Vaughn squirmed as I took hold of him, though in that moment I could do nothing but shake him and glower into his eyes. He tried with all his strength to push me off; I stumbled back from them both.

'You contemptible swine – to hell with the both of you! You moved that girl's body, staged it for your own measly purpose! You,' I pointed at Vaughn then, 'for some misplaced loyalty to this charlatan! For your previous failures as an officer of the law. To hell with you, wretches alike.' I squared up to Vaughn, who cowering away, collapsed backwards into his seat. I looked down upon them.

'Mark my words: in my eyes, you are as guilty as the killer.'

'We had no part in any murder,' Cummings moaned, his head in his hands, looking down towards the floor. 'You must know we had no part.'

'Perhaps not in the deed itself, for you both lack the guts to do such a thing. Believe me I know that, but you have played your part, unknowingly conspired for the guilty man. All this time I assumed Betsan was killed in the woods before being staged by the mill. I've given greater consideration to those who work in the woodlands, who would know where to keep her. It means so little now for she could have been killed anywhere in this rotten village.' I leant in close to both of them.

'Were it up to me, you would both hang beside the killer on the gallows.'

I couldn't tolerate the sight of either of them grovelling anymore. I had no desire to pack away my camera equipment, still standing from my earlier interviews. I took hold of my exposed plates and those developed from the mill, before striding out of the hall.

'I'm sorry, Inspector,' Vaughn called out in haunted tones. 'I'm s-s-so sorry.'

'Stay where I can find you,' I replied. 'If either of you try to leave, I'll hunt you down and shoot you where you stand.'

24

At the Bottom of a Glass –
June 23rd, 1904

I felt distraught as I walked back onto the Twyn. I was angry, of course, full of wrath, but neither fully describe my feelings then. I felt lost, like I had come to nothing after all my time spent thinking on and enquiring into the murder of Betsan. I was failing her, and for that I felt worthless.

I had not a single solid suspect. Cummings had the greatest motive, Geraint perhaps was the lover scorned. I doubted either man was guilty (of the murders, at least). In truth I knew nothing, for nothing in this place was certain. The murders could have both been random. The children's deaths could have indeed been carried out by some twisted vagrant, passing by the village. Betsan's brutal killing could have been motivated by something completely beyond all that I knew and enacted by the most unlikely of people. Until perhaps an hour previous, I assumed that the killings five years ago and now were connected. Now I was adrift, and so too were all my theories.

I had to search for Geraint, though my will was completely shattered. With no idea where he may have gone, I decided first to look at the inn, as foolish as that may seem. Perhaps it may be of surprise then that as I stumbled into the sunken patio and stepped through the inn's small door, I found the man, slouched in a stool at the bar. He was necking some spirit as I came over to him, waving to Solomon for the whole bottle. Solomon, in turn, gestured at me subtly.

'Come on, for God's sake,' Geraint slurred. 'You think I've had enough? D'you?'

I pulled up the stool beside him. 'I told you to stay in the hall.'

Geraint snorted. 'Why? S'you can arrest me for something I didn't do. The woman I love is dead and you're happy to put it on me.' He waggled a finger in my face, his elbow slipping on the bar as he did. 'I told you everything. I want you to find the real killer but instead you want to place blame on the easiest person you can get. I'm … I'm dull but not an idiot.' He reached a flimsy hand out for Solomon's bottle and I, dropping my photographic plates onto the bar, stretched over and took it. Solomon didn't protest, and quietly moved away.

'If you cared for her so much,' I said to Geraint as I refilled his glass, 'you could have contacted someone. The police from Glamorgan, from Cardiff. No matter what fears you had, you could have reached out for help.'

He sunk another drink. 'Look what good it would 'ave done me. They send some highbrow chancer like you who hasn't got a clue who did it and wants to pin it on me. I'm not an idiot.'

I didn't take great offence, as in that moment I agreed with him. I was moving backwards, the killer becoming ever more elusive. Geraint's grief felt as much then as my own. Though I wanted to, I struggled to muster any words of hope or encouragement for I was destitute of them. Instead I poured Geraint another drink, reached over the bar and grabbed any glass I could find. I sipped quietly on whisky as my mood only darkened.

It was approaching half past eight, and neither Geraint nor I said anything till the hour hand on the bar's clock struck nine. I still drank the first glass I had poured myself, pulling out the developed negatives from the mill and looking upon them absentmindedly. Geraint was dangerously close to passing out.

'On my first enquiry as an investigator,' I uttered, more to myself than Geraint. 'I was in South London. The Yard were after some racketeers who were shaking down local businesses. In truth it was not a complex enquiry. A merchant's office was torched and my photographs along with other evidence from the scene led me to the guilty party. But I remember walking alone, realising that I was relying upon my own wits, my own intellect.' I was becoming quite melancholic, staring down at the developed pictures as though they were the first I had ever taken. 'It was such a lonely feeling, daunting really. Of course, after that my confidence only grew, my arrogance as well. Now ...'

I fell silent. Solomon was nowhere to be seen, the hatch to his cellar open, though I had not even noticed him go down. Geraint was pulling himself upright though his eyes were half closed.

'Now I feel like my daunted, lonely self all those years ago. I've let an illness get the better of me. I've seen things ...'

A flash of dreadful flame, a spectre with hollowed eyes.

'... that I cannot be certain are real or false.' I meant to speak of Betsan's ring to Geraint but couldn't say the words aloud. The negatives had shown me the ring, an ethereal band of light in a picture. I tried not to think of it, for it scared me too much. If the ring had been real, what else from those pictures ...

'She wasn't perfect,' Geraint blurted then, his head lolling as he spoke. 'She had her moments, was fiery with me.' His hand crashed against my shoulder and he leant his forehead against mine. His breath was near combustible.

'I never meant to row with her that day. My last words to her were angry.' Tears began dripping onto my shoulder. 'If I'd known it would be the last time I saw her, I would've just taken hold of her an' run. Run away from this bloody place.'

The man was broken beyond any comfort. It seemed best to take him home.

'Tomorrow, should this storm pass, I will do what I can to alert the authorities. I – we – need more help to find the killer.'

Solomon remained out of sight though it didn't seem to matter; no doubt he would guess I was taking Geraint home.

I stood, finishing the small remainder of my drink. I left my photographic plates on the bar as Geraint fell backwards from his stool. I was able to grab his limp body.

'I'm … I'm just glad it was my brother who told me. Heart o' gold, my brother.'

I nodded as I tried to wrestle the man upright.

'Come to me and told me. Was barely awake. Thought it just a bad dream. But it came from my brother, all he wants is people to be happy.'

I nodded again and set Geraint's arm around my shoulder. It wasn't until we reached the inn door that I fully realised what he had said.

'Your brother told you?' I stopped, taking Geraint's arm from around me after which he fell against the door frame. I managed to haul him back towards the bar; he was barely awake.

'Geraint,' I shrugged him, before tapping his face. He looked at me with a start. 'Your brother told you? He told you about Betsan's body?'

'He's a good man, is Lewis. Wants people to be happy. He's not smart but good in other ways.' Geraint made some strange motion with his hands. 'He's a craftsman.'

'And he told you of Betsan's body? What time was this?'

Geraint garbled something inaudible before closing his eyes again. I managed to rouse him a little.

'I don' know. Was early, just before dawn maybe. I think he was down the mill when they found her.' He scratched at his face. 'He woke me up, told me … about, told me she was dead. Didn't say where though. He got upset and just won't talk when he's like that. I was running 'round. Running 'round trying to find out. I wasn't even awake properly when he told me – my day off.'

I let Geraint slump onto the bar then and frantically thumbed through my notebook. Excitedly I turned to the page I had marked with Johnathon Miller's name. I read through the few small notes I had made; I wanted to be certain.

'Edward and Will. They were the only ones with Miller that morning. They found her just after dawn.'

I tried rousing Geraint once more but to no avail, reaching then for the bottle and splashing some of the whisky in his face. He grunted as his eyes opened slightly.

'Lewis works for Miller, correct? What does he do for him?'

Geraint mumbled. 'He's a good man. Great with his hands.' He closed his eyes momentarily. 'Father. Our father taught him to make things proper, carve and things. That's why John keeps him.'

He closed his eyes again. I tried to think of any way Lewis could have known about Betsan's body before it was discovered by Miller. Perhaps Geraint was wrong; perhaps Lewis had told him later in the day, when word had spread throughout the village. If Lewis had told Geraint before dawn, there was only one way he could have known Betsan was dead …

Carvings. By Geraint's reckoning, Lewis was good at carving things. It struck me then plainly.

'Geraint. Geraint!'

The man was insensible. I spoke loudly straight in his ear.

'Soldiers, Geraint. Does Lewis carve wooden soldiers? Would he make them down the mill?'

Geraint roused enough to curse me.

'I don' know. He's his own man.'

The developed plates were laid out before me. I cast an eye over each one quickly, squinting to look at the tools on the workbench. In the corner of my second image, one I had taken from the centre of the room, I eyed the cans of paint and brushes. Next to it was a chewed-up piece of wood, at least that's what I had first thought. It took on more of a form as I looked at it, a head perhaps, atop shoulders.

'Your brother knew of Betsan's death before her body was found. He made the soldiers that Solomon's children played with, had with them when they died.'

I grabbed up Geraint roughly and began dragging him to the door. Solomon must have emerged from the cellar then, asking out of sight what I was doing.

'He lives down the hill, down Elm Grove Road, yes?' I had taken Geraint's address when I had questioned him but could only vaguely remember.

'The last but one cottage,' Solomon called after me, bewildered.

I didn't reply as I clattered Geraint through the front door. I managed to coax him out of the patio, and the rain of the storm seemed to wake him enough to walk.

'I need to sleep,' he kept repeating as we trudged quickly down the hill. It was not far, and by the time we came to his rather bare and unkempt front garden, he was stumbling without my aid.

'Get inside,' I implored him. The front door was not locked, and I bundled past him into the cottage. Like the telegraph station, we came straight into the kitchen, though there was no adjacent room. The stairs were to our right and calling out Lewis' name I traipsed up them. I searched through the rooms above; the house was completely deserted. When I returned downstairs, Geraint had collapsed onto the hard-stone floor. He was barely conscious, though I fell to his side and spoke loudly to him.

'Your brother, Geraint. Where is he? Where would he be?'

Geraint didn't wake, and it was only when I shook him roughly that he prised his eyes open.

'Where is Lewis?' I repeated desperately.

'I don't know. He stays out ... sometimes. I'm not his mother.'

He fell asleep once more, but it didn't matter. I leapt up and began sprinting back to the Twyn. I had no real idea where Lewis could be, but fancied he was down at the mill. It was the only place I could think to look.

Lewis was connected to both the murders. Lewis was surely the killer.

25

The Silent Brother – June 23rd, 1904

As I trudged along the woodland path that led to the mill, the forest imposed itself upon me. This was no June evening like any other, for it seemed the darkest depths of a winter's night. I knew it was not normal, knew then that nothing of this village was.

The trees loomed larger than ever they could. Unseen eyes watched me, of man or beast or any other foulness I could think of. I turned constantly, looking over my shoulder for any sight of what may stalk me. Heavy walls of darkness confined me to the solitude of my contemptible imagination, and soon, the dreaded *Calon Farw* was nipping at my heels, trying desperately to consume my very soul.

The driving rain drummed through the foliage; the undergrowth murmured with all the strange noises of twilight. The slightest movement startled me, and all the while I was talking to myself in a harsh whisper, trying to calm my nerves by any means, clinging to my Enfield. I had to find Lewis Davey, I had to find him to end all this.

Much of the way was flooded, the small stream that separated the winding path from the forest, breached and overrun. In places, the water came up beyond my shins, and I waded and stumbled, falling badly at one point, so that I landed hard on my shoulder. I cried aloud, but with hurried effort, splashed for purchase and scrambled on, ignoring the pain spreading down my left arm.

I guided my way along the path to its very end coming to the stout stone bridge before the mill.

I caught sound of a terrible creaking noise.

I began swirling and searching in the darkness. With my good right arm, I aimed the revolver, my heart erupting. My dreadful excitement, my fears, were getting the better of me. I began moving across the bridge slowly; as I did, the strange creaking noise grew louder. The bridge itself stood just above the floodwater, though here it gushed quite swiftly. The mill was in sight, its white paint standing out a little in the gloom. As I stepped ever closer, the creaking sound grew louder, reaching its climax as I came within a few yards of the mill's black door. In my foolishness, I thought it Betsan, luring me towards her.

Something moved nearby. I was paralysed, terrified of what may leap towards me. Only then did I realise the mill water wheel was spinning and creaking.

I sighed heavily, furious at myself. I had to get a hold of my senses, focus on Lewis and dispel all nonsense of ghosts no matter how hard it was to do so. I moved alongside the mill wall, slowly creeping towards the round window which that day past (a lifetime ago) I had seen Lewis board up himself. Through a fine crack between two timbers, I saw a faint light flicker.

I thought what next to do. If indeed Lewis were inside, I had an element of surprise, something of an advantage. There seemed no reason for him to think I was coming to the mill. Yet still I couldn't take that chance. I had to apprehend Lewis then and there, giving him no opportunity to thwart capture and evade me.

Taking a deep breath, I laid a hand against the mill's black door. I felt it give a little. Still gripping my revolver and in one motion, I pushed hard so that it swung fully open. I half expected to see Lewis, sat upon some rickety chair, drinking from a brown bottle of ale, a callous smile spread across his lips.

Instead I stepped into a warm, well-lit room, the air heavy with dry mill dust. As I inhaled, I coughed and spluttered. Disorientated I looked about. A little way to my left, I saw a figure, seated at a workbench, gazing toward me in complete bemusement.

Lewis Davey flinched as I aimed my Enfield straight at him.

'Hold there, man! Make one false move and I'll put you to the floor.'

'Sorry! What do you mean?' He spoke queerly, with a heavy lisp. He didn't raise his arms but almost climbed onto the workbench in complete alarm. He knocked a few tools – a file and some small wood chisels – down onto the floor. He was shaking his head in complete confusion before I said another word.

'Let's make this easy. You'll surrender yourself now. I have no shackles, but I am not afraid to use this.' I shook my Enfield a little. 'You'll come with me back to the village.'

He continued to scramble along the length of the workbench, knocking over more tools and hunks of wood as he did. I followed him with my gun and called loudly. He hunkered down to the floor by the wall, a little distance away from the actual millstone. I aimed at him through the thick axles and greased cogs. He buried his head in his arms, holding his left hand out to me with the palm raised.

I couldn't understand him as he mumbled.

'Speak up! Don't play the coward and talk to me plainly.'

He didn't look over to me as I moved closer towards him. His hand was shaking badly. I realised he was calling for his brother.

'He's not here. Look to me, face the charges I bring to you.'

I stood then right over him. He slowly turned his head, one small eye gazing up at me. His round face was flush, shuddering in what was clearly abject terror. I saw him cling to something with his hidden hand.

'Show me what you have. Move slowly.'

He shook his head. 'It's not, it's not finished.'

I was taken aback by that. 'What?'

'It's not finished. I was finishing it.'

He caught me off guard, my tone losing all its fired aggression.

'Show me,' I said, trying to muster some sort of command. 'And move slowly.'

He shook his head at first. I thrust my gun a little toward him and with a whimper he began to move. He slowly showed me his hand. Clasped tightly in it was a small wooden soldier, the exact type that Solomon's children had had. It was as I had suspected – he was their maker. The soldier's rifle was not fully whittled and formed. The craftmanship was nevertheless quite extraordinary.

'It's not finished,' Lewis repeated, crying now.

'It doesn't matter.' I dropped my arm a little. 'Lewis Davey, I'm here to charge you with the murder of Betsan Tilny.' I needed evidence for the children's murders five years previous; whilst Lewis making the soldiers was a connection, it was loose and not enough. I was determined to get a confession from the man.

'I didn't ...'

His voice trailed off and he turned his head away from me. I moved a step closer to him.

'You may deny it, but you can state your case when the Constabulary arrive. I have evidence to support my charge – you knew of Betsan's death before her body was even discovered. You weren't down the mill when she was found yet told your brother she was dead. You couldn't tell him where the body was however because it had been moved from the common, the place you left it. Don't play the fool with me.'

He turned slowly towards me, his beady eyes wet, his face and lips shivering. He began looking around the room, growing more and more panicked as he did.

'Where's Geraint? Where's Geraint!'

His speech was laboured, slow. I felt myself lower my gun completely.

'Your brother isn't here, Lewis.' It was becoming hard now to maintain my steely composure. 'He can't help you right now. You'll have to come with me, it's a serious charge, man.'

'Geraint. I didn't do anything. Where's Geraint?'

He was quaking now uncontrollably, his nose dribbling, his short frame writhing in the corner of the room. He dropped the wooden soldier and turned his body, beginning to scratch at the stone wall, as if trying to tunnel away from me. I didn't want to step any closer to him, minded that this may all be some elaborate charade. It didn't seem that way, though. Lewis was only becoming more and more erratic.

Finally, I went to him. I crouched and placed an arm on his shoulder, turning him roughly towards me. He wailed and tried to turn his head from me. I took hold of him by both shoulders and spoke slowly to him.

'I know you killed Betsan, Lewis. I know it. Geraint told me. You came to him, before dawn, woke him and told him Betsan was dead. That was before Johnathon Miller discovered her. You couldn't have known she was dead then unless you had some part in her murder.'

He began to rock back and forth.

'It's not what happened. It's not what happened.' He seemed barely able to speak, his strained words coming to me between rasping breaths. It was as though he were convulsing before me.

I tried to shake some sense into him, but that only did to worsen his panic. I began to hush him then, doing all I could to calm him down. It was strange; I had convinced myself only a short while ago, that the unstable man before me was a brutal, heartless killer.

'All right then. All right. Tell me what happened. If you deny the charge, tell me why I should believe you.'

His breathing was only a little better, though he began to talk with some clarity.

'I didn't want to see her. I keep seeing her – I keep seeing her!'

He began hitting at the side of his head, and it was all I could do to drop my gun and grip hold of his wrists. He was stronger than I so that I keeled over awkwardly and let go of him completely. He stopped hitting himself then but clutched at his legs and buried his face in his lap. He began rocking, as I, quite shocked and exasperated, sat watching him.

I collected my Enfield after a moment and pocketed it. It seemed clear I wouldn't need it.

Lewis began to quiet down. I wondered what best to do. After a little while sitting in silence, I reached for the carved wooden soldier on the floor. Gently I tapped at his knee until he raised his head just enough to look at me, I held the soldier out to him. He took it gently and gripped it tight, rocking still but far more serenely.

I realised then how ill he was, not an illness of body but one of mind, the kind of illness that makes men slow. He was like a child in the body of a grown adult. Slurred talking; not fully developed. Whether he was capable of murder seemed uncertain, though even children can pull the wings from a fly.

'I need you to talk to me, Lewis,' I said softly. 'It may be hard, but you have to tell me. If you didn't kill Betsan, you have to convince me.' I felt quite wicked as I lied to him then. 'It will be all right, even if you have. But I need you still to tell me.'

He held the little soldier close to him.

'I didn't. I didn't. I was here, I was here making—' He held the soldier out to me a little.

'You were here, making your soldiers?' He nodded. 'Were you here all night?'

He nodded again. 'It's quiet. When Mr Miller is not here, it's quiet. He doesn't know I'm here at night.' His voice grew panicked again. 'Don't tell Mr Miller, don't tell him.'

I recalled how Miller had spoken to him when last I had come down here. *Fool*, he had called him. *Fool.*

'So you were here, making the soldiers. Then what?'

He spoke without any pause for thought. 'Before daytime, I left, I went to the woods. It's quiet in the woods. I like to see daytime come when I'm in the woods.' He pointed one shaking hand in the direction of the Cwm Sior. 'It's quiet at daytime in the woods.'

I nodded reassuringly. 'You left before dawn? You left here before dawn to go into the woods?'

He smiled a little. 'I like the woods, when daytime comes.'

'All right. Then what?'

He opened up a bit more then, wiping at his face as he spoke. 'I went to the woods and saw someone. Two.' He raised his free hand and held two fingers up at me. 'One was the policeman.'

My heart sank. As did I, for all my excitement at the prospect of catching the killer left me, replaced by my exhaustion and weariness. It overcame me in an instant, and I felt myself dropping, as though I were falling through the floor.

'Constable Vaughn. You're talking about Constable Vaughn?'

Lewis nodded. 'I saw him and someone. I hid, and they ran.' He began to grow upset again and I found myself reaching a hand out to comfort him. 'When they ran, I wanted to find them. But then I saw... I saw her, hurt. She was hurt!'

He started sobbing into his arms, but before I could say another word, he looked up at me again.

'I was scared. I was scared and wanted Geraint. I wanted Geraint, so I ran. I ran and told Geraint.'

He yelled out then before moving and falling against me, crying on my chest as I quietly put an arm around his shoulder. This was no suspect; it was trauma personified. It needn't take an investigator to know that Lewis was no killer. He continued to talk as I cradled him on the floor.

'I didn't mean to make Geraint sad. I didn't mean to, I didn't.'

'You didn't, Lewis. You did no such thing. I'm sorry I scared you. You don't need to be scared.' I wanted to comfort him some more and gently took hold of the wooden soldier. 'You make good soldiers. You've made these a long time?'

He nodded. 'I make them. I used to make them for children. Gave them to mothers, fathers. All left now. All the children. They all left and now I have no one to give them to.'

'Did you give them to Solomon? To his children?'

Lewis mumbled. 'No children. No children. I gave them to mothers and fathers with children.'

I patted his shoulder. 'I know. I know. There are no children now.'

What a fool I was.

There we stayed upon the floor of the mill whilst the storm whistled through every crack in the masonry. In time, Lewis began to calm and grow still.

He was not the killer. But that was little comfort to me.

26

In Plain Sight – June 23rd, 1904

I was able to convince Lewis to come back to the village with me. He took his soldier with him, and as we walked I repeatedly spoke to reassure him.

'You don't need to be frightened, Lewis.'

We moved slowly, though I had no real idea of the time. We saw no one as we came back into the Twyn and walked down Elm Grove Road. The door of Lewis and Geraint's cottage had seemingly slammed shut, though as we stepped inside, Geraint was still sprawled on the kitchen floor. Lewis rushed to his side with a great deal of concern.

'Geraint. Geraint!'

Geraint began to stir and grumble.

'What's going on? What's the matter, Lew?'

'It's fine,' I said, standing just inside the doorway. 'Your brother—' I didn't really know how to explain. 'I'll need to speak to both of you in the morning. Make sure you're here.'

I bade them goodnight, and walked out of the cottage, closing the door behind me. I stood in the road and looked up at the sky, rain trickling down my face. Had I the energy, I would have screamed and cursed myself hoarse. But I didn't. I merely stood staring up at darkness before plodding miserably back to the inn.

I was tired of being wet, tired of the wind whipping through my coat. I was tired of the village, in that moment tired even of my work. I wanted rest and simply to wake up at home in London, recalling all this as a dream, before it quickly slipped from consciousness and I was left with no inkling or memory of this dreadful place. I was at the end of my tether; that in many ways was an even greater defeat than having a killer still roaming free.

The gas lamp had been snuffed out by the elements, and not a speck of light shone anywhere in sight. I was able to make my way to the inn, though nearly fell into the sunken patio and fumbled at the door. A single gas lantern was lit inside, stood stoically beside Solomon. He jumped up as I came in, his hands fidgeting.

'You were some time with Geraint. Is he all right?'

I only shook my head. 'Not really. I would have a drink and then go to bed.'

Solomon obliged. He was wearing little more than a vest, his braces hanging loose around his legs. He looked as haggard as I. He fetched me a drink and told me it was brandy. I took a good swig.

'I'm sorry, Solomon, for all this really. I'll need to get word to the Constabulary in Glamorgan or Cardiff tomorrow.' I was rubbing my left arm, my shoulder throbbing from where I had fallen on it. 'Whether this storm rages on or not. I'm afraid I'm done.'

He leant on the bar before me, exhaling deeply and fidgeting some more with his hands. He didn't look at me but spoke in his quiet manner after a minute or so.

'I know. I know you did your best. And if the Constabulary come, they will too. I'm sorry to say this, but I don't think they'll find the man.' He shrugged and stepped away. It was perhaps the last kick I needed, the disappointment of a bereaved father.

I nodded, for I believed he was right. I moved from the bar toward the little door and the stairs. Solomon replaced the bottle of brandy and busied himself absently. It seemed he didn't want to look at me.

'Thank you, for all your hospitality,' I said. 'I'll make sure you have full payment in the morning.'

With that I downed the last of my drink. My hand twitched as I set the glass on the bar. It tipped to its side, and before either Solomon or I could stop it, it fell and smashed on the floor behind the bar.

I apologised, tiredness now getting the better of me.

'It's fine, it's fine.' Solomon knelt down, collecting some of the shards. I meant to leave for I was sure I was causing the man great grief. As he came back up, I saw something gleam faintly around his neck. I hadn't noticed it before; it had been tucked just below the hem of his vest. Now it hung before him as he spilt some of the broken glass onto the bar.

'What's that?' I asked, trying to maintain the calmness in my voice.

He glanced at me confused, before following my eye line and looking down at his chest.

He took hold of the thin ring on the end of a silver metal chain.

'Oh this!' His voice was more jovial than mere moments before. 'Was my wife's. I just couldn't let them bury it with her. Too precious.'

The ring was clearly of no great value, not adorned with any small jewels or the like. It was thin, dull and ill-shaped. I had seen this ring before, only then it had shone brightly in a developed negative. It had been made for slender fingers. *For Betsan's fingers.*

When Solomon looked back at me I managed to feign a smile.

He reciprocated. The silence hung for too long between us. I wanted desperately to reach for my gun.

'These things are often too important to lose.' I tapped my hand lightly on the bar. 'I should get some rest.'

He didn't reply. As I stepped through the door, I stopped myself. As foolish as it seems now, I wanted to be rid of any doubts. It took such an effort to maintain my composure and turn to stand before him once again. I spoke as nonchalantly as I could.

'One thing dawned on me earlier – perhaps it is relevant. The soldiers, the wooden ones your boys had. Would you happen to know who made them?'

His crooked smile remained. 'Can't say I do. Is it important?'

He knew nothing of Lewis' craft, had never received anything for his children. *His children – he had no children.*

I shook my head. 'Perhaps. I'll pass on my thoughts to the Constabulary tomorrow.'

Without another word I stepped away. I maintained a steady pace as I came to the bottom of the stairs and climbed a few upwards. Everything was pitch black. I took out my Enfield, pulled back the hammer.

When I turned something hard struck me in the jaw.

Then there was only deeper darkness still.

27

The Finest Act – June 23rd, 1904

I heard shuffling and the dull thud of a heavy weight as I shifted
in and out of consciousness. Words were uttered, quiet yet harsh,
biting and cruel. Something clattered and as I came around, I
noticed the stale smell of bitters, the rotting of dank wood. I felt
cold and damp all over. A pain that started as a needle point, a
prick of hot lead being pressed against the skin of my upper left
shoulder, began to spread and deepen in intensity. I writhed and
groaned as I tried to relieve myself of the growing discomfort. It
was then I realised my hands were bound behind me, the knots
of rope around my wrists so tight, they had near stopped the
circulation to my hands and fingers.

My jaw had been struck; it throbbed mercilessly. I tasted dried
blood across my teeth and gums. My neck was stiff, and as I
slowly opened my eyes, I realised I was looking down at the floor.
A floor I recognised – the floor of Solomon's cellar.

'What... what's happening...'

Bloodied saliva drooled from my lips. The shuffling, the clank-
ing and knocking stopped suddenly. Footsteps slowly drew near,
until a figure loomed before me. A pair of raggedy boots was all
I could see as I stared down at the floor.

The cold steel of a gun barrel was pushed under my chin
and raised steadily, forcing me to look upwards. Solomon looked

down at me. His expression was cold, void of all emotion. Empty is perhaps the more fitting word, for in that moment it was as though nothing of a soul, or heart, or conscience dwelt within him.

His eyes gleamed, bold and bright by contrast to the dark and shrouded room. He looked at me with a hunger, with a perverse and deathly lust.

'What the hell are you doing, man?' I was confused, my words slow and slurred.

Solomon's lips twitched ever so slightly.

He turned and stepped away. I watched after him, though it took a great effort, the pain from my jaw and head disorientating my vision. My neck and shoulders felt weak, and my head began to loll forwards as he reached the very shelf where I had developed my photographs on the other side of the cellar. He set my Enfield down with a clink and took hold of a large basin. When he threw the contents of cold water across my face and body in one quick thrust, I recoiled and gasped to life properly.

He didn't say a word, turning his back to me and focusing on something I couldn't see on the shelf. Shocked by my sudden start, I twisted my neck to my left and right, spotting a few candles propped and balanced on some crates and unopened barrels. I began recalling all that had happened: Lewis, the mill, returning to the inn, Betsan's ring around Solomon's neck. In a moment of anger and panic I cursed at him repeatedly, pulling hard at my wrists, writhing in the chair and even trying to stand though to no avail. He barely seemed to notice.

I tried to compose myself amidst all the pain and fury.

'*You*. You all along.'

He didn't turn to me.

'This – all of this – won't end well for you, Solomon.' I winced as I spoke, the very act of speaking causing fresh pain to pulse from my jaw. Still, Solomon didn't turn to look at me. He was working to fix something, tinkering quickly.

I began twisting my hands awkwardly to feel at my bonds. A thin rope had been wrapped around both wrists numerous times; I splayed and stretched my fingers.

'They'll come for you in time, man. Whatever you think you're going to do, they'll come for you in the end.'

'How does this work?' Solomon said quietly, frustrated. His heavy husk of a body blocked all sight of what he was working on, though in that moment I noticed my camera stand, fully erected close to the shelf. My case was lying open on the floor alongside it; my camera and few remaining plates had been removed.

'Tell me how it works,' he said again, his voice now louder. He turned to look at me, holding a glass quarter plate in hand. There on the shelf I spotted my camera, lying haphazardly on its side.

I didn't answer him, but spoke with all the conviction I could muster.

'Whatever you think this is, Solomon, you're done. If you kill me, more and more police will flood this village. You won't be able to hide for ever—'

He smacked a hand down hard against the shelf.

'*Tell me* how this works, or I'll make your end much slower than it needs be!'

His face was flushed, the sweat from his brow dribbling down like molten sulphur in the dimmed candlelight. His hand moved towards an array of tools and implements. I eyed a pair of tongs, a hammer, a thin butchering knife.

'How did you get my camera? What do you want with it?' I tried with great effort to hide the fear in my voice, knowing that I had not succeeded when Solomon smirked thinly.

'I want to take your picture, Inspector.'

To this day I shudder when I think of the way he looked at me.

'I won't tell you anything,' I found myself uttering, 'until you tell me about Betsan. About the murders of the children.'

His smile vanished in an instant. He reached clumsily across the desk, set his hand upon the handle of the hammer and thrust it in my direction.

'I just couldn't hide it from you in the end. Wearing that little bitch's ring right under your nose was just too tempting!' He took a step towards me, holding up the ring he still wore around his neck. 'You really want to know what happened to her, don't you?'

I didn't answer, holding his gaze in silence. After a moment he stepped back to the little shelf and lazily tossed the hammer down. He continued to fiddle and poke at my camera, trying in vain to insert the glass plate, his oafish hands pulling and prising at wood and brass latches.

'You should tell me how this works, Inspector,' he said calmly. 'In truth you owe me your life.'

I was baffled by what he meant. 'Because you haven't killed me yet?'

He shook his head, his face expressionless once more.

'Because I could have killed you before. Because if I hadn't stopped what I was doing, you'd be dead already.'

He set the camera down gently and began staring into the corner of the room. He nodded his head, clearly deep in thought, though I had no idea what was going through the man's mind. He muttered something under his breath and began pulling, rather indelicately, on his lower lip.

'How are you feeling now, Inspector? Has your fever passed?'

He still wasn't looking at me, yet the way he stared absently across the room filled me with near as much dread as when he glared straight into my eyes.

'This is all over, Solomon,' I groaned in earnest. 'Whether you kill me or not—'

'When I first heard that an Inspector was coming to the village, I was *worried*,' he cut in, his voice distant and hushed. 'I'd wanted just to kill you. Cummings asked for you to stay here and the idea came to me.'

He nodded some more, his cheek quivering as his lip curled in a dreadful smile.

'I felt quite excited the day you arrived. Truth be told I felt happy. *I'd never poisoned a man before* – not the way I usually do things.'

I looked at him in bemusement until the truth of it all dawned on me.

'You ... you've been poisoning me?'

He didn't answer, his smile only widening.

It all made sense then – the suddenness of my illness, the severity of my fever. I'd thought it mere coincidence, an unfortunate case of luck that I had become so ill at the near outset of the enquiry. How foolish I had been for not seeing it sooner. How foolish I had been for so many things.

'The fever, the bloody fever was all your doing!' Anger took hold of me and I cursed aloud, much to Solomon's pleasure. 'How did you do it? My food, my drink, no doubt?'

He nodded, setting his gaze on me then.

I shook my head, clenching my eyes shut.

'The hallucinations, everything I've seen ...'

'A side effect I'm afraid,' Solomon muttered dryly. 'The belladonna plant is called deadly nightshade for *so* many reasons.'

He stepped over to me quickly, moving around the chair and roughly grabbing hold of my bound wrists. I turned my neck painfully to watch him in my peripheral vision; I saw him crouch downwards, before feeling a clammy hand slowly move up my back to the base of my neck. His fingers rubbed my skin gently.

'You were so scared in your room, Inspector, the night you came to this cellar and made your photographs.' He squeezed my neck lightly, and it was all I could do to keep still and not wriggle desperately from his awful grip. 'Did you really think she was with you in the room that night, or the next? Did you really think you were with a ghost?'

'Why keep me alive?' I muttered, holding my voice steady, pushing aside any thoughts of this madman standing over me as I lay, near death, in bed. 'Why not simply kill me then?'

Solomon didn't answer for what felt an age, his hand pulsing on the back of my neck, his breath grazing softly against my skin. He stood up suddenly and moved back towards the shelf and my camera. I tried to hold in a sigh of relief.

'Interest,' he replied then simply. 'You were interesting. And *this*,' he pointed at the camera. 'I needed to know more about this. Seeing you down here, seeing those pictures of Betsan's body…' With his back to me he fell silent and continued prising at my camera, opening the rear compartment with some force.

'You'll break it doing that,' I said quite truthfully to him.

He hit his hand down against the shelf again before grabbing at the hammer. For a moment I thought he would be unable to contain his rage and would bring it down onto the camera, smashing it into a thousand pieces. But he didn't, instead holding it steady as he yelled across the cellar to me.

'Tell me how this works!'

I shook my head gingerly. 'Tell me about Betsan.'

It was rash of me to try to barter, though in that moment something seemed to snap inside the man. He cackled, wailed aloud and hit the side of his head with his free hand. He came back across the room towards me.

'What do you want to know?' he chuckled, doing all he could to contain his laughter. 'Do you want to know what it felt like strangling her, or whether I started burning her whilst she was still alive?'

His body shuddered as he spoke gleefully. His eyes fluttered each time I unwittingly pulled at the bonds around my wrists; the corners of his mouth trembled. He enjoyed my struggle, my pain, and I tried my best to conceal it then, for I wanted to give him no satisfaction.

'Try to get comfortable, Inspector—'

'I am *no bloody Inspector*,' I growled, glaring towards him, spitting blood from my mouth.

'That's right,' he said with feigned astonishment. 'You wanted me to call you Thomas, didn't you?'

Our conversation in the bar upstairs, what I knew now was all a sham. I'd let my emotions get the better of me, sitting across from a supposed father in grief, a broken man reliving the greatest trauma. How small and meagre I felt then at the manner to which I had been conned, how easily I had been dragged into the lies of Solomon's wicked charade.

'Whose children were they, Solomon? Was there a reason you killed them?'

He pulled absently on his lower lip and shook his head.

'The Morgans. Nice family, *nice wife*.'

'Did you enjoy seeing them grieve too?'

He nodded enthusiastically. 'They didn't stay very long after it happened. Too afraid, I think. I was lucky, really – Vaughn is an idiot; some of the labourers gave me an alibi unknowingly.'

I shook my head despondently. 'Were they the first you killed?'

Solomon cackled dreadfully. 'I lived in London for many years, Insp— *Thomas*. Sorry. Lots of *things* to do in London.'

He pointed at me with a wry smile. 'No doubt we were both there at the same time.'

I didn't say a word.

'When father died, I returned here, took over the inn. Found it hard to shake old habits, though...'

His smile vanished in an instant. He glared at me with anger and scorn, pointing the hammer he held in his hand towards my camera behind him.

'I want to know how this works! I want it!'

I admit I lurched at his sudden change in demeanour. I shook my head, nonetheless, doing all I could to learn more from him.

'I'll show you in good time, Solomon, first you tell me about Bets—'

He lunged forwards, grabbing me by the hair and shoving me so that I, and the chair I sat on, clattered to the floor. Standing over me he bent down and yelled in my ear.

'I tell you what to do, Thomas! I tell *you* what to do.'

I was stifling a scream, for I had landed hard on my shoulder and the pain was now excruciating. Solomon pulled up the chair roughly and began dragging it across the stone floor to the shelf; he barked and cursed as we moved. There, he made me face the camera, striking me hard against the back of my head with his open palm.

'Now then, before this gets any nastier, tell me how this works.'

I breathed in deeply, my entirety shaking.

'Not until you tell me about Betsan.'

He finally nodded in resignation. Calmly he set down the hammer on the bench and reached for my revolver. He placed the cold barrel to my temple. I did all I could to hold still – if this was my end I wouldn't scream or plead for mercy. It would give Solomon far too much satisfaction. Even as he twitched his hand, as though he were about to pull the trigger, I didn't bat an eye.

'She came to the inn, you know,' he said, amusedly, pulling the gun away from me. 'Came to me that night.'

I craned my neck and looked at him. He was toying absently with the revolver, the wicked smile returned to his face.

'You need to be careful with that,' I said flatly.

'I didn't lie to you completely,' he continued. 'The inn was full till about nine that night. I was just tidying everything away when Betsan came in. She seemed a little upset, was looking for Geraint. When I said I hadn't seen him I offered her a drink to calm her down. We sat talking for a little while. When I tried to be *nicer* to her, she got nasty.' He gestured to the cellar around us. 'It wasn't long till I'd managed to get her down here.'

I closed my eyes and shook my head. She'd been murdered here, right below the place I'd slept, right where I had sat and developed the pictures of her corpse. I looked about the floor.

'I had to conceal the scorch marks; nearly choked myself to death burning her like I did. And the blood, of course.' Solomon nodded toward a stack of barrels on my left before setting the gun down on the shelf. He tapped delicately on the top of my camera. 'If I'd had this, I could have shown you how she looked the moment before she died.' He sneered, before grabbing at the back of my neck and gripping tight. 'You'll show me how this works now.'

'I can't,' I grunted, 'not with my hands bound.'

He struck me hard on the back of the head once more.

'Do you think me a fool? Do you think me that stupid?'

'The chain,' I grimaced, for the blow to my head had made me jar my shoulder. 'The mutilation. You did all that for show, all that for fear?'

Solomon shifted the chair with force so that I looked straight at him. He knelt his lumbering body down to my level. Still in his grubby vest, I smelt the perspiration rise off him as he leant in ever closer to my face.

'You feed off it in time, Thomas.' He spoke with a renewed air of calm, of civility. 'When you kill as often as I have, you begin to *need* the fear. I wanted to cut her up into pieces but—' he shrugged. 'I left her on the common where everyone would find her. I was surprised to learn she had been found down by the mill.' He ran the back of his hand across my cheek. 'Did you ever get to the bottom of that?'

I held my tongue.

'I guessed it might be Cummings' doing. He's a snake, that man.'

'But why Betsan, Solomon? Why the children?'

He sighed, letting his hand fall to his side 'Do you believe in God, Thomas?'

I frowned, confused.

'I think I do,' he continued. 'God wouldn't have made me the way he did had he not wanted me to do what I do. And the day with the children, the night Betsan showed up here, all alone. *Fate*. Complete fate.' He ran a finger along his throat. I'd seen him do it before, when we had sat in the bar, talking of 'his' murdered children. I recoiled from him, trying to pull my wrists apart then with no real care or thought. Solomon beamed.

'Whether you show me how this camera works or not, Thomas, I'm going to kill you. I'm going to kill you and hide in plain sight, just as I have for years, just as I will continue to do. People never suspect the bumbling bar man, the silent fool.'

He stepped away out of sight. I wriggled and squirmed, twisting and turning my wrists to find any give, any loose end of thread that I could pinch with my fingers. I heard a rattle of metal, turned my neck painfully to see Solomon as he dragged a chain out from one dusky corner of the room. He let it fall to the floor just by his feet, before bending over to untangle some of the heavy links. The hem of his vest lifted, and there, just above his left hip, I noticed a few clear scratch marks. Betsan's defence wounds, no doubt.

'Now then,' he said quite casually, returning to the shelf and his array of loathsome tools. 'I'll ask nicely one last time.' He took hold of the thin butcher's knife. '*Show me how this camera works.*'

With the greatest effort I stayed quiet. Solomon nodded with an air of disappointment.

'This shan't be pleasant for you, Thomas.'

He moved around me, grabbed at the chair and dragged me a short way from the shelf. Before I knew what was happening, he struck me hard against the face with the back of his meaty hand. I was dazed, my ear ringing; he spoke just at my side.

'…it drives you quite mad – eats away at you – when you try to fight that urge.'

He stepped before me and swiped the blade close to my eyes. I lurched backwards. He swiped again, again and again, drawing closer with every quick thrust. With his final swipe, he aimed the knife lower, pushing the blade towards my throat and holding it against my skin. I winced, as the jagged edge pricked my flesh and sent a thin trickle of blood down to my collar. The look on the man's glossy face alarmed me. His skin darkened before my eyes. The veins in his neck throbbed quickly. I could see the depths of his enlarged pupils and felt every tremor of his excitement. As he pulled the knife away from me then, I really thought my time was up. I saw the face of my father in that moment, telling me to be brave, not to cower or falter at the last. I waited for the death blow that would slice open my throat.

It didn't come. Solomon stepped backwards away from me. He licked his lips as he did.

He began pawing through his tools. 'Where is it?' he growled after only a moment. He cursed before traipsing slowly up the stairs without so much as a glance over his shoulder. With the creak of the hatch opening, I stifled the urge to cry out for help.

Alone, I gasped and began to breathe heavily. I was engrossed in panic, my body charged, each fibre of my being struggling to break free. I looked about me, to my feet and the wall close to my left side. I still wore my coat, but knew that even if I could move, there was nothing in my pockets of any use. *My gun*. It was surely my salvation. I pulled at my wrists, the skin now rubbed raw. In dismay, I tried to stand, and awkwardly managed to take a few creeping steps towards the shelf. It was no use, though; my body was weak and in one desperate moment, I felt myself fall awkwardly to my side. I tried to stand but couldn't, cast my eyes about the room in some vain effort of finding something that would help me. I twisted and bent my fingers and wrists in such an excruciating way, yet all was hopeless. I was at the whim of a complete madman.

I groaned into the cold stone floor, broken, beaten. It was such a pitiful way for all things to end.

The few small candles, dotted around the room, began to flicker. Barely at first so that I thought it merely water dripping from the ceiling, catching the small exposed flames. It lasted only an instant, and whilst then it was hardly something I noticed, it is a moment I am for ever drawn back to in the darker hours of the night, when my mind wanders and reflects on that dreadful encounter in the cellar.

I heard a crash and clatter above. I looked at the shelf, saw the handle of my gun. Water dripped to my right. I watched sullenly, drip after drip, splashing quietly against the floor I would surely die on. Solomon was talking to himself, now close to the open hatch. I waited in morbid anticipation for his return. He cried out, seemingly in mock triumph, before returning with heavy footfalls down the wooden steps. He stopped when he saw me sprawled upon the floor.

'It will be over quicker, Thomas, if you tell me how this camera works.'

'Go to hell,' I stammered, a last pathetic attempt at defiance.

He moved quicker into the cellar then, dropping a shovel at the foot of the steps as he marched over to where I lay. He carried a meat cleaver in his hand. With some effort he hauled me from the floor, though returned immediately to my camera and began hacking the cleaver repeatedly into the wood of the shelf. I admit the outbursts made me reel.

To my shock, my fingers touched upon a loose end of rope around my wrists. I was barely able to grasp it between the thumb and forefinger of my right hand. As I pulled, delicately at first so as not to arouse Solomon's attention, I felt my bonds loosen, ever so slightly. Cautiously I wriggled my hands. Steadily, only a fraction at a time, I was able to prise my wrists apart. Anxiously I continued to tug on the loose end whilst all the while, Solomon jabbered and grappled with my camera. I watched as he set the quarter plate in, as he lifted and began fixing it to the stand, the lens aimed straight at me. With ever more frantic movements, I pulled and prised until at last, I could feel the bonds give and knew they had been loosened completely.

My body shook. I felt quite delirious.

I had some chance now to overcome my captor, though it would not be an easy task. My shoulder still ached and my vision remained unfocused. Solomon was bigger in stature and heavier in weight; I couldn't fight him for that would be foolhardy.

My gun – I needed to get it away from Solomon. It was my

best chance. I could take him by surprise, shove him aside and make a short dash for it. That seemed my only real choice. I thought little on it, for I needed to act quickly.

'You're of a type, Solomon,' I said then, trying to quell the fear in my voice. 'I've seen it often enough; a weak child, I imagine, likely the disappointment to your father.'

I was rambling but had gained Solomon's attention. He stopped adjusting the camera and eyed me darkly.

'Either that or he buggered you. It's a sad fact but most killers share that in common; abusive fathers. It's why they kill, to regain control, impart their power on others.'

'Watch your tongue,' he snarled viciously.

'What surprises me, however, is that you chose such weak victims, targeting even children, in fact. Most killers challenge themselves, or so they think. They pick ever more difficult prey, at least the ones with any ounce of bravery do.' None of this was true of course, but I had to goad Solomon towards me.

'You're quite weak in truth. You think yourself clever when any fool could do what you have done. You think yourself special for bringing fear to a remote village full of superstitious people? That's nothing. Not like *The Ripper*; he made the whole of London cry out in terror.'

Solomon was shaking his head slowly, trying to brush off what I was saying.

'That was special,' I continued. 'Unlike you, he'll be remembered.'

He grabbed the cleaver, ripping it from the shelf. He started stepping over to me slowly, brandishing it before him. I could see his knuckles were white as snow as he grasped hold of the hilt.

'You think you're smart,' I spoke on brazenly. 'You think you have a power over others. You have no power. None will think of you in the years to come. You're a killer of the helpless. In time, the authorities will catch up to you and you will no doubt surrender before they can shoot you like a dog. They'll bury you in an unmarked grave, along with every memory of you. No one will ever know who you were.'

Solomon began raising the cleaver as he came within a few feet of me. I could see his fury, his rage. I forced myself to wait for the moment he would strike.

'No one will remember *you*, Thomas,' he howled. 'I'll bury you so deep!'

'You're angry because you know it's true. I know what a waste you are—'

It all happened quickly then, a blur. Solomon raised the cleaver higher looking to bring it down upon me. Before he could, I bowed my head, and ignoring the pain from my shoulder, brought my arms out from behind me and leapt out of the chair to tackle him. His gasp, as I surged and knocked him backwards, seemed more from surprise than anything.

We collapsed onto the floor, though there he had the upper hand. Swiping out with the cleaver, he nicked my arm lightly. I cried out, managing to scramble away from him as he swung at my face.

I made for the shelf and my gun. He clearly knew my intention, rising quickly and stepping towards my revolver as well. He swiped clumsily through the air and clattered against my body. I reeled forwards, falling again to the floor just before the shelf. As Solomon slashed downwards, I rolled away, scrambling to my feet and moving back towards the chair.

He now stood between me and the gun, but his excitement got the better of him. He left it and charged with no thought or great skill, thrashing out with the knife in anger. I managed to avoid his first, wayward swipe, before hitting him hard with my good right arm. He lost his grip on the cleaver as he stumbled backwards, it falling to the floor. I took a step forward but to no avail. Solomon was unnerved; he moved backwards and with his eyes fixed on mine, fumbled for my Enfield.

He aimed the gun at me, the hammer already pulled back. He straightened his arm and I readied myself for the shot. I made sure to keep my eyes open to the last.

Solomon's face, split with a smile of total contempt, changed suddenly. His gaze shifted for the briefest moment; he looked past my shoulder. He lowered the gun slightly, his arms slumping.

I leapt forwards and took him off guard, trying to wrestle the gun from his grasp. He reacted quickly, shoving at me with his free hand. I managed to pull the gun clean away from him, though in that moment he knocked me off balance. I fell backwards hard, fumbling to take hold of the handle as he in turn lunged down onto me. We jostled and wrestled, his heavy hands swinging at my face, I in turn thrashing at him.

Still clenching the barrel of my Enfield, I managed to connect the butt with Solomon's jaw. He reeled, clawing then towards the cleaver, crying out as he did. I rolled away from him in terror, took hold of the gun proper and fired, the blast of noise deafening in the confined space. My Enfield smoked as Solomon lay dead upon the floor.

I yelled and let go of the gun. The candles in the room seemed brighter than they had before. Clenching my injured shoulder, I stood unsteadily and looked around.

I was alone, with Solomon's corpse lying at my feet.

28

The Passing of the Storm –
June 24th, 1904

I awoke, to quite the pleasant whistling of birds singing outside the inn window. It seemed such a foreign sound. As I lifted my head from the wooden table, my hand still loosely holding my gun, I noticed the brightness of the room around me. The sun was beaming, casting every corner in warm, golden light. I felt a little dazed, wincing as a sharp pain from my shoulder coursed up my stiff neck. In spite of this, everything was serene, worlds away from the chaos and furore of the storm.

I stood slowly and moved over to the bar area, knocking into a few chairs as I went. Nervously I stretched over and looked behind the bar to the hatch leading down to the cellar. It was closed, as I had left it.

The fight, my single gunshot. The moments I had sat bound in the chair, the sharpened edge of Solomon's blade pushed against my neck, or the barrel of my gun held against my temple. I tried pushing all such thoughts from my mind.

Uncertain as to what to do but compelled to be in the morning air, I left the inn and stood in the sunken patio outside. The day was glorious, rich blue skies unblemished by a single wisp of cloud. The trees of the Twyn had been battered however, branches snapped, limbs torn away exposing fresh bark. It was clear that some of the cottages and other properties had been damaged by the freak weather as well. Slate roof tiles lined the dusky road; a window opposite where I stood had been smashed.

There was no one in sight. I stepped out of the patio and looked towards the town hall. I doubted Cummings or Vaughn would still be there; they had likely struggled back up Britway Road to Cummings' estate.

I walked down the length of the Twyn. I began to see a few people stirring within their homes – curtains being opened, doors unbolted. It wasn't long before I heard voices and saw a small huddle of men gathered outside the church with its three simple spires. There were five or six; they fell silent as I approached and didn't say anything as I stood beside them. They eyed me with the same infuriating suspicion that I had grown accustomed to. Today, I was in no mood to stand for it.

'I need to contact the Glamorgan Constabulary, or Cardiff, whichever is easier. They are needed immediately.'

It was the ironmonger I had interviewed two days previously who spoke first.

'What's happened?'

'A man is dead. I need the police here at once.'

The men looked from me to each other.

'Who?' the ironmonger asked me.

'It is none of your concern. I need someone at the station – the lines will have to be cleared today. I can't wire anyone so that's the only way we'll be able to make contact.'

Nobody stirred. I spoke angrily then, pointing to a man on my left.

'You. Get down to the station and be on watch. If a steamer comes, you flag them down. Tell them a killer has been apprehended and they need to get the police here as soon as possible. It doesn't matter which way the train is headed.'

The man remained rooted to the spot.

'Well, come on, move!'

He hurried away then towards the station. The expression of those he left had changed completely. They looked at me with some alarm.

'The body of Betsan Tilny. It lies in rest at Michaelston as I am sure you know.' I turned from one man to the next. 'I'll need her brought here in all haste. Take a cart.'

The ironmonger shook his head uneasily. 'Mr Cummings, and Constable Vaughn—'

'Have no say in this village anymore,' I interrupted. 'This is no enviable task, but it must be done. If you would like, you can speak to the police when they arrive; I'm sure they will be keen to hear of your refusal.'

The men, visibly aggrieved, made no complaints. They stepped down the Twyn without a word, their heads all bowed.

I took a deep breath, looking upwards and feeling the warmth of the day. It was going to be a long one.

The village awoke slowly, but by mid-morning, word had spread. A small crowd of men and women gathered on the Twyn, some smoking and muttering quietly, others sitting and watching, concern etched into their faces.

By then I had returned to the inn and found Solomon's keys, blessedly tucked safely behind the bar. I had no great desire to head down into the cellar and search about his corpse. With these I had locked up the inn completely, before spending two hours or so flitting from place to place.

I had gone to Geraint and Lewis' house; the pair had been awake though Geraint had looked in no fit state. I had done him the courtesy of explaining what had happened, watching as he broke down in a mixture of anger and shock. Lewis consoled him softly. I left asking only that they kept the circumstances quiet until the police had arrived. By then it wouldn't matter much.

Next, I made my way to the Beacon House, though en route I met Jacob Clyde, the Postmaster. He tried prying into what had happened.

'Never you mind,' I said brashly. 'I need you to track down Coun— Mr Cummings and Mr Vaughn. Tell them only that I seek them and that the enquiry has been closed. If they are not at Cummings' residence make sure to search for them.' I waved him off and he left obligingly.

At the telegraph station, Mrs Wilkins was as curt with me as she had been when last we met. Her husband was in attendance, though, and he seemed quite the opposite.

'Sorry I haven't spoken to you yet, Inspector; I've been busy with the telegraph lines.'

He was not a young man, his hair turning grey, the wrinkles around his eyes prominent. He stood nearly a foot shorter than his wife and I.

'It's fine, Mr Wilkins. How are the repairs coming along? I need to alert the authorities of what has happened here; I have sent a man to the station but that may not do.'

Mr Wilkins hesitated as he thought. 'They're not good. The lines were down all the way up the turnpike and may be even further along to Michaelston. It's much sturdier from there but there's no guarantees.'

'Can you get men to assist you in the repairs?' I asked. He shrugged and nodded. 'See to it and do what you can.'

He seemed amenable and happy to help. I left with my thanks, before heading to the General's estate. I was not there long, relaying to Harriet what happened the previous day.

'This may all mean nothing to the General, but I assume you will now need to deal with his affairs.'

'I will,' Harriet spoke regretfully. 'In many ways I am glad. Arthur is not a perfect man but loves this place dearly. It would kill him knowing what was really going on.'

I had nothing to say to that and left a little while later wishing Harriet my best.

That took me to mid-morning, whereupon I returned to the Twyn and the gathering crowds of nervous faces. Jacob Clyde was waiting; he informed me that Mr Cummings and Vaughn would remain at Cummings' estate until needed. I decided that this was probably for the best; it was better they weren't present and causing a fuss amongst the villagers.

I wasn't sure what to do then, as a few voices called out to me, sheepishly at first but then with greater authority. All in attendance were anxious, desperate to know what had happened. I gathered the small crowd a little and spoke to them candidly.

'My enquiry has unearthed the perpetrator of Betsan Tilny's murder, as well as the murders of the young twins five years ago. I hope that officers from the local Constabularies will arrive here today, at which point they will no doubt begin speaking with some of you. Please ensure you answer them as honestly and clearly as you can.'

'What of the spirit!' a man called out.

'Who was it?' a woman asked from the back of the crowd. 'Where are they if they are guilty?'

I saw Solomon's lifeless body lying on the floor, his cold, merciless eyes staring up at me. I chose not to answer.

'Please ensure you speak with the police frankly.'

A voice began yelling from further down the Twyn, and as I and the rest of the crowd turned, the young man I had sent to the station came running towards us.

'The train line,' he said breathlessly. 'It's been cleared this morning. Train just came through. They stopped, and I told 'em what's happened. They're going to send for the police in the next town over.'

I spent several hours back in the vacant inn then, knowing it would be some time until the Constables arrived. I went to my room, opening my case to pack away my things. I gathered all the torn and scribbled diary entries I had on the little table, tucking them away in my case, before covering them in my worn and dirty clothes. This was quite a childish act but one I did unconsciously. I didn't want to look upon them.

I set about searching through the drawers of a little davenport and two cupboards in Solomon's room. I found a small mahogany box, tucked neatly behind hanging trousers and Sunday shoes. Opening this, I discovered a heap of newspaper clippings which I began to thumb through slowly.

It was grim reading, each small, dog-eared piece of paper, telling its own miserable story. A body found cut up in a back alley. A woman found strangled in her bed. Drunken vagrants stabbed through the chest where they slept. A spate of disappearances over the course of some months. Crimes committed primarily in London, though some enacted in Oxford, Bath and Bristol. The oldest was dated at eighteen ninety.

It was short work laying out each clipping on the floor, plotting the course of Solomon's despicable career. The crimes became more violent, the victims' bodies left in ever more gruesome and grotesque states of depravity. There were names I recognised, cases I was aware of but not privy to at the time. To my horror, I realised I had indeed worked on one case, in the winter of eighteen ninety-four, though it had been far earlier in my career and I was not an investigator at that stage. That was little comfort though – a misplaced sense of guilt washed over me. Had I known then, I could have stopped him. Had I known then ...

There was a diary in the box. On the first page were a list of names, locations and dates, each correlating to the clippings spread out before me. Beyond this, I saw the terrible extent to which Solomon had documented each of his murders. Page upon page of hand-scribbled notes, sketches of bodies bound and screaming, lists of tools used, details on sordid desires and fantasies. I tried to look upon it as I would any other piece of evidence. I found no sign of my photographic negatives but did happen upon a few small brown vials. They were all unmarked, though it was not an outlandish assumption that they contained the belladonna poison Solomon had laced into my food.

Taking a few sheets of letter paper from the davenport, I returned to my room and began writing my initial report. I was succinct, recalling the actions I had undertaken in my first few days in Dinas Powys and the manner in which I had fallen ill. I made no mention of spirits, or spectres, or things scratching in the night. I merely noted my whereabouts and questioning, that evidence had been collected in the form of photographic negatives, though these were currently missing, no doubt taken by the killer. I outlined the enquiries I had made following my speedy recovery, noting what I now knew to be the nature of my poisoning. I detailed all the illicit activities I had uncovered; Cummings' and Vaughn's reprehensible deeds I spoke of fully, as well as my recommendations for what action should be taken against them.

I struggled to write of my final discovery – Solomon wearing Betsan's ring. It first appeared to me as a band of light in a picture, nothing more. How could I explain that, the manner in which I had learnt of it? After a few minutes of thought, I outlined that Geraint Davey, Betsan's fiancé, had testified such a ring was missing. He had given me a description and finding a ring of said description about Solomon's person, I had questioned the man about its origin. I needed then to provide a summary of my time captured in the cellar.

I finally stated thus: Solomon had failed to bind me adequately to my chair. After some time in which he confessed all his crimes to me, including the murder of Betsan Tilny and the murders of two children five years previous, he had attempted to kill me. At this point, free of my bonds, I was able to overcome him, grappling my pistol and shooting him with one fatal shot. I outlined in brief my actions that morning, stating how I had sought the assistance of the Constabulary.

It was not long, only three pages. I intended to write something far more significant in the days ahead, but this would do as a preliminary. I read it back once, twice. I continued to read through it again and again in fact.

It all made sense to me then. What I had written was the truth. The entirety of it. It felt so uplifting.

I thought first on my negatives. I had developed them in the height of fever. I have no doubts of my skill or the techniques I employed during development, but it would be more than plausible, *nay completely likely*, that my poor condition made me see all manner of strange things in those pictures. I had 'seen' the girl's ghost lunge at me, raging, an inferno, in the cellar of All Saints church – was it not just as likely I may see the very same thing in the negatives I had taken? Could it be that lacking any opportunity to look upon those images again since my fever had passed, I may simply have reinforced the absurd notion that something awry, unnatural, had lingered in them?

How then did I come to know of the ring? It was made plain to me (or so I believed), in the very negatives I now cast doubts on, present on Betsan's wedding finger. This visage had come to me in the town hall, upon which I had questioned Geraint, who confirmed such a ring was indeed real. Was that the case, though? I was still quite unwell, in need of rest. Perhaps the idea of the ring – like everything else – had come from the depths of my imagination, concocted in this false pretence of 'what I had seen in the negatives'. Was it such a coincidence that Geraint, as smitten as he was, should have asked Betsan to marry him, giving her a ring, a common custom that almost all men adhere to upon seeking engagement? In short, was it such a leap, the conclusion that I had come to? Could the existence of a ring, one that was missing at the time, not simply have been a 'hunch', a result of years of investigatory experience on my part?

It seemed very plausible.

Understand in the warm light of that day, so far removed from the madness of the previous few, my thinking then went beyond simply trying to convince myself. I genuinely started to believe these conclusions, for they were well reasoned, logical. Everything I thought I had seen was mere fantasy, delusions brought on by my combined stress, illness and lack of sleep. I was reflecting on an enquiry that had been one of my most bizarre; any man would have been affected in the manner in which I was. Most would have simply left the village after a day, realising that their illness was getting worse, afflicting them and hampering any enquiry. My stubbornness had perhaps been my undoing, but it seemed to matter little now.

My duties were done. I was in need of recuperation, of a well-earned leave of absence. All talk of ghosts and ghouls would be left behind, and as with the day I had awoken from my fever, I began to laugh a little. Bexley the Crypt Inspector – the name was growing on me somewhat.

I was revived, rejuvenated. Sitting at the table I couldn't help but feel a sense of pride and one of relief. My world was rebalanced, returned to its status quo. I would leave this place and lead the life I had before my arrival. I let the image of Betsan's spectre linger in my mind, thought hard on it as I stared at the milling villagers out on the Twyn.

Then I let the image fade, for in truth it was nothing but nonsense.

At three o'clock, a troop of officers arrived. I had been waiting for them on the station, and seeing the steamer approach, had beamed with sheer delight. They were Glamorgan Constables, and they piled onto the platform briskly. They were normal, nothing out of the ordinary. Like the little steamer with its fireman and driver. They were normal too. It was such a joy to reconnect with the outside world, with things that were all so familiar.

Their Sergeant introduced himself and at times like these, a reputation such as mine is not a bad thing. He was aware of who I was, as were several more of the men.

'I've read about your work in the London papers,' Sergeant Davis said kindly. 'Surprised to see you down here.'

'It was by request of your Chief Inspector.'

Davis laughed at that. 'He kept that one quiet. So, what's all this of a murder?'

Davis turned to the engine driver and told him to hold at the station. I led the troop of Constables up to the Twyn, explaining in brief what had transpired.

I shan't detail here the following hours as it seems unnecessary other than to say thus: Betsan's body was brought back to the village, upon which the Constables took ownership. Solomon's body was brought out from the cellar, to quite the shock of the villagers in attendance. Both bodies were then taken to the steamer. Cummings and Vaughn were brought down from the estate and formally charged, in my presence, with conspiring to pervert the course of justice (among other things). Vaughn was too ashamed to look at me. Cummings, in a makeshift gurney carried by two men, spat hellfire as he was taken away. The train left with both men and the bodies to Cardiff, scheduled to return later in the day.

Many of the gathered villagers were questioned; Sergeant Davis and I sat to review my draft report and the evidence I had in the form of Betsan's ring, the children's possessions and Solomon's deplorable diary.

'The photographs you took,' Davis asked me. 'You can't find them anywhere?'

I shook my head. 'Solomon likely took charge and disposed of them. Probably thought it would help conceal the truth somehow. It matters little – there's enough evidence here to outline what really happened. These names,' I held up the diary, 'will need to be corroborated, but I have no doubts each is of a man or woman murdered or missing, with a case file still open.'

'It's hard to believe,' Davis mused. 'How could a man get away with all these killings for so long?'

I couldn't think of an answer to give.

I thought of how I had escaped my bonds.

'We will need to collect more evidence from Mr Cummings' estate regarding some of his illicit business practices, and there are others who conspired with him. The girl's mother must be informed as well...'

The hours slipped by, afternoon turning to evening. Davis was going to remain in the village late into the night, along with half of his Constables. I made no secret of my desire to leave. He understood and with the aid of a young officer sporting a rather flamboyant moustache, I took my case and camera equipment down to the station.

It was nearly half past seven. The sun was still shining brightly, descending in the clear sky. The train was due to return in a little while. The young officer remained with me, passing small talk and enquiring about what had happened. He commented more than once on my clear relief, to which I concurred. I was happy to be rid of this place, to be returning to a city, to a little normality.

Normal. Everything would be normal again.

The steamer trundled towards us, and quite oddly I laughed with joy. The officer smiled as I took hold of his hand and shook it vigorously. He helped me bundle onto the train with my case and camera equipment, shutting the carriage door before waiting to wave me off.

I went to sit, the carriage deserted. I felt foolish and laughed again. The whole while I had been carrying my preliminary report in one hand. I had meant to leave it with Sergeant Davis; in my haste I had clearly not.

I opened the door of the carriage and the young officer stepped to me, still smiling beneath his fulsome moustache.

'Forgotten something, sir?'

'Yes, yes, quite foolish of me.' I handed him the three-page document. 'This is my preliminary report. It is rough, but I intend to write a comprehensive follow up. See to it that it arrives on the desk of your Chief Inspector Brent, with my regards.'

The young officer's expression changed then. 'Beg pardon, sir?'

I frowned. 'The report. See to it that it gets to Chief Inspector Brent.'

The officer looked from the papers in his hand to me with some confusion.

'Sir. There is no Chief Inspector by that name.'

I shook my head, a little irritated. 'Well, of course there is, man. He requested I come here in the first place. His letter is somewhere about my person.'

I began checking through my pockets, though I had a feeling it was in my case. I set my hand upon something soft and pulled out the ragdoll, the one Betsan's mother had given me. I had forgotten all about it. Its little face, with its blank expression, looked up at me. The steamer's whistle bellowed out.

'Sorry, sir. With respect, I have worked at the Constabulary for the last five years. There is no such Chief Inspector by that name. I don't know anyone by that name, in fact.' He looked from me to the engine and acknowledged a voice that spoke to him. 'They're pulling off now, sir. I'll see to it that Sergeant Davis gets this.'

He pushed shut the door of the carriage, me standing motionless. I watched as he and the platform, and the village of Dinas Powys, drifted away into the distance, before moving out of sight entirely. Only then did I take to a seat, the little ragdoll still in hand. A few minutes later I dropped it to my side and began pawing through the pockets of my coat, fumbling then for the clasps of my case and rummaging clumsily through its contents. Tucked neatly in a side pocket I found the letter I had received. I read through it quickly to the name typed and signed at the very bottom.

Chief Inspector Taliesin Cedwyn Brent.

I had not been mistaken. I sat back and pondered as the train rattled on.

The young Constable was surely confused. There was no other explanation for it. I tucked the letter in my coat pocket and looked out of the carriage window as the world drifted by. It was not long till we came to Cardiff, the blue skies of eve dulled by the dry haze of dust and dirt. We passed by the rows of terraced houses, young children still at play, their voices wailing and crying out in wild ecstasy. In the distance, large ships were visible, cargo being lifted from their bowels by monstrous steel cranes. People moved in horse-drawn carriages and carts down thin cobbled roads, and I even spotted a new automobile, a rare sight if any. As we alighted at Cardiff station, I saw the clerks and businessmen, stationmasters, pedlars, colliers from the valleys in the north.

All normal. Nothing out of the ordinary. Yet still I felt a growing unease.

Like Dinas Powys before, I wanted to leave this city. Without thought I asked of a train to London. The last for the day was leaving in fifteen minutes. I moved to the platform, taking nothing in around me. The young Constable must surely have been wrong. There was no other explanation.

Yet he looked at me with such certainty.

It wasn't long before I was sat on a long, fine carriage headed to London. It was not empty; a man and a woman in their mid-fifties, a gentleman in a fine suit with a slender briefcase. A few others, though there was plenty of seats to choose from. I sat as far away as I could from anyone else.

There is no Chief Inspector by that name.

The young Constable had seemed so certain.

As we pulled away, I took out the letter and read through it repeatedly, noting the date it was sent, the address, all manner of minor things. I recalled that Vaughn had received a similar telegram from Chief Inspector Brent, informing him that I was soon to arrive and the services I would carry out. He would attest to it, and two lots of correspondence would be more than enough to prove I wasn't mistaken.

I looked out the windows as we sped away from Cardiff. Soon we were immersed in the rolling landscape, the beauty and tranquillity of a calm summer eve. All so normal.

Something dreadful dawned on me. It niggled away at first until I gave it my full attention.

Cummings and Vaughn had never wanted me in Dinas Powys. They had never wanted me knowing what they had done. They'd never wanted anyone outside the village knowing what had happened. They'd wanted only to keep the murders quiet.

How then did the Glamorgan Constabulary come to know of the murders in the first place?

Brent had written to Vaughn, telling him of my arrival to assist in the enquiry. Brent had written to me, asking for my services. Neither I nor Vaughn had made any contact with him before this. Brent had had no way of knowing.

I only wanted everything to return to normal.

Terror began to well up inside of me. Betsan in the negatives. Betsan coming to me in the church cellar, Betsan in my room and watching me from every shadow.

Betsan. Betsan. Betsan. I tried to think none of it real.

I took a pencil from my pocket. I wished then I had found my negatives to look upon – they would be irrefutable proof.

Betsan. Betsan. Betsan.

There is no Chief Inspector by that name.

How naïve I'd been to think none of it was real.

I only wanted to return to normal.

I scribbled Betsan's full name below Taliesin Cedwyn Brent. I began to scratch out matching letters from each name. Terror made my hand tremble.

How could I have believed that none of it was real.

I scratched away the last letters, the pencil falling from my fingers as I did. It was plain to see now. The letters from one name matched up with the letters from the other. My trembling hand grew more unsteady. The elderly woman with her husband laughed. Normal slipped away from me.

Betsan Ceridwen Tilny – Taliesin Cedwyn Brent.

They were one and the same. Betsan had brought me to the village. Betsan had brought me to find her killer.

I looked back out the window.

We charged through green pastures. Labourers moved lazily at the end of their working day. It was worthy of a John Constable painting.

It was tainted for me for ever.

Credits

Sam Hurcom and Orion Fiction would like to thank everyone at Orion who worked on the publication of *A Shadow on the Lens* in the UK.

Editorial
Bethan Jones
Emad Akhtar
Francesca Pathak
Lucy Frederick

Copy Editor
Jon Appleton

Proof Reader
Linda Joyce

Contracts
Anne Goddard
Paul Bulos
Jake Alderson

Design
Debbie Holmes
Joanna Ridley
Nick May

Editorial Management
Charlie Panayiotou
Jane Hughes
Alice Davis

Production
Ruth Sharvell
Hannah Cox

Marketing
Jessica Tackie
Lucy Cameron

Publicity
Alex Layt

Finance
Jasdip Nandra
Afeera Ahmed
Elizabeth Beaumont
Sue Baker